Will the Real
Carolyn Keene
Please Stand Up

Also by
Christine Keleny

Historical Fiction:
Rosebloom
A Burnished Rose
Rose From the Ashes

The Red Velvet Box

Memoir:
Living in the House of Drugs

Will the Real Carolyn Keene Please Stand Up

Christine Keleny

CKBooks

The names in this book are accurate as far as the information I could find could tell me. The situations they are in are purely fictional, though the majority are based on information written about these people and their lives.

Many of the letters or portions of letters (in italics) come from the Edward Stratemeyer collection at the NYPL and are the sole property of Simon & Schuster along with the excerpt from the original printing of *The Secret of the Old Clock* and the name: Nancy Drew. Special thanks to Simon & Schuster for their use.

Keleny, Christine.
  Will the real Carolyn Keene please stand up / Christine Keleny.

  pages ; cm

  Issued also as an ebook.
  Includes bibliographical references.
  ISBN: 978-0-9892152-4-4 (softcover)
  ISBN: 978-0-9892152-5-1 (hardcover)

  1. Keene, Carolyn--Authorship--Fiction. 2. Drew, Nancy (Fictitious character)--Fiction. 3. Ghost writers--Fiction. 4. Mystery and detective stories--Fiction. 5. Historical fiction. I. Title.

PS3611.E4464 W55 2014
813/.6   2014944044

Copyright 2014 by Christine Keleny
Published and designed by CKBooks Publishing
Cover art: Earl Keleny and selfpubbookcovers.com

To my husband Andrew.

I couldn't have done this
without you.

One ∽

"Hello, Mrs. Adams."

"Hello."

"May I call you Harriet?"

"I prefer Mrs. Adams, if you please," Harriet said, a bit put off at the man's presumption.

"I'm sorry," the man said, suppressing a grin. "Mrs. Adams, can you take a look at a copy of this article for me?"

The man in the impeccable, navy, pinstriped Brooks Brothers suit and tie walked over to Harriet Adams in the witness box and handed her a sheet of copy paper. Harriet was just as dressed out. She never left home without the proper outfit for the occasion: hose, shoes, and purse that matched her dress. She had gotten out of wearing hats but still felt naked without one. The man stepped back a respectable distance and looked down as if he were examining the floor, giving Harriet some space and time to examine the paper he had just given her.

Harriet adjusted her glasses. Perspiration was causing them to slip down on her nose, and if they didn't sit just right, she had difficulty seeing through her bifocals. She examined the paper as requested, then looked back up.

"Yes?"

"Can you tell the jury, Mrs. Adams, the title of the article you just read?"

Harriet looked slightly perturbed at the man for his seemingly inane request but complied, reading off the top of the first sheet. " 'Nancy Drew's author - she's no mystery.' "

"Can you tell us when that article was written and by whom?"

Harriet pursed her thin lips, her coral-colored lipstick cementing her lips together for a split second. Harriet glanced over at the judge, who nodded for her to follow the lawyer's request. She looked back down at the paper once more. "*San Antonio Express News*, August 7th, 1977. "

"Do you remember being interviewed for this article, Mrs. Adams?"

"Well, of course I do," she said, her indignation rising further. "I may be eighty-seven, young man, but I'm still the principal owner and operator of the Stratemeyer Syndicate, and I have been for fifty years!"

"That's quite a feat."

"I should say so. I took over my father's company at a time when a woman in the publishing business had never even been heard of."

2

"You and your sister Edna, that is."

"Yes, yes, my sister helped for a time," Harriet replied, waving off the notion as something insignificant. But it wasn't insignificant and Harriet knew it. In her mind this young man was being insolent, and she wasn't going to quibble with details. "But our mother was an invalid at the time, and Edna primarily took care of her while I ran the company."

"But initially, Mrs. Adams, you tried to sell the company, did you not?"

Harriet looked at him and blinked repeatedly, initially flustered by the comment; apparently this young man had done his homework. Harriet quickly regained her composure. "You must understand the circumstances at the time; I was married and had four children, the youngest just five. And as I've said, my mother was basically incapacitated. She had suffered a stroke a year earlier and had migraines and other ailments for years. She needed someone at her constant beck and call. It was the logical thing to do."

"So when was the last time you had worked in your father's company, before his death, I mean?"

Harriet looked at the man sideways, eyes slit in determination. "What are you implying, young man?"

The lawyer strode confidently over to the jury box, letting the two rows of men and women sitting behind the rail think over the implication of his question before he spoke.

"What I am saying is that in 1930, when your father died, you knew nothing of the book business or how to write books," he said directly to the jury.

He turned accusingly in Harriet's direction. "In fact the

only work your father, Edward Stratemeyer, allowed you to do for the Syndicate was some editing of already written stories. And that was fifteen years before his death! He thought the company would die with him, didn't he Mrs. Adams?"

The lawyer leaned in toward Harriet and grasped the rail in front of her. She could see from the faint sheen on his skin that he was perspiring too. "Didn't he!" he repeated for emphasis.

There was a murmur in the gallery, as the implications of his words traveled through the rapt crowd.

This court case was the most anticipated legal proceeding in the book world in 1980. And this witness, geriatric or not, was whom everyone was waiting to hear. Grosset & Dunlap, a firm that had been in the book publishing business for eighty-two years – and thus a big weight among the New York book publishing houses – had leveled an unprecedented $300 million lawsuit alleging breach of contract and copyright infringement against Mrs. Harriet Stratemeyer Adams and the Stratemeyer Syndicate. Everyone who was anyone in the book world wanted to hear what Harriet had to say because this case was focused around the most admired, read, and productive girl sleuth in the literary world: Nancy Drew.

The suit actually started after Harriet had finally had enough of her dealings with the company. Harriet's junior partners: Nancy Axelrad, Lorraine Rickle, and Lieselotte Wuenn, had convinced Harriet to drop Grosset & Dunlap because of what they viewed as the highway robbery that was being perpetrated by the New York publishing giant – and had, in fact, been taking place for years. Grosset & Dunlap had

4

worked with Edward Stratemeyer or his family since 1908, and it was, in part, because of this seventy-one year history – and the fact that they were willing to work with Harriet and her sister after their father's death – that Harriet was loath to push the issue. But Nancy's 50th anniversary was just a year away, and Harriet's junior partners knew something had to be done to keep the company solvent. The company was down to three major publications compared to twenty-two at the time of Edward Stratemeyer's demise.

The issue was royalties. The junior partners in the Syndicate encouraged Harriet to negotiate with Grosset & Dunlap, as she had done numerous times in the past, but with one trump card up her sleeve: change the royalties the Syndicate received from the current paltry rate of four percent – the same rate they had given Edward Stratemeyer seventy years before – to the graduated rate where the percent increased as the number of published books increased or the Syndicate would go elsewhere. Use of a graduated rate was part of any current publishing contract, and the Syndicate wanted to be treated as everyone else.

Grosset & Dunlap called Harriet's bluff and refused to amend their current contract. The Syndicate would not capitulate, so in 1979 they signed on with Simon & Schuster, allowing them to publish all future Bobbsey Twins, Hardy Boys, Dana Girls, Tom Swift, Tom Swift Jr., and Nancy Drew series.

The Syndicate lawyer stood from behind his table. "I object, your honor. The prosecution is badgering the witness."

The judge looked at the defense attorney then to the prosecutor and gave him a stern look. "I concur, Mr. Williams. As important as this case may be to you and your client, you are not trying a murder case. Mrs. Adams and her family are respected, longtime residents of this community and should be treated as such. Please keep a civil tone when addressing the witness.

"Yes, Your Honor."

Harriet's eyes danced with satisfaction. His Honor had one thing correct; they were longtime, respected residents of the area, New Jersey to be exact, and her father was the most prolific, successful creator of stories for young readers that the publishing world had ever known.

What he didn't have correct, however, was that this *was* a murder case, or at least a case tantamount to murder in Harriet's eyes. If she lost this suit with Grosset & Dunlap, her family's business would die, a business that not only brought up millions of girls on the adventures of Nancy Drew and had fans the likes of Barbara Walters and Ruth Bader Ginsburg, but also popularized the boys' book adventure series with long standing series such as The Rover Boys in 1899, Tom Swift in 1910 and the much loved children's series The Bobbsey Twins in 1904, plus innumerable others. This included the hijinks of Frank and Joe Hardy: the boys' mystery series Edward first published in 1927 and, right along with Nancy, was still going strong, thanks to Harriet. Wasn't Nancy's popularity proven at the gala, fiftieth anniversary party put on by Simon & Schuster for Nancy Drew just this last April? It had taken place at the chichi Harkness House on Fifth Avenue in New York, no less, and was the talk of the town.

So Harriet was determined not to let her father's legacy die. She had saved it in 1930 after his death, and she was determined she would do it again.

"I'm sorry, Mrs. Adams. Let us continue."

Mr. Williams adjusted his tie. "Can you please read the highlighted section of the article before you?"

Harriet picked up the paper again and found the item that Mr. Williams had asked for. She read the small section, looked back to Mr. Williams then started reading aloud.

" 'Adams took over the writing of the Nancy Drew series, wrote outlines for the other series and farmed them out to ghostwriters.' "

"Now if you would, please read the publication and date of *this* article," Mr. Williams said, handing Harriet another sheet of paper.

"The *Quad-City Times*, Sunday, February 17, 1980."

The man strode over to the jury box and turned back toward Harriet. "Can you read the highlighted section of *that* article, please?"

Harriet adjusted her glasses and examined the paper. " 'Under the pen name "Carolyn Keene," this delicate, plucky, 87-year-old great-grandmother has authored 57 Nancy Drew stories since 1930, a little more than one cliff-hanging, globe-trotting and, yes, covertly educational tale a year.' "

Harriet put the papers down in her lap and looked up at the prosecuting attorney.

"And what you do think of that, Mrs. Adams?"

Harriet picked up the paper again, looking at her smiling face in black and white gazing back at her. "I think her description is quite lovely."

"But this is not true, is it Mrs. Adams. Both of these articles state that you wrote all of the Nancy Drew stories, but you did not," he said, the young man's voice getting louder.

"In fact, there is someone in this very courtroom who can prove, beyond a reasonable doubt, that she is the true writer of Nancy Drew from Nancy's inception in 1930 to Volume twenty-five in 1948, then one last volume in 1953."

Mr. Williams then turned and pointed out a slight and elderly woman sitting behind the prosecution's table in the front row of the gallery.

The chattering in the room resumed as all eyes turned toward the woman, who at seventy-five was much younger than Harriet. And she looked it; the woman's posture was that of a twenty year old, and her eyes were bright with mischief as she stared pointedly at Harriet.

Harriet stared back. She had only met her twice, the last time was thirty years ago when Mildred Benson and her second husband had stopped by unexpectedly during a trip to New England. She wouldn't have recognized her if Mr. Williams hadn't pointed her out, but Harriet knew who she was. She knew very well who she was. But it had been years since Harriet had corresponded with Mrs. Benson. In fact, the last time was when Mildred's second husband had died. She hadn't heard directly from her since.

A bead of sweat rolled down Harriet's side.

"Let me explain," Harriet said.

Harriet sat forward in her chair. Harriet wanted to set the record straight. She wanted to make everyone understand. "Mrs. Benson may have written some of the original Nancy stories – and she did so off of my father's then my own outlines, mind you – but I'm the one who created and wrote the Nancy that everyone knows today. It's because of *me* that she's still alive!" she said with conviction. "I knew what my father would have wanted for Nancy. I grew up in his home. I knew what influenced my father and what he stood for. They are the same things I stand for."

"Please elucidate for us, Mrs. Adams."

Harriet sat back in her chair and took a deep breath. She set her lips and looked off into the distance, letting the memories flood in.

Two ∿

(1887)

"I'll be right back, Maurice," Edward said, tucking the wrapped parcel further under his arm.

Maurice looked briefly up from his desk, about to shoo off his youngest brother with hardly a glance, but something caught his eye and he looked back up at Edward.

"What do you have there?" he said, placing his pencil on the ledger in front of him.

Edward hesitated. He knew Maurice didn't think any more of his extracurricular activity than their father did. He had heard the speech many times before. "Writing is no occupation for a man," his father would say. "You can't support a family on that." And at twenty-five, Edward was definitely considered a man. He had yet to devise a way to show his father, or the rest of his family, how he was going to make money from this passion of his. But with his brother Louis's help, he was hoping he was finally on his way.

Maurice reached out his hand and motioned for Edward to hand over the package. Edward sighed and reluctantly complied.

Maurice examined the address. "Library of Congress? What are you sending to the Library of Congress?" he asked, opening the brown paper as if his question was a rhetorical one.

Edward lifted a hand, about to protest this breach of privacy but quickly gave up the idea. Maurice wasn't the oldest of the Stratemeyer children, but since he was older than Edward – by eight years – and was a favored son – running a tobacco shop as their father had done until just recently – Edward knew better than to try and usurp his authority, even though in Edward's eyes this presumed authority was only in Maurice's head. Maurice pulled out the multiple-page, handwritten document and read the cover letter. "The Complete Libretto of Love's Maze?" he said, incredulous. "A comic opera?" He chuckled and shook his head.

He put down the cover letter and examined the title page, then looked back up at Edward. "And you and Louis are in cahoots on this, are you?"

"Can I please have that back."

Maurice shoved the papers back in the brown wrapping, not bothering to rewrap it, and held it up to Edward. "When will you get your head out of the clouds, Edward? You're not a boy writing your one cent magazine stories any longer. And that story paper of yours a few years back was a flop, as well. I could have predicted that. You're twenty-five, for God's sake, and you work as a clerk for a mere $12.50 per week."

"For you!"

"My point exactly."

Maurice picked up his pencil and started to write. Edward placed the play squarely in the paper wrapping, tied the string back around it, and tucked it back under his arm.

Maurice looked up before Edward turned to leave. "You need to find a wife, Edward, and move on with your life. I've given up on Louis. At thirty-one, he's going to be a bachelor all his life, but you still have some time.

Edward turned and looked at himself in the reflection of the glass door. Edward Stratemeyer was not what a woman might consider a "catch," but he was no slouch, either. He stood approximately five feet seven inches and was thin but not wiry. His longish face, large bushy mustache, and oval spectacles (that covered his blue-gray eyes) all set squarely in his stiff, white collar, bow tie neatly in place. His hair was starting to recede, but it was quite thick and he kept it well groomed. Edward was fairly pleased with the figure that looked back at him in the glass. Though he didn't consider himself a ladies' man, he considered himself a man with a vision, and he hoped one day he could find someone to share that vision with him.

Edward squared his shoulders and reached for the door, his myriad book ideas starting their almost constant tromp through his head. Edward *was* making plans. In fact he wished he had time to put in writing all the stories he had mapped out in his mind. But Maurice was right; there was the small problem of money. Edward had saved up a fair amount the last eight years working in his father's, then Maurice's, tobacco shops. This was after completing two years of private study in rhetoric, composition, and literature after high school – a complete waste of time, according to his father, (Heinrich) Julius. He had plans, all right, but he didn't feel like bothering Maurice with them. Edward knew his brother wouldn't approve, anyway.

Edward tightened the grip he had on the manuscript under his arm. He turned back to Maurice. "You'll be happy to know, Maurice, that Louis and I are already working on a second play. Once we sell these two, we'll be well on our way."

Edward left without waiting for a reply.

Maurice looked up and shook his head in disbelief then returned to his ledger.

Unfortunately for Edward and Louis, neither play made it to Broadway or even a second rate playhouse, despite the rubber that was worn off the soles of their shoes as they ran them around Manhattan, pitching to anyone willing to listen.

Edward's first break came a couple of years later when he received a letter in the mail.

"Mother! Mother, you must see this! Arthur Winfield is a success!" Edward called out from the hallway in their home, holding his letter up in triumph. He looked in the kitchen, then the parlor, finding his mother sitting by the window, needle in hand, darning a sock. Edward handed her his letter. She read it eagerly.

"How wonderful, Edward! I knew you would do it. Though I wish you would have written it under your own name," she said with a touch of petulance.

"We've discussed this before, Mother," he said in soft repremand, "that's not how it's done. But look, they sent along this check." He gave her the check to examine as well.

"Seventy-five dollars! My, that's quite a wage for one story. Won't your father be surprised."

"Surprised about what?" Julius said as he strode into the room.

Anna handed her husband Edward's check. Noticing who it was made out to, he turned to his son. "And what is this about?"

"From my story, Father. The one I had been 'wasting my time on' lately."

" 'Victor's Bright Idea,' or some such nonsense."

Edward smiled in amusement. His father knew the title; in fact, Julius had read the whole story, a small secret his mother had shared with him after Edward had sent it off to the publisher.

"Victor Horton's Idea," Edward corrected him, going along with his father's feigned ignorance. "It's going to be printed as a serial in a children's broadsheet called *Golden Days, Golden Days for Boys and Girls* to be exact, out of Philadelphia."

"And they paid you for a story about a boy who runs off to find fame and fortune but doesn't manage to find it?"

"That very one."

"Amazing." Julius strode to the fireplace and pulled the metal screen away from the opening. He bent down and started loading the grating with small bits of kindling. "That's commendable, son, but you'll have to sell a lot more of those to make a living."

"I plan on it, Father. I plan on it," Edward said, beaming. He kissed his mother on the cheek and streaked out of the room, bounding up the steps to his bedroom and his small writing desk. He had new plans to make, and he wanted to get them all down in writing.

(1890)

"I've made up a few things for you, dear," his mother said, handing Edward a large basket as she blinked to keep her tears from falling.

"Mother. I'll be all of five miles from here," he said, taking the obviously heavy load from her hands.

"But you'll be on your own, and who knows when you'll get a decent meal again. You know how you forget to eat when you get busy writing."

Edward gave his mother a kiss on the cheek and glanced over at his father, who was standing at her side. "Thank you, Mother, but I doubt I'll have much time to write, at least for a while, anyway. The store will keep me quite busy, I'm sure."

"Well, your father can come by and help out anytime the need arises. Can't you Julius?" she said, looking up at her husband. Her offer was more of a statement than a question, however, and the look on her face left no doubt in anyone's mind to that fact.

Without a response to his wife, Julius stepped off the stoop and turned Edward toward the waiting cab.

"Good luck, Edward," his sister, Anna, called out to him.

Edward turned back to the porch. It was filling with his remaining siblings, his four brothers, and the passel of nieces and nephews that had all come to the family dinner his mother had planned to see him off.

"Let me know if you need anything," Maurice yelled.

Edward waved to them all. It was quite the spectacle and even brought out a few of the neighbors to see what all the commotion was about. At the ripe age of twenty-eight, the baby of the Stratemeyer family was finally leaving the nest.

"Remember, the family dinner is every Sunday afternoon!" he heard faintly in the distance. He turned back around again to lift a hand in acknowledgement to his mother. She had brought out her white handkerchief and was waving it in the air.

"Your mother's right, Edward; I can help out whenever you need it. I don't know much about selling stationery, but a shop owner is a shop owner. Just drop me a line," Julius said in a low voice as if his wife could still hear him.

Julius stuck out his hand to his son. "Good luck."

Edward took his father's strong hand in his and smiled.

Julius was in his seventies, but he still had quite a bit of the strength he once had while working in the California gold rush in the 1850s. Edward always admired his father for that. Edward excelled more with pen and paper than with his hands or on the playing field, but he always admired those, like his father, who had more physical prowess. "Thanks, Dad. I've learned from the master."

Julius placed his hand on Edward's shoulder, and with an approving squeeze, he smiled back at his son. Edward heaved the basket into the back seat of the carriage and sat in next to it. He stuck his head out of the window to wave one last time to his mother, his sister, and his father, the only ones remaining to see him drive off.

"Where to, Sir?" the taxi driver asked.

"Four-twelve Broad Street, Newark," Edward said with a self-satisfied grin. Edward had rented a one bedroom apartment above the store that he was leasing on Broad Street, a stationery store that sat to the East of multiple institutions of higher education including the New Jersey Law School, the Seth Boyden School of Business, and the Newark Institute of Arts and Sciences. A perfect location, Edward thought, so close to all the young men and women who would need writing paper, ink, and pens to write home to their loving families. The store would also sell newspapers and magazines and, Edward envisioned, eventually the dime store novels similar to the one he had just sold to the book publishers Street and Smith.

The title of the short story was "*Match*," and despite its brevity, he was quite proud to be working with such a large

17

New York publishing house. He had two more short stories in the works that he hoped they would accept, as well. Not only had the *Golden Days* editors bought his first story, they had given him a very good piece of advice: "I think you would become a good serial writer if you were to know just what was required, always remembering that each 'to be continued' must mark a holding point in the story." Advice he used in the "*Match*," and something he would pass on to other writers under his tutelage at a much later time in his life. Something he could not even imagine as he stepped out onto the curb and stood in front of the large glass windows of his stationery shop.

Edward leaned in to pay the cabbie. "Don't forget your basket," the driver reminded him.

"Oh, yes! Thank you."

Edward retrieved the basket and set it next to him on the sidewalk. He looked across the street at the grassy commons area called Military Park. This triangular-shaped piece of land on the edge of the city had, until some twenty years earlier, been a training ground for the military. It was three blocks long along Broad Street, two blocks in length on the opposite side, along Park Place, and a block wide on the side that faced the Passaic River, a dirty waterway that ran along the East side of the city and eventually wound its way to Newark Bay, a major shipping port for New Jersey.

Edward smiled and turned to face the row of shops behind him. He looked up at the large wood placard above the storefront. "Stationery" was all it said in large block letter and in small text underneath "Magazines, Newspapers,

Periodicals." Edward stood with his hands on hips admiring the sign until someone coughed demurely, obviously trying to gain his attention.

It was a woman, and when Edward didn't look down, she cleared her throat once more.

"Excuse me," the woman finally said. Being subtle was not getting the young man's attention, so the woman decided a more direct approach was needed.

"Do you know when this store will be opening?"

"What?" Edward stammered, finally realizing he was being spoken to.

It was a bad habit Edward had; his thoughts would wander so far from the world around him, the real world would completely disappear from view until something or someone brought him back to the present. When he came back around and saw a fair, petite young lady standing before him, he couldn't help but smile.

She was a good four inches shorter than Edward and a year or two his junior he surmised. She was fashionably dressed in a black, puffy-sleeved jacket over a high-necked, taffeta dress of soft sea-blue that billowed like a stiff waterfall to the sidewalk. The matching satin bow and ostrich feather on the woman's hat above a modest brim attempted to draw Edward's eyes upward, but the alabaster skin of her face, that shone as if it were lit from within, transfixed his gaze there.

The young woman blushed at his extended stare. *Is he going to answer my question or is he just going to stare at me all day?* she thought, peevishly.

When he didn't answer her question, she finally felt compelled to repeat it.

"Do you know when this stationery store will be opening? The sign on the door just says, opening soon." she asked again, pointing toward the building and stepping closer to it, in part for emphasis, in part to put some distance between herself and the odd, sanguine-looking gentleman.

"Oh, why yes! I would expect any day now."

"Any day now," the woman repeated slowly. *That's an answer but not much of one,* she thought.

"Perhaps I'm asking the wrong person. You just appeared as if you were familiar with the establishment."

"Oh, I am! I am!" Edward said, stepping closer to the woman. "It's my shop."

The woman looked at him in astonishment. Admittedly, he looked the part in his coat and top hat, but his demeanor was not like any shopkeeper she had ever known.

Edward took off his hat and bowed his head in respect. "I'm sorry. Where are my manners? I should introduce myself." Edward placed his hat in his left hand and held out his right to the woman. "My name is Edward Stratemeyer. I've just moved here from Elizabeth."

The woman touched her gloved hand to his and promptly withdrew it. "Magdalene Baker Van Camp," she replied, with a diminutive nod.

"Very pleased to meet you," Edward said.

They stood and stared at each other until Magdalene broke the silence. "Well, I'll come by in a couple days, then," she said, not sure how to end this awkward encounter.

20

"Please do!" Edward beamed. "I should be open bright and early tomorrow morning. No, on second thought, perhaps Tuesday. Yes, I better say Tuesday."

Magdalene couldn't help her amusement at the scatterbrained young man. *I can't see him lasting more than a month,* Magdalene thought as she nodded her good day and hurried on her way.

Edward watched the bustled dress and the lovely woman who wore it seemingly float down the sidewalk – the dress appearing to move on its own accord as she turned the corner and disappeared out of sight.

Edward dropped his hat back on his head and clasped his hands in satisfaction. "I'm going to like it here, I think." He picked up his basket and, with a spring in his step, turned toward the door of his second floor flat. "I am going to like it, indeed."

Three ∾

The bell on the door of the stationery shop jingled, bringing Edward's attention to the doorway. He smiled and stepped over to greet the woman who walked in.

"Maddie!" he said with a smile, coming around the counter to greet her.

Magdalene looked briefly at Edward, looked down then immediately back toward the elderly woman who stood with an exasperated look on her face at the counter where Edward had just left her. Magdalene tried to stifle a smile at the pleasant though ill-timed greeting as she almost imperceptibly inclined her head in the older woman's direction.

Edward eventually caught the meaning of her posture and turned to face the indignant woman.

"Oh, I am so sorry, Mrs. Webster. Please forgive me,"

he said, making his way back around the counter to stand in front of her.

"I'll be with you in a moment, Miss," he said to Magdalene, then turned and attended the lady at hand.

Magdalene busied herself by picking up a *Ladies Home Journal* and leafing through it.

"Well, I think that is all I need," Edward said as he closed his notebook.

"Thank you so much, Mrs. Webster." He came around the counter and ushered the still- miffed elderly matron toward the door. "I would expect your order back in about a week."

Magdalene set down her magazine and looked up at them. The woman looked haughtily back at Magdalene, sneered at Edward, and left without so much as a "Good day."

Magdalene giggled when Edward turned to face her. "Oh my, Edward. Is that what you have to face every day?"

The couple crossed the room toward each other then held hands. "Oh, don't mind Mrs. Webster. She's a pussy cat when you get to know her."

"She's some sort of cat, no doubt."

Magdalene leaned toward Edward, waiting for the customary peck on the cheek. Edward happily obliged.

"Are our invitations in yet, sweetheart?" Maddie said.

Edward led her over to the counter then went around behind it and brought out a small box. He ceremoniously set it in front of her but didn't let go of it.

"Well, open it you fool. You are such a tease, Teddie."

"Special order for her ladyship," he said and, with a flourish, pulled the cover off the box to reveal a set of gold embossed ivory cards set neatly in a pile. Maddie brightened and held a card up to read.

Mr. & Mrs. Silas Van Camp
And
Mr. and Mrs. Heinrich J. Stratemeyer
Cordially invite you to the
Wedding of their children,
Magdalene Baker Van Camp
To
Edward Stratemeyer
The twenty-fifth of March,
In the year of our Lord, 1891

Maddie looked back at Edward, a pleased look on her face. "They're lovely, Edward." She reached across the counter to grasp his hand. "I only hope your father makes it to the ceremony." Maddie's expression changed to one of concern. "How is he doing?"

"He's fine, dearest. The medication the doctor gives him seems to calm him, and Mother says he sleeps a fair share of the time, so they're managing."

Maddie gave his hand a squeeze.

"But enough about that," Edward said. "I want to hear how your writing is coming. Did you bring me a sample as you promised?"

Maddie looked down, embarrassed by the fuss her fiancé was making. She knew Edward was the real writer.

The poems and short prose she dabbled in was for ladies gatherings, not for the general public.

"You're sweet, dear, but it's *your* writing we need to focus on. Once we're married, I can do the bookkeeping for the shop as I do now for the Yeast Company so you'll have more time to work on that novel you're always talking about."

Edward came from behind the counter to stand next to Maddie. He took her hand again and kissed the back of it. "Come March, you are going to make me a very happy man, Miss Van Camp, a very happy man."

(1892)

Edward leaned back in his wooden desk chair, the rusty springs squeaking from the pressure. There was a crease between his brows as he stared at the half-typed page.

"Richard is on his way to New York, but it shouldn't be that simple. No self-respecting boy would want to take a train unless something potentially exciting could happen."

Edward brought his index finger up to his lips, his expression one of deep thought. Suddenly, his face lit up and his fingers flew to the round, white keys once more.

A sudden jar at this instant caused Richard to pitch forward from his seat. Then, before he realized what had happened, the car tilted, then turned completely over on its side.

The rhythmic flap, flap of the typewriter's metal arms swinging into place on the strip of ink-infused cloth, printed out the next exciting scene in *Richard Dare's Venture; or, Striking out For Himself,* Edward's first attempt at a full length novel.

"Dear...Dear," the feminine voice said again, though Edward did not hear her.

Maddie had been trying to get Edwards attention for a few minutes now, first with a subtle wave of her hand, then with a soft clearing of her throat. She hated to startle the man. But this preoccupation wasn't unusual for him; her husband was singularly focused when he was working on his stories. If he wasn't talking to himself – reading his story out loud – he might be moving around the room, pantomiming what his characters might be doing on the page. She knew that this role playing was important to Edward, just as his research was important to him, whether it was out of a book or from a trip to a particular local. It was all to ensure that the reader would feel the nuance of the situation in the story, feel as if they were part of what was going on for the characters, whatever their age might be.

And normally, Maddie wouldn't disturb her husband at his work. Edward had sold nearly ninety boys' stories in the short time she had been with him, in addition to working in the store every day, and keeping his mother happy through his frequent correspondence and attendance at the family dinner every Sunday afternoon. But today was another matter.

Maddie was about the call out to him again when a pain gripped her, making her stop and taking her breath away. She let out a reflexive gasp and propped herself with one hand on the door jam. She made her way haltingly over to her husband's desk. She eyed him, bemused by his concentration but still disturbed by a pain that she wasn't expecting and that she had never experienced before. Still, it took him a second to finally see her standing there.

"Oh! Hello, my love. I didn't hear you come in."

Edward stood and reached for the only other chair in the room. "Here. Sit," he said, ushering her into the wooden chair. He sat opposite Maddie and held her hand. "And what does my lovely wife need this fine day?" he said with a smile.

His smile soon changed to fright as his wife gripped the side of her chair and squeezed his hand with a strength Edward didn't know she possessed.

"Dearest! What is the matter? Shall I get the doctor?" Edward stammered, partially rising to his feet.

Maddie held him firm, relegated to the interminable and painful silence until his wife was able to speak. She looked up at her husband, then down at their feet; both pairs of shoes were wet and dripping.

The couple stared into each other's eyes. "I think you're going to be a father," Maddie said calmly.

Edward looked down at the multiple folds of taffeta covering the large bulge in Maddie's lap and dropped down to kiss her hand and hold it to his cheek.

"Dearest! You are not going to believe this!" Edward said,

rushing into the nursery. But one look from his wife and Edward's exclamations were stifled and he stood rooted to the floor.

Maddie put a finger to her lips, never skipping a beat as she rocked their daughter, Harriet, in the white, lacy layette. Maddie leaned over to ensure that the now chubby babe was indeed asleep, then stood and ushered her penitent husband out of the room.

She closed the door silently then turned toward Edward. "All right, dear. What is all the fuss about?"

Edward handed her a letter, beaming with satisfaction. Maddie read it, her face brightening as she read. She wrapped her arms around her husband and kissed him sweetly on the cheek.

"How wonderful, Teddie!" She looked down at the letter again. "An editor of the *Good News* story paper and for Street and Smith Publishing, no less! They must have been impressed by how well your stories are coming along."

"During the interview, they seemed to imply the wide variety of my work was an asset, as well."

"Well, you can pen a mystery as handily as a western."

"It's all in the research, my dear. It's all in the research."

Maddie grasped Edward's arm and led him away from the nursery door. "And the fact that you're a boy at heart," she teased.

Edward patted her hand. "Well, that too," he said with a grin. "But that little secret is just between you and me."

"My lips are sealed," Maddie said. Then she reached up and kissed Edward full on the mouth.

Edward was surprised by the gesture, but readily succumbed to his wife's advance and took her in his arms, taking in the full measure of her.

Edward sat at his desk at Street and Smith and looked at the story that he held in his hands. He knew the gentleman who had written it. He had seen him drop it off with the receptionist himself. But he thought William Mather had been the author of the Billy Sill stories, so Edward was perplexed when Jonathan Worthington dropped off the next installment in the series for him to review. He wasn't sure if there had been a mistake, but he decided he ought to make sure. He walked up to the door of the editor-in-chief of *Good News* and rapped quietly on his wood paneled door.

He heard a muffled "Come in" from the other side, and Edward let himself into the room.

Mr. Maplecrest sat behind a large, oak desk puffing on a cigar and looking over an open copy of the boys' story paper laid out in front of him.

"Hello, Eddie," he said amiably. "Have a seat, my boy."

The manager of *Good News* was a large man, and despite his amiable demeanor, Edward knew he was a shrewd businessman. He knew Mr. Maplecrest had earned the gray hairs that graced his temples and the wrinkles around his eyes, just as easily as he had filled out his waistcoat.

The chief editor pulled out his watch and opened it to look at the face. "It's only ten in the morning, Eddie. I don't usually get questions from you until at least past noon," he said with a grin.

"I think there has been a mistake, sir, but Agnes says I am incorrect. But before it went any further, I wanted to run it by you."

Mr. Maplecrest leaned onto his desk. "Very wise of you, Edward. Better to be safe than sorry, I always say. What is it, my boy?"

"Nancy gave me this story, the latest installment in the Billy Sills series," Edward said, handing the typed story pages to Mr. Maplecrest. "William Mather is the author of that series, but I saw Jonathan Worthington hand it to Agnes just this morning."

"So did you look at it?"

"I did, and it appears as if it is Mr. Mather's work."

Mr. Maplecrest took the papers from Edward but didn't look at them. He leaned back in his chair with a chuckle.

"I would hope so," the large man said and took another puff on his cigar. "I've given him the formula to follow. If he values his continued employment with us, he'll continue to follow it."

"Formula?" Edward stammered. "I don't understand."

"We need our serials to follow a particular pattern, the tried and true writing formula I've created. It ensures continuity of the story, as in this case, when our previous Mr. Mather decided the fee we paid him was no longer suitable."

Edward's boss leaned his elbows back on his desk. "You understand why, don't you?"

Edward stared at the large man a moment, not really

looking at him but rather looking through him. He eventually refocused on Mr. Maplecrest's face, a look of understanding in his own.

"So that you can replace him and our readers won't know the difference!" he said in triumph.

"Exactly!"

"Is that also the reason for the pseudonyms? I always thought that was to protect the writer's identity."

"And to protect our bottom line. If we had to cut a popular serial such as Billy Sill every time we lost a writer, we'd be out of business before you could say Jack Robinson!"

Edward blinked his surprise at the information being shared, both at Mayer's reason for departure and the fact that the nom de plumes were used not only to hide the true authors but for the benefit of the company.

"But you have never mentioned this formula in relation to my stories, sir, other than the page length you require."

"I haven't had to, Eddie. You're smart enough to know what our readers want and you're able to do it consistently. That's why I hired you as an editor, my boy!"

Mr. Maplecrest handed the story back to Edward and stood to usher him out of the room.

"So now you know our little secret, and I am sure you will keep it under your hat."

"Yes, sir. Of course, sir," Edward said, nodding his head in ascent.

"Wonderful," the man said, cigar still in his hand. "Keep up the good work," he finished, clapping him roughly on the back.

"Yes, sir."

The editor closed the door, leaving Edward staring at the worn and cracked finish, wondering in the back of his mind when he too would be deemed too expensive for the publishing house.

(1894)

"Ed. Edward, come down, please."

Maddie pulled on the cord at the base of the steps, ringing a bell attached to it a story up in Edwards writing room. It was a mechanism her father had rigged up when Maddie grew too large while carrying their second child and could no longer easily negotiate the steps to Edward's study.

Edward looked up at the swinging bell and put down his ruler, a makeshift sword in his latest swashbuckling adventure.

He came to the head of the steps and peered down, not wanting to come down if Maddie just needed him to answer a question or help with a decision about the household.

"Yes, dear?" he said down the steps.

Maddie held a brown paper package up for him to view.

No words were needed. Edward was down the steps in a flash.

Maddie handed him the parcel, matching his smile with hers. Edward eagerly unwrapped it, letting the paper and string fall to the floor without thought. He held the book in his hand, running his palm over the rough, burnt-rust hardcover with loving care. He handed it to his wife and stood behind her, looking over her shoulder as she examined it.

"Look there, Teddie," she said, pointing to the black type across the top. " 'The Stratemeyer popular series!' "

Edward chuckled. "Yes, all two of them."

"First, Richard Dare and now, Luke Foster." Maddie turned and looked up into her husband's eyes. "I know there's another boy lurking in there somewhere."

Edward grinned.

"I hardly have the time, with my new position at *Young Sports*, in addition to editing at *Good News*, and with the new baby…"

Edward's smile easily turned sour as he spoke.

"Dearest." Maddie lightly touched her husband's cheek. "Come and sit with me. We need to have a chat," she said, grasping his hand.

Maddie led Edward into their small parlor and sat with him on the stiff sofa.

"I hate to see you this way, darling. You're working yourself too hard. You do all this editing and outlining of stories for other writers at these story papers leaving you little time for your family or even your own writing. I think you need a change, dear."

Edward gazed at his wife in amazement. He had been thinking those very same thoughts, but with the new baby on the way, he felt he dare not mention it to her.

"Well…I've actually been thinking…" he started. He stood and walked over to the fireplace mantle then turned to face his wife. "What would you think of me starting my own boys' paper?"

Maddie's eyes widened in surprise. She wasn't sure what the solution to her husband's frustrations were, but starting his own publication wouldn't be her first choice.

"I'd have to think it over, I suppose."

Edward stepped eagerly over to her side and sat back down, grasping her hand in his and gazing into her eyes. "I wouldn't think of making a change until after the baby is born, of course."

He stood again and started pacing the room.

"I'm learning so much at my editing positions. And now that I have the rights to many of my stories back…"

"Yes, but you paid almost twice as much to get those stories back as what they paid you in the first place, Edward. How is that sound business?"

Edward sat back down next to his wife. "I know that doesn't sound logical, dearest, but you'll see. I can put those paper serials together and put out book versions of those very same stories, making up that cost in no time and with very little effort on my part," he said, eyes sparkling with promise. "They're already tested by the boys, so any publishing house will be sure to snatch them up for print."

"Oh, I see. That is a good idea."

"And I was saving the best for last." Edward walked over to the bureau and took a stack of papers off the top. He brought them over to his wife and set them on her lap.

"Do you remember those questions I was asking

you about the names of the articles of ladies' clothing and milliners?"

"Yes. You said it was for a story you were working on, though what kind of boys' adventure story would need that sort of information, I wouldn't dare to know."

Edward set the stack of papers down on Maddie's lap. She picked them up and read the cover page. "*Out on the Town* by Edna Winfield." Maddie looked at Edward, perplexed. "Winfield? Winfield? Why does that sound familiar?"

"You might be familiar with Arthur Winfield, of Victor Horton fame."

Maddie tilted her head and stared at her husband. Then the light of recognition appeared on her face.

"Seriously, Teddie? You're Edna?" Maddie said with a small snicker.

"It's a romantic serial for the *New York Weekly*."

Maddie's smile widened.

"And they're asking for four more stories, and maybe more."

"But you already have eight books in that new book series of yours. What's it called?"

"The *Bound to Win* series, and its ten books, but never mind about that."

"But with the economy such as it is, I think we are just barely recovering from the stock market debacle not even two years ago. Frankly, I'm surprised the publishers can keep their heads above water and still purchase your work. Buying books can't be foremost on a parent's mind these days."

"But that's the thing! I *do* continue to sell my stories,

and it's because of the children not their parents. They save up their bottle and birthday money, plus the few coins that get tossed their way here and there, and they're able to buy my books so they can check in on their favorite characters. Really, Maddie, I think it's the children that might pull the publishing houses out of their slump. I really do."

"Well, you do continue to sell your dime novels, so many now I think I've lost count." Maddie fell back against the back of the sofa as if truly exhausted by her attempts at keeping all of Edward's numerous published works straight in her mind. "Honestly, Teddie. I don't know how you manage all this and still run the store, and with little help from me of late," Maddie said, caressing her growing belly.

Edward went down on one knee. "But with this new series, Edna dearest, I'll need your assistance more than ever."

Maddie's eyes shot open, taking in the import of his words. "Edward, I haven't written since before we married. I wouldn't presume…"

The edges of Edward's large bushy mustache curled up ever so slightly, a trait Maddie found hard to resist.

She leaned forward and playfully pinched his pointed chin. "How can I ever say no to you, Edward Stratemeyer?"

"Splendid!" He rose and measured off the room again with his long strides. "Then I'll tell the paper that I'm in, and we can start planning our own paper. We'll call it…we'll call it *Bright Days*. Yes, I think that will do. Sends the right message, don't you think?"

Edward's arms were working almost as much as his mouth, directing his words as any good symphonic conductor as he walked the length of the small room and made his plans. "And I'll contact Mr. Alger for a contribution. He says he's not writing much these days, but I know Horatio has a story or two in him still. He's like me, it's in his blood. And then there's Adams… " His voice trailed off when his words could no longer keep up with his thoughts.

Our paper, indeed, Maddie mused. She could see the wheels turning in her husband's mind. Maddie was used to this by now, hearing a word here and there when he wanted to emphasize a point to himself. Maddie dutifully listened, continually amazed at the energy of the man. There would be very little "we" in this plan. *But all the better*, Maddie thought. *I'll have my hands full as it is.* Then she let out a small squeak as a small hand or foot made its presence known.

ℱour ∾

(May 1898)

The two small girls were nestled snugly in their shared bed, Harriet, seven years old, Edna, just three. Downstairs a small fire was burning in the parlor grate to push out the chill of the April rain as the happy couple spent a quiet evening together reading, Edward with his paper, Maddie with her book.

"My, this sounds like quite the battle," Edward said from behind the news print.

Maddie put down her book to listen.

"We have been in this war with Spain for, what, a month now and we've already won a decisive battle in Manila," Edward explained.

"Manila? Why are we in Manila? I thought we were in Cuba. The atrocities that those Spanish are perpetrating on those poor souls… starving them out, the deplorable detention camps…" Maddie shook her head in disgust.

"Manila is a strategic move, dearest. The United States wants to make sure the Spaniards in Manila are occupied, so they don't come to their comrades' aid in Cuba."

"Hopefully it will all be over soon and just another battle won for the history books," Maddie said.

Edward set down his paper and stared at his wife. "Maddie. That's a wonderful idea! I'll write another historical!"

"But I thought you were writing about the Revolutionary War."

"True. But how better to bring our own young men up to date than to write about the battle that is going on at this very minute? I think it's a wonderful idea! With the stationery store closed and *Bright Days* a thing of the past, I have the time. I just needed another idea."

Edward stood up, walked over to his wife, and kissed her on the cheek. "Thank you, my dear. I think I'll start on it immediately."

"But it's after eight in the evening, Ed."

"Have to strike while the iron's hot, my dear!" he said with glee.

Edward started out of the room but stopped and looked at the paper still in hand. "Do we still have last week's papers? I need to get some material about the battle."

"I think they've been used to start the fires, dear."

"Then I'll have to make a trip to the library first thing in the morning."

❦

"Are you a famous writer now, Father?" Harriet asked Edward as he tucked her and Edna into bed.

"I wouldn't say just yet, sweetheart."

"But at Christmas dinner I heard Uncle Louis say that your Manila book has sold over six thousand copies. Six thousand is a lot!" Harriet's corkscrew curls bobbed gaily as she nodded her head with admiration.

"It is a lot, isn't it?"

"Is your story about Grandpa Julius and the gold rush going to sell that many copies?" she asked, her eyes wide with anticipation.

Edward sat down on the side of the bed and moved a stray curl off of his young daughter's forehead. "Actually, my next book is about the Alaskan gold rush that is going on as we speak!" he said, playfully tweaking her nose.

"Do you know where Alaska is, Hattie?"

"Yes, we learned all about the forty-five states in school last year."

"The gold rush in California that your grandfather was in started in 1848, many years ago."

"Oh," Harriet said with a pout. "I wanted to hear about Grandpa Julius." Harriet crossed her arms across her chest imitating Edward's posture when he was disappointed with something Harriet or Edna had done.

"Young ladies such as yourselves wouldn't have any interest in the difficult life of a 49er. How about I tell you about what happened to Mr. Bobalincoln. Do you remember from two evenings ago? He and Mr. Whistler had just gotten their buggy stuck in the mud."

Edna's curls bounced as she nodded her head in assent. She couldn't take her thumb out of her mouth to answer, or her arm from around her dolly, who was tucked in tight beside her, but Harriet's features were unmoving.

Edward smiled sweetly at Harriet and tried not to laugh. "But…it *was* an interesting time, the California gold rush."

Harriet's face brightened instantly.

"All right then." Edward hesitated, quickly forming the story in his mind. "It was 1848 when your grandfather stepped onto the large, metal boat that would take him to the Americas. The boat was the biggest thing he had ever seen."

"How big, Poppa?"

"As tall as this house and twice the length!"

Harriet's eyes widened.

"He was thirty-two years of age at the time, and he spoke only German. It was a long journey across the wide open ocean." Edward moved his hand in a wide sweep, emphasizing the vastness and expanse of the water. "And excited as he was, he was also quite afraid. He carried just one cloth bag with him and his violin. The bag held his Sunday clothes and a Bible his mother had given him."

"The Bible in your study?" Harriet asked.

"That very one!

"And in his breast pocket he had his most prized possession," Edward touched the object in his vest pocket, "his father's pocket watch, a gift for his trip to America."

Harriet reached for his father's watch fob and drew Edward's heavy watch out of his waistcoat pocket. She ran her finger lightly over the intricate swirls and loops cut into the gold cover. The two hardly heard Edna's sucking sounds as she dozed contently beside them, pulling hard on the thumb in her mouth.

January 4, 1899

My dear Mr. Pendergrass,

I have sent along the outlines of three stories I would like published. It is a boys' adventure series as my previous works have been, but not of a historical nature as my most recent publications.

This series follows the lives of three brothers Dick, Tom, and Sam Rover whose mother is deceased and whose father is away exploring Africa. (Exploration runs in the family). So the boys are sent off to their uncles and eventually to a boarding school and left to their own devices.

I will not be publishing under my recent pseudonym, Captain Ralph Bonehill, but my previous nom de plume of Arthur M. Winfield. I would expect each story to be approximately 48 - 50,000 words.

I will continue to publish my boys' historicals but feel that a pure adventure series may be longer lasting (less apt to lose favor) and more easily

continued (more books in the series) if it is not written
around specific times or events in history.
  I eagerly await your reply.

                                    Sincerely,
                                    Edward Stratemeyer

Mr. Pendergrass picked up the first outline and thumbed through the three typed pages.

"Twenty-eight chapters is a decent length," he said to himself. "But the title…? Mr. Pendergrass read the heading on the first page: *The Rover Boys at School; or, The Cadets of Putnam Hall.* "Not particularly inspiring. But I suppose they have to start somewhere."

He rifled through the other sheets. *Well, at least the titles improve,* he thought. The next book was titled *On the Ocean; or, A Chase for a Fortune,* and the third in what he called his breeder stories was *In the Jungle; or, Stirring Adventures in Africa.* It was Edward's habit now to put out three stories of one series at once, and if those sold well, he would keep the stories going – or breed other books. If not, the idea could be easily dropped and something else put in its place. Edward was rarely in want of ideas.

He picked up the first outline and read through the cast of characters.

Anderson Rover: Widowed, mineral expert, gold
      mine proprietor, and traveler, made his
      wealth from California mines.
Richard Rover: AKA Dick, age 16, studious.

Tom Rover: age 15, fun-loving, mischievous.
Sam Rover: age 14, the athletic brother, Tom's ally
in his pranks.
Uncle Randolph Rover: gentleman farmer, studies
and experiments in horticulture, married
to Aunt Martha.

The list and descriptions of friends, teachers, and relatives continued down the page, illustrating Mr. Stratemeyer's ability to make his stories varied and interesting.

Mr. Pendergrass started through the outline.

Anderson Rover, a widower, has left his three boys with his brother while he goes to Africa to expand his already significant fortune. The boys are soon bored and sent off to boarding school – Putnam Hall, a military academy – and get into mischief.

Chapter 1 – Introduces the Rover boys,
uncle, and aunt.
Explain why the boys are going to boarding school: mother died of fever, father went out west and made an even bigger fortune than he had before his marriage but he grows restless, decides to mine in Africa. Leaves the boys with his brother. He is not heard from for some time so Uncle Randolph plans to send the boys to boarding school.

Chapter 2 – An Encounter on the Road
Dick is accosted by a tramp who takes his pocketbook
and his father's watch.
Tom and Sam come to the rescue, get the pocketbook
back but not the watch.
They all chase the tramp to the water. The tramp gets
in a boat, the boys find an old log. They make chase.
Tom falls off the log and gets hit by a tree branch. Dick
jumps in to save him. The tramp gets away. The boys
make it to shore but Sam, still on the log, is heading
for the falls.

"Now that's a Stratemeyer adventure," he said and gathered the papers up again. "Interesting though, the boys are quite well off: a father of wealth who is conveniently absent; the boys being sent off to a boarding school. A bit different from the poor boy tales he's done in the past." Mr. Pendergrass hesitated. "But then who doesn't admire people with means or at least have aspirations for such." He knew, as any New York book editor did, how well Mr. Stratemeyer had done with his Dewey at Manila book, and was sure he had more of the same on the way. But to change gears as Edward was doing with this new adventure series, to not put all his eggs in one basket, as it were, was complete genius in Pendergrass's mind. And ambitious. But he would let his readers decide if they liked Richard, Tom, and Sam Rover. Mr. Pendergrass knew the reading public was the ultimate editor, and he was happy to put the final decision to them.

Edward had sold some of his stories to the publisher

W.L. Allison under the "Working Upward Series," so Pendergrass knew Edward had more than one poker in the flames. Mr. Pendergrass mused about having such an insightful, hardworking man on his own staff and made a mental note to offer Edward a position as editor.

Mr. Pendergrass looked back down at the outlines. "If only Stratemeyer sold his story rights. We'd make a mint on these. I'm just glad he came to us to publish them. Sell these for a dollar a hard cover and we'll still make a pretty penny, as it is. I'm sure he'll go for the four percent royalty rate. They all do, no matter how good they are. They can't publish without us and they know it," Mr. Pendergrass said with a self-satisfied grin.

"I'll let him know right off that we'll publish," he said.

The editor pulled a clean sheet of note paper from the neat stack in one of the many slots on his desk and dipped his metal writing tip in the ink jar.

Five ∾

(1899)

Maddie was in her finest black silk dress and an understated black hat so as not to draw attention to herself. She put her gloved arm around her husband's as they filed solemnly out of St. John's Episcopal Church with the rest of the small gathering of Alger's friends and family.

Horatio Alger was a king in Edward's eyes; his characters, Richard Hunter of the Ragged Dick Series or Julius from Alger's Tattered Tom Series, were among Edward's best childhood friends. His characters had such pluck and fortitude that it was hard not to like them. Alger was considered the grandfather of the boys' serial, and Edward had always attributed his love for the written word to Alger and William Taylor Adams – AKA Oliver Optic – who had also died just two years earlier.

Fresh from Alger's funeral service, Edward felt even more compelled to complete the final request of this favored author. He had completed Adams' last work after his death, and now he had been asked to do the same for Alger. He had met with Horatio just a few weeks ago and was given two almost completed stories: *Out for Business; or, Robert Frost's Strange Career*, and *Falling in with Fortune; or, The Experiences of a Young Secretary,* in addition to outlines for five other stories that Alger requested Edward complete for him. Alger's lung condition was getting the better of him, and he couldn't finish them himself.

Edward was honored beyond speech, of course, despite the fact that both Alger's and Adams' books were not thought of as literary works and were criticized for being formulaic. Edward never forgot what Alger had said to him one evening over cigars and brandy: "I've found out what the boys that read my books like, and I'm not going to risk disappointing my boys and having them feel that I've fooled them for the sake of winning a reputation for versatility."

It was also a feather in Edward's cap to have his name attached to a work of Alger's, though at the moment, he wasn't quite sure he was correct in that assumption.

Edward leaned down to whisper in Maddie's ear. "Don't you think it odd, Maddie? There was hardly anyone at the funeral."

"I thought the same thing myself," she whispered back. "It is a sad state of affairs when such a writer, a man who obviously had a passion for writing and was a leader in his genre, is so easily forgotten."

Edward lifted his eyebrows in acknowledgement and the realization that he too was a writer much like Alger. He wondered absently who would be at his own funeral, if he would be remembered for what he had written, or if he too would be left as a notation in some obscure writer's journal or a name on some college English paper. He squeezed his wife's hand and led her to their waiting carriage to take them to the train station and back to New Jersey.

Harriet heard the neighbor's chickens clucking wildly, their feathers rustling as she sat reading and swinging on the bench swing in her back yard. She knew something was wrong at the Adams' home even though she couldn't see what was going on from where she sat. She set her book, *The Swiss Family Robinson*, down beside her and ran over to the fence to see what the commotion was about. When she stepped closer, she saw Russell Adams, a boy just a year or two her senior, bent over and running after the ruffled birds, taking after one for a time then another, switching haphazardly to a different bird when he couldn't catch the first. Harriet bent over in laughter at the sight. Russell heard her and stood up to see who was making fun of him. That's when he spied Harriet and her sister, Edna, looking over the fence at him, and he scowled.

"Having a bit of trouble, Russell?" Harriet snickered. Edna covered her mouth to stifle a laugh. "You make about as good a chicken farmer as you do a scholar."

Russell put his hands on his hips. "I know more than you do."

"That's because you're in a higher grade."

"Well, if you're so good at catching chickens, Miss Smarty Pants, how 'bout you come over and show me how."

Harriet looked at her sister and grinned.

"Hattie, you better not. Mother's not feeling well, so we're supposed to be still."

Harriet waved her sister off, hoisted her skirt up to her knees, and jumped the fence.

"Hattie!" Edna yelled to her sister's back as loud as she dared.

Harriet turned around and put a finger to her lips to quiet her sister. Edna looked at the house to see if anyone was looking, then ran to the back of the yard and through the back gate, heading to the Adams' chicken coop.

Harriet opened the door to the coop and stepped inside. Edna ran up to the side of the coop and hung onto the wire, ready for the show.

In a gentlemanly manner, Russell bowed slightly at the waist and motioned Harriet toward the birds, who were back to pecking absently at bugs or missed grains of corn in the dirt. Harriet licked her lips and got into a crouch.

"Be careful, Hattie. Don't let them scratch you!" her sister called out.

Harriet ignored her sister and crept closer to the birds. She moved slowly into the midst of the small group, being careful not to ruffle any feathers, and picked out a colorful rust and gold hen as her target. When she got to within a few feet of the bird, she lunged. Suddenly, there were chickens, dust, and feathers flying everywhere. Edna covered her mouth in horror.

"Oh, Hattie!" She ran over to where her sister lay perfectly still, face down in the dirt.

Russell ran over as well and was about to reach to help her up when Harriet turned, and with a smile of triumph, thrust out the dazed bird in Russell's direction.

"I've got it!" she said, spitting stray feathers and dirt out of her mouth.

Russell held his middle and laughed until the water came to his eyes. Edna looked at her sister, covered in dirt from her chin to her button shoes and couldn't help but laugh, too.

"Harriet Stratemeyer, you do take the cake," Russell said with amusement.

Harriet smiled with satisfaction. "Well, are you going to take the chicken or not?"

Russell took the bird from Harriet and put it under one arm. He held out his other hand to Harriet and helped her to standing.

Harriet tried to brush off her white blouse and green skirt but soon gave up. He mother would be upset with her, but it wouldn't be the first time. The two friends stepped out of the coop, Russell holding the door open for Harriet to step through first with Edna close behind. Edna ran up to the chicken in Russell's arm and stroked its iridescent head as it blinked complacently, ignorant of what was in store.

"So what did you need to catch the chicken for, anyway," Harriet asked as they all headed for the Adams' shed.

"For dinner," Russell said, without skipping a beat.

Harriet and Edna both stopped in their tracks. Russell turned around and looked at them.

"What did you think we did with them?"

"I thought you had them for eggs," Harriet said with some dismay.

"We do. But when they get too old to lay, we butcher them. Want to come see how it's done?" he said with some amusement.

Edna grasped her sister's arm in fright at the thought and stared at the beautiful chicken sitting quietly under Russell's arm.

"Russell Adams you are not only ignorant, you're cruel." Then Harriet turned on her heel and stomped away, Edna trailing right behind.

"Where do you think your chicken dinners come from?" Russell yelled out to Harriet. "You silly girl," he said to himself.

Even though Harriet Stratemeyer was a perpetual tease and a show off on top of it, Russell couldn't help but admire her gumption.

Only Edna turned back briefly, a look of horror on her face.

Russell shook his head, opened the door to their shed, and stepped inside. Moments later the sound of an ax being brought down hard into a block of wood was heard followed by a minute of frantic ruffling of feathers, then all was silent.

"I want a tablecloth just like yours," Edna whined, protruding her bottom lip as far as she could.

Edward looked over his paper at his daughters playing on the floor and was frozen in place. He dropped his paper to the floor and walked over to them, staring down at what had been keeping them occupied and quiet for the last two hours. He stood transfixed, hands on his hips.

Both girls looked up at their father, waiting for him to tell them to pipe down. Their mother had another migraine, and they had been told by Mabel, their new housekeeper, to find something quiet to do.

"I'll make her a tablecloth, Father," Harriet said, assuming her father had come over to intervene on Edna's behalf.

Edward crouched down, examining the girls' handiwork. When their father didn't speak, both girls looked at each other, puzzled. He looked up at them, then back down at their little village without uttering a word.

What lay before him was a row of shoebox houses, three of which were low, one-story dwellings, the fourth, the one that Hattie was working on, was set on its short side and divided into three different floors. There were doors cut into the sides of the boxes and windows with swatches of tissue or fabric glued in place for curtains. Upholstery-like fabric was cut in ovals or rectangles for floor coverings, pasteboard tables, and chairs. Beds finished off the rooms. Their father examined every detail.

Finally Edward spoke.

"This is quite amazing. Did Miss Mabel help you with this?

"She found us the boxes and some of the scraps we needed for dresses and rugs and things," Harriet said.

"How long have you girls been working on this?"

"A few days," Harriet said. "We bring it out whenever Momma has to lie down."

"And who are these ladies?" Edward asked Edna, pointing to two pasteboard figures with cut-out paper skirts and blouses attached to their stiff frames.

"That's Betty and Bridget. They're twins," Edna explained.

"Brilliant!" Edward exclaimed clapping his hand together. "Then they always have someone to play with."

Edna nodded her head in agreement, but looked at her father with some surprise, unsure why this excited him so.

Edward looked back down at the pasteboard village and smiled. He had been mulling an idea around in his head for a new series and this pasteboard village was helping narrow his focus This new series would be a significant departure from his latest series, The Rover Boys, even though The Rover Boys had really taken off, even more so than his boys' industry stories. With Edward's industry stories – *The Young Auctioneer, Bound to be an Electrician, Shorthand Tom the Reporter, Fighting for his Own* – even though some of the same characters showed themselves throughout the various books, the protagonist was always a different fellow. Those stories didn't seem to garner the loyalty The Rover Boys had.

The rapid popularity of The Rover Boys made Edward realize having the same boys in story after story kept the reader's interest longer. The readers seemed to gain a friendship, as it were, with Dick, Tom, and Sam Rover and wanted to follow them along in each new adventure.

But there wasn't much out there for the younger set, or even much specifically written for young girls. Edward had often seen Harriet with one of his own worn copies of Alger's Ragged Rick books in her hands and thought, with a slight pang of guilt, that besides the very popular *The Wide, Wide World* by Susan Warner, some stories by Louisa May Alcott: *Little Women* and *Eight Cousins*, and Anna Sewell's *Black Beauty*, there was little for young girls to read, besides the stories written for boys. And Edward had gotten fan mail from girls as well as boys in the five years his Rover boys had been around, so he knew girls liked a good adventure as much as the boys.

But creating books for girls went against Edward's better judgment. He knew that girls started reading at around age seven, and by twelve years of age they tended to move onto more adult women's novels, which were more readily available and frequently helped prepare the girls for their role as women. But looking down at his two girls, now nine and eleven, Edward couldn't help but want to write a story just for them. That and the fact that his wife had been encouraging him to do just that for a couple years now.

Edward kissed his girls on the forehead and left for his study. He sat down at his desk and glanced at the typewriter but thought better of it. "The noise would bother Maddie," he said out loud. Instead, he set the typewriter gingerly on the floor, pulled out a sheaf of paper, and opened up his inkwell. He placed the end of his pen to his lips in thought.

"If I am to cater to a wider range of girls, I should have two sets of twins instead of just one, one younger set and one older. Yes! But the twins…the twins will be paternal so there can be both a boy and a girl. That would allow for adventures for both the boy and the girl characters. Brilliant!"

Edward wrote down a title: *Twin Bobbseys*. He studied the words a moment then drew a line through it and wrote: *The Bobbsey Twins*. Edwards smiled in satisfaction.

"Now for some characters."

Edward thought a moment longer then scratched out a couple names.

Frannie and Freddie Bobbsey

"Let's see." Edward tapped his pen to his lips again. "Let's make them…four. That way, they have many years ahead of them and they will appeal to the younger set." He quickly wrote down their age then added two more names and ages to his list with hardly a hesitation.

Nan and Bert Bobbsey - eight years

He looked at the names of the four-year-olds again and crossed out Frannie. He thought a moment and replaced Frannie with Flossie.

"Now, they can't be wanting for anything, so they would

have a colored nanny. Let's call her Dinah." Edward added the name to his list. "And with such young children reading these stories, I should think both parents are present."

Mr. Bobbsey - successful businessman, owner of a lumber company
Mrs. Bobbsey - kept their home

Edward wrote down a few more names, friends for each set of twins. Then he went to work on volume one.

The Bobbsey Twins were very busy that morning. They were all seated around the dinning-room table, making houses and furnishing them. The houses were made out of pasteboard shoeboxes, and had squares cut in them for doors, and other long holes for windows, and had pasteboard chairs and tables, and bits of dress goods for carpets and rugs, and bits of tissue paper stuck up to the windows for lace curtains. Three of the houses were long and low, but Bert had placed his box on end and divided into three stories, and Flossie said it looked exactly like a "department" house in New York.

There were four of the twins. Now that sounds funny, doesn't it? But you see, there were two sets. Bert and Nan, age eight. Freddie and Flossie, age four.

Nan was a tall slender girl, with a dark face and red cheeks. Her eyes were a deep brown and so were the curls that clustered around her head.

Bert was indeed a twin, not only because he was

the same age as Nan, but because he looked so very much like her. To be sure, he looked like a boy, while she looked like a girl, but he had the same dark complexion, the same brown eyes and hair, and his voice was very much the same, only stronger.

Freddie and Flossie were just the opposite of their larger brother and sister. Each was short and stout, with fair, round face, light-blue eyes and fluffy golden hair. Sometimes Papa Bobbsey called Flossie his little Fat Fairy, which always made her laugh. But Freddie didn't want to be called a fairy, so his papa called him the Fat Fireman, which pleased him very much, and made him rush around the house shouting: "Fire! Fire! Clear the track for Number Two! Play away, boys, play away!" in a manner that seemed very lifelike. During the past year Freddie had seen two fires, and the work of the firemen had interested him deeply.

Writing away feverishly, Edward didn't even hear his wife enter the room.

Maddie gazed over Edward's shoulder and lightly touched him on the arm. "I see you're hard at work."

Edward set his pen down and turned toward his wife. "Are you feeling better, my dear?" he said, grasping her hand. He quickly rose and brought a second chair closer to his desk for her to sit.

"I am. Thank you."

Maddie leaned over and picked up the paper Edward had been working on.

"Twins. How clever of you, Ed."

Edward sat and picked up her hand once more. "I wanted it to be a surprise. It's a child's book. A book for young girls, primarily," he said, beaming.

"Oh, Edward. How wonderful! The girls will be thrilled."

"A little late for Hattie, perhaps, but Edna should enjoy it."

"It's a start," Maddie encouraged. "You'll think of something for Hattie before long. I'm sure of it."

(1904)

The girls made themselves comfortable in the train car as Edward looked after their luggage. A week at the seaside with three women, even though two were under the age of thirteen, meant a plethora of luggage. Edward tipped the porter then joined his family inside the train.

"Where are we going, Father?" Edna asked. Harriet already had her copy of *The Mystery of Edwin Drood* open on her lap.

"We're going to Ocean City."

"How far is that?"

"I suspect about a three hour trip, so we'll be there before dinner," he said, tapping her affectionately on the leg.

"So is it by the ocean?" Edna asked.

Harriet lowered her book and looked at her sister cross-eyed. Edna stuck out her tongue in response.

"Now that's enough from you two," Maddie admonished.

"The proprietor of the Ocean Plaza Inn said we can see the ocean from our front porch," Edward said.

"So we'll get to swim?" Edna said with relish.

"We will, indeed. And there are miles and miles of boardwalk along the ocean for my lovely Maddie." Edward picked up his wife's gloved hand and kissed the back of it.

"What else is there to do?" Edna asked.

"There's fishing!"

Edna furrowed her brow at her father. "No. I mean things for *me* to do."

"Well, let me see."

Edward pulled a folded brochure out of the side pocket of his linen suit jacket and opened it with a flourish. He took his spectacles out of his breast pocket and read over the offerings. "It says here there's a pavilion with a replica of the city of Jerusalem inside of it.

"The whole city?"

"That's what it says. Then there is the tent colony," Edward said, waiting for Edna to question him.

"A tent colony? What's a tent colony?"

"Well, besides the proximity to the ocean, Oceans Grove is known for its camp meetings, meetings where people come to listen to preachers and sweat in their good clothes."

Maddie slapped Edward playfully on the thigh. Edna covered her mouth and giggled.

"Anyway, many of the faithful can't afford to stay in nice hotels like we're doing, so many years ago they set up tents to live in and they never took them down." Edward looked down at the brochure. "It says here there are over one hundred tents in the colony."

"I wish we could stay in a tent," Edna said.

Edward and Maddie exchanged glances. "I don't think your mother would enjoy the amenities."

"What are amenities?" Edna asked.

"Never mind," Maddie said.

"Ah! And then there's Beersheba's Well."

At the odd name Harriet lowered her book just enough to see over the binding. She had been half listening to her father, not wanting to seem too interested in this trip to the seaside. She had wanted to stay with her friend, Dottie, but had been told this was a family vacation and everyone in the family was required to come.

"Who's Beersheba?"

Edward looked down at the paper in his hand. "It doesn't say, but the well goes down four hundred and twenty feet. That is going to be some mighty cold water."

"Wow!"

"And last but not least, The Great Auditorium."

"What's that?" Edna asked.

"It's an open-air auditorium that seats ten thousand people."

At this, Harriet put her book down on her lap. Now her father had her undivided attention.

"Are there going to be ten thousand people there when *we* get there?" Edna asked.

"I doubt it, dearest. It probably only fills when they have their camp meetings, and I made sure there are no meetings scheduled while we're visiting.

"But..." Edward hesitated. "I do know there will be at least four people in the auditorium this coming Saturday, and I suspect a few more, when we sit down to see John Phillip Sousa and his band!"

At the mention of Sousa's name, Edward pulled a set of tickets out of his jacket pocket and waved them in front of his face.

Now he had everyone's attention, even his wife's.

"Sousa?" Maddie exclaimed, clasping her hands together. "Really, Edward?"

"The one and only!" he said with pleasure at his wife's reaction to his surprise.

"Who's Sousa?" Edna asked.

"You know the marches your mother listens to on the phonograph?"

"The band music?"

"Indeed."

Maddie wrapped Edward's arm in hers. "I'm so glad you are getting into the spirit of the trip, Edward. You have been working way too hard of late."

"You are quite correct, my dear. I've got so many stories running through my head and outlines piled up on my desk, I need to clear some of that away. It's made me realize the need to finally set up that syndicate I've been thinking about for so long."

"That's a wonderful idea," Maddie said. "Then you can hire writers to write stories for you."

"My stories," he quickly interjected. "They would all be my stories, or at minimum my outlines written under new pseudonyms. That way I can ensure quality and gain the flexibility of having others helping me out."

"Is that why you wrote The Bobbsey Twins under Laura Lee Hope?"

"Exactly! And when I incorporate, I can hand the twins off to another writer and continue working on my other ideas."

"Such as..."

"Besides getting the Dave Porter stories that I mentioned to you up and running, I thought I'd start a series of sea adventures or even a hunting series. What boy doesn't like to hunt or, if they are city boys, wish they could hunt, maybe even wild game in Africa? Now wouldn't that be an adventure!"

Edward looked back at his girls. Edna was looking out of the window. Harriet was back behind her book.

"But enough of that. This is a vacation, after all."

Edward bent down close to Edna's ear. "Who would like to start a story?"

Edna turned to her father, beaming.

"I get to start this one," Harriet said. Despite having her nose in her book, she had heard her father's whisper to Edna. The girls coveted the privilege of starting one of Edward's impromptu stories. It was a game they had played since the girls were old enough to read for themselves. They played it particularly on cold, winter nights in front of the fire or sitting on the front porch after Sunday dinners at Grandma

Stratemeyer's. One of the girls would look at something in her surroundings and start out the story. It used to start out with "Once upon a time..." but as they got older, the game was to try and pick a beginning that would stump their father. It rarely worked with Edward's vivid imagination, but they relished the opportunity to try. The girls had also started to incorporate their own characters and plot twists into the story when Edward seemed at a loss for where the story should go next. Harriet noticed he did this more often of late, and she suspected he hesitated on purpose, wanting his daughters to do more of the story telling.

Harriet closed her book and scanned the train car. It was occupied by mostly middle-class families or young couples, some gay and talkative, obviously heading for a vacation spot, but others were more solemn, the trip probably one they took every day to and from work. Finally Harriet spied the perfect character. It was an elderly gentleman with a bushy, salt-and-pepper mustache with large, curly handlebars. He looked of foreign descent and was writing with some concentration in a small, black book that he held close to his face as if to shield the contents from others. Harriet had read her share of Sir Arthur Conan Doyle of late, so her mind easily went to the creation of a mystery.

"I've got it!" she said with zest. "Mr. Morris Montague was on a train heading to our nation's capital. He was checking the notes he had written down in his notebook related to the odd telephone call he had received just two days earlier from Senator John..." Harriet thought a moment. Maddie was about to intervene when Edward put a hand up to stop her. "Senator John Kean," Harriet blurted out. Her parents glowed with pride when she remembered the name of the current New Jersey Senator.

Edward looked around the train car and saw the gentleman Harriet had picked as her subject. Just as with his own fiction stories, he had taught the girls to pick things in their environment or things they might have recently read in a book, to work into their stories as he did with his own stories. He knew that fiction, partially based in fact, had that much more of an impact on the reader.

"Ah, yes!" he said raising his index finger. He hesitated only a second before continuing the tale, long enough for Edna to discover who he and Harriet were looking at. "Mr. Montague had a private detective agency in New York City and was renowned for his investigative prowess."

Edward never dumbed down the stories he wove with his daughters, as he sometimes did in his boys' book series. If there was a word that his children didn't know, he preferred to explain its meaning, or if it was a particularly difficult one, he'd have them look it up before he would continue. A task they groaned at every time.

"The senator had contacted him about a particularly sticky situation that needed his immediate attention. The phone call from the senator was cryptic but to the point."

Edward stopped talking, as if he was thinking of what was to come next. He looked over at Edna, who per the story game rules they had devised, was the next to add to the story line. She was so enthralled with what her father was saying that it took her a moment to realize it was her turn to interject.

"Oh, me…! Yes. Um…Senator…"

"Kean," her mother added.

"Yes. Senator Kean had said that…that a capitol page was missing, his page, in fact, and he needed to find the boy before…he spilled the beans."

"Spilled the beans? What would a lowly page know that was worth spilling?" Harriet said with obvious distaste.

"Yes! Spilled the beans," Edna said with more conviction.

"Indeed," Edward said in agreement. "There had been a secret vote on the House floor the night before, and the page was on his way with the voting results to President Roosevelt's office when he vanished into thin air."

All three faces looked eagerly to Edward for the next installment of the story.

The carriage pulled up to the curb and stopped. The children looked out the window to see where they had stopped. Their father had suggested a Sunday drive before heading over to the Van Camps for dinner, but he didn't tell them where they were going.

"This is it!" Edward said with almost childlike glee, exiting the carriage and holding open the door for his daughters and his wife.

Maddie looked out the door of the carriage before

Edward assisted her down. "Is this a publishing client of yours?"

Edward pulled a calling card out of his breast pocket and handed it to Maddie.

Magdalena B. Van Camp Stratemeyer
168 N. Seventh Ave
Roseville, New Jersey

Maddie looked up at the number on the three-story, Queen Anne house that stood before them.

"Edward...this isn't our home, is it?" Maddie said with some trepidation. Edward was known for his surprises, but buying a home without her seeing it first was something she would not expect of him and would be hard pressed to agree to. It was a lovely looking home with a large front porch and a four-sided turret that ran the full three stories of the home.

Edward grasped her hand and kissed it. "It could be."

"Really, Father!" Harriet said excitedly.

"Oh, Father, it's wonderful!" Edna said.

"It's up to your mother, of course."

Maddie looked hard at her husband. They had been talking about moving to a bigger home; the girls were getting older and it would be nice to give each of them their own room. And Edward's business continued to grow; his home office was shrinking by the day. But it would be hard to quell the girls' excitement if the house didn't fit Maddie's standards. She wished he hadn't put her in this position.

"Well, let's see what it looks like on the inside, then your father and I need to talk."

Edna grasped her mother's hand and pulled her toward the front stoop. Harriet had already tried the door and had found it open. They all waited for Edward to catch up.

"It's all right. I made arrangements with the owners to take a private tour," Edward explained as he pushed the door open and ushered them into the large front hallway.

To their left a deep maroon carpeted staircase ran to a second-story balcony. A parlor was to their right and a hall leading to the kitchen ran straight in front of them. Edna ran into the parlor. "It's got a fireplace for Mother," she yelled from inside the room. The other three stepped past the double, wood-paneled sliders to see an empty, spacious room with a high ceiling and yellow, and somewhat faded, patterned wallpaper. The fireplace had a rose-marble facade and a darkly-stained, wooden mantle that matched the crown molding and large baseboard that surrounded the room.

Harriet was drawn to the sun streaming in through the three large windows in the corner turret, and she sat on the padded bench that encircled the intimate space.

"This would be perfect for reading, Mother. Don't you think?" she said, caressing the worn, wine-colored, velvet cushions.

Edna led them through the formal dining room, a butler's pantry, and into the spacious, bright, white kitchen.

"It's so large," Maddie said.

"I thought we could employ a cook. And it has a fully

furnished washroom in the basement!" he said, opening a side door to a dark stairwell leading to the basement.

"I want to see the bedrooms!" Edna said, running out of the opposite door and into the front hallway.

Maddie leaned in toward her husband. "Can we afford a cook, Edward?"

"I think we can," he whispered back.

The family could hear Edna excitedly clomp up the steps ahead of them. By the time they reached the top of the stairs, Edna had rushed back into the second floor hallway. "There are three bedrooms!" she said as she grasped her father's hand. "Does that mean Hattie and I get our own rooms?"

"Unless your mother wants her own room." Edward said in jest.

Edna gave him a perplexed look.

"Of course I don't want my own room, dear. You know your father; he was just teasing."

Edna disappeared back into one of the rooms. "This one is mine!" she yelled from inside.

"I'm the oldest, Father. I should get to choose first," Harriet complained.

"We don't even own the house," Maddie reminded her.

"But we could," Edward said again. He walked over to a door in the middle of the hall and opened it, revealing a steep set of wooden steps. "I want to show you this, Maddie," he said, extending his hand and ushering her through the doorway and up the steps.

The couple stepped up into a room with half walls covered in a small, flower-patterned paper and steep pitched ceilings that came together in a peak in the center of the room. This room also had a turret as the two rooms below, though the windows here were three-quarter size of the ones on the other two floors.

"I thought this could be my writing study," he said, his mind already envisioning it occupied by his writing desk, book shelves, and the upholstered chair facing the windowed turret, the chair he frequently sat in when he was sketching out book ideas.

By this time Harriet and Edna were in the room, as well, checking out the attic space and looking out over the rooftops of the neighbors' homes nearby.

Maddie walked up to her husband and clasped his hand in hers. She trusted Edward when he said that they could afford this home and the extra help she would need to run it. She had some money from her family, of course, but she knew that her husband's syndicate had been doing well enough that he had hired on his first ghostwriter, a pleasant man by the name of Howard Garis. He was to write Edward's new Motor Boys series. It happened that Mr. Garis also lived in Roseville and his wife, Lillian, was a writer, as well. She and Maddie had hit it off right from the start.

Leave it to Edward to be ahead of the curve, she thought when Edward had told her about the new book series. Touring cars had been around for a while, of course, but they were still a luxury item that most could not afford. What better thing for a boy to aspire to than owning something only the rich could afford. She didn't see the appeal of these smelly, noisy machines, but she knew her husband coveted having one and it would just be a matter of time before they owned one of their own.

"You like this house, don't you, dear?" Maddie said.

Edward squeezed her hand. "Only if you do, dearest."

"Let's purchase it then."

A cheer erupted from both of the girls, startling their parents, who didn't realize they were standing right behind them listening in.

"Would you like more tea, Lillian," Maddie asked, reaching the china tea pot painted in delicate, pink roses.

"Yes, please," she said, holding out the matching china cup. "And if I am to call you Maddie, then you must call me Lilly."

Maddie inclined her head in affirmation then put the back of her hand on the tea pot to check for warmth. "Oh, it's cold. Let me get it warmed up for you."

"Fran," Maddie called in the direction of the kitchen.

A moment later Fran, the family cook, stuck her head through the open parlor door. "Yes, ma'am?"

"The tea is cold; could you warm this up for us, please?"

"Of course, ma'am," she said, taking the tea tray into the kitchen.

"I'm so glad Howard was willing to help Edward with his writing. I think the Motor Boys series is going well, and I know Edward appreciates the help."

"When Edward first visited us, what was it, nine, ten years ago now, I suggested he might enjoy writing for your husband. But you know how men are. It took him this long to decide I was correct, not that I'd remind him of that fact, mind you."

Maddie smiled discreetly.

"I hear you're a writer yourself, Lilly. Edward tells me you worked at the *Evening News* before you married Howard. Is that where you met?"

"It is and now neither of us work on the paper. Howard became so busy writing his own stories that he had to quit. I think that was two years ago already. Have you read his latest tale? It's in the paper as a serial. "

"Oh, yes!" Edna piped up, eager to contribute something to the conversation. At sixteen, sitting quietly still didn't come all that easily for Edna, but her mother understood her youthful exuberance and let the interruption slip by. Both Edna and Harriet sat together on the settee, observing the older women closely. "It was a lovely story about a gentleman bunny; Uncle Wiggly I believe was his name."

"That is correct. I read and edit for Howard, so I've been privy to the next few installments to the story. I think the children are really going to enjoy it. Don't you agree, Edna?"

"Oh yes," Edna said, her hair bow bouncing as she nodded her head with earnest. "It's for small children, really. But it's still a lovely story. Did you read it, Harriet?" Edna said, turning to her sister.

"I have not, but I will make a point to now that I know Mr. Garis is the author."

"Harriet, your mother tells me you are going to continue your education past high school this fall. How wonderful. Do you know yet which school you will be attending?"

"Not yet, but Father has narrowed it down to Barnard and Wellesley."

"Two very fine schools."

"And Miss Edna, are you at Barringer with you sister?

Edna's bright face instantly drooped and she dropped her chin almost to her chest.

"We thought preparing Edna for college ahead of time would be easier on her than what her sister will have to do to prove herself this next summer," Maddie explained.

"We had started Edna at Centenary Collegiate Institute, a boarding school in Hackettstown, but…" Maddie looked at Edna as if looking to her daughter to give her the appropriate words to use, "but it turns out Edward and I just couldn't do without her, so we brought her back home again. Now she's at Miss Townsend's right here in Roseville and is doing quite well," she said cheerfully.

Edna looked up and smiled, liking her mother's explanation of her present situation more than the real one. Edna had tried to enjoy herself at the new school, but in truth, it was she who missed her family and the attention that Miss Fran and Roland, their chauffeur, gave her as the baby in the family. In addition, it was difficult to adjust to all the rules and the challenging coursework at Centenary. Miss Townsend's personal attention was much more to Edna's liking.

"Oh, that reminds me, Hattie. Please try and remember

to talk to Miss Townsend about taking that extra French class this summer. We want to make sure you fulfill your language requirement no matter what school you get into."

"Yes, Mother," Harriet said. She was as anxious as her mother about all the exams she would be taking over the summer. She wanted to make sure she could start college in the fall without having to take extra preparatory classes at the college before she could start her real coursework. Harriet was fairly confident in herself, but she was not at the top of her high school class, and she wanted to start out right her first year of college.

Fran walked into the room and set the tray down in front of Maddie.

"Thank you, Miss Fran."

"Dessert is ready in the dining room, ma'am."

"Oh, wonderful. Thank you."

Maddie filled Lilly's cup with tea and turned toward her daughters. "Edna, would you please go upstairs and tell your father and Mr. Garis that dessert is served."

Edna sprang to her feet, glad for the excuse to leave the difficult conversation behind.

As per Edward's house rules, Edna stood in the hallway and rapped on the door to her father's study. However, she had learned that her father was usually so engrossed in his stories that he wouldn't hear her, so she did not to wait for his response. As she ran up the steps, Edna heard commotion above her. She entered the room with caution and was stopped in utter surprise. The two men in their dress jackets and ties, watch fobs swinging, lunged and parried with wooden rulers as if they were in the midst of a serious sword fight. They were moving in slow motion, dissecting their every movement, as if choreographing a movie picture scene.

"You see, Howard. Tom Swift will be an expert swordsman, marksman, and mechanic, a real gentleman inventor and world traveler," Edward said, not stopping their well-rehearsed dance. "I think you'll enjoy filling out Tom's more mature exploits than the hijinks of the Motor Boys."

Neither man noticed Edna was in the room until she giggled.

Both men froze in place then dropped their fighting stance. "I think we have a critic, Howard," Edward said with a grin.

"It's just humorous to see grown men fighting with rulers."

"Did it look authentic?" Edward asked with sincerity, coming over to his daughter's side.

"It would be better with real swords," Edna said.

"True. Remind me to talk to your mother about that."

Edna giggled again, knowing this wasn't the oddest request Edward had made to her mother.

Edward turned back to Howard. "You see, old friend, I could really use the help. I've got the new Webster series out, and I'm continuing with Ralph in the Railroad series, Dorothy Dale, Jack Ranger…Well, you probably know most of them.

At any rate, what do you say; this one would be all yours. You'd work from my outlines, of course, but you'd be in on it from the start," Edward said, placing his hand on Howard's shoulder.

Howard stood a minute in thought, tapping the ruler lightly against his thigh. He had his own stories to write, after all, and Stratemeyer's insistence on giving up all rights to the works he wrote for the Syndicate and the use of a pseudonym instead of his own name as author chafed him a bit under the collar. But Edward's stories were sound, not literary works of art mind you, though neither were his own, and with two children and a wife to support, it didn't seem prudent to turn down work. *Let's see, I currently write a book every three weeks. If Edward pays me a hundred dollars per book, that's an extra…sixteen hundred a year*, Howard thought. Plus with Edward's active mind, Howard knew the work would be steady.

"All right, old man," Howard said, extending out his hand.

"Splendid!" Edward exclaimed. "I'll have the first three breeder outlines sent to your home tomorrow."

"Tomorrow's Sunday, Father," Edna reminded him.

"Ah, you are correct, my dear," he said, wrapping his arm around his daughter's shoulders. "What was I thinking? Your mother would string me up to a yardarm if I did any business on the Lord's day."

Edna nodded in agreement.

"Oh, I almost forgot. Dessert is served."

"We are being summoned, kind sir," Edward said, taking the pseudo weapon from his friend with a bow.

Edward set the rulers on his desk and held out his arm for his daughter to take. "Miss? Shall we?"

Edna snickered and grasped her father's arm.

Edward stopped before they headed down the steps. "Don't forget to ask your wife about helping out with The Bobbsey Twins. I read her *Two Little Girls* book just the other day and thought it quite charming. I think she'd enjoy a series like the Bobbseys with so many characters to keep busy."

"I'll talk to her about it tomorrow and get back to you."

"Splendid, old boy. Splendid."

Six 〰

(Ladora, Iowa, 1911)

The red-haired girl in the fourth row of school desks slid a copy of *Tattered Tom; or, The Story of a Street Arab* out from inside of her desk. She looked up to see if Miss Baker was watching and without turning around, poked the book into the knees of the child behind her.

"Hey," Arnold said without looking at what was being shoved his way.

The girl turned around momentarily and glared at him, then snapped her attention back to the front of the room.

Miss Baker looked up at the noise, but when she saw all heads down, the second graders working diligently at their desks, she continued on with her grading.

Arnold soon felt the same poke, but this time he took the book and tucked it up underneath his shirt. Not a minute later another jab had him taking a note from the girl in front of him, her long, red plaited rope of hair not moving an inch during the stealthy pass. He opened the note hastily and tucked it under the work assignment on his desk. It took him a minute before he felt brave enough to slide his work aside enough to see what was written beneath.

The hut, noon.
Bring rover boys!
- Mildred

The hut was a run-down, wooden structure at the back of the school yard that had once housed yard tools. Now it was the official hangout for the boys during recess. Mildred had been let into the group because none of the boys had the guts to exclude her. She was the best pitcher they had for pickup baseball, and Mildred didn't act like a sissy when she accidentally got hit with the ball. Besides, she was the only girl they knew who liked a good fight. And what boy didn't think they could best a girl in a fight, or at least want to try, anyway.

A group of five boys had been sitting in the hut eating their lunch when Mildred arrived.

Mildred knocked twice on the weathered, gray doorframe, waited a second then knocked twice again – the secret signal for entrance. The burlap sack was moved to one side and she stepped inside.

"So'd ya bring it?" Mildred asked Arnold.

Arnold motioned for a boy next to him to bring out the

goods. The boy reached behind his back and handed her a paper sack. Mildred pulled out a copy of *The Rover Boys in the Jungle; or Stirring Adventures in Africa* then placed it back inside the bag. She put it in the canvas satchel she had over her shoulder and set the bag on the floor.

"So, same rules as last time. If you hit me twice above the waist, I get to keep it two weeks, if you hit me only once or only below the waist, I get it for a month."

Mildred held out her hand to Arnold, who shook it firmly.

"Deal," he said.

Mildred coveted books, any books, really. She would even leaf through the textbooks in her father's library when she was desperate for something to read, though he mostly had medical books for his practice as a physician in Ladora. And even though Mildred's mother, Lillian, regularly had Chautauqua education assemblies in their home, Lillian had very few books of her own. In desperation, Mildred would sometimes try to read the Protestant newspaper her mother received every month, the *Protestant Press*.

Mildred's first book was Beatrix Potter's *Peter Rabbit* from the school library, and she had loved that book so much that, after completing first grade, she spent hours copying the whole book down by hand because she knew she wouldn't have access to it over the summer months.

So when the boys in her second grade class got tired of loaning her their books, she came up with the idea of winning the books from them. Mildred had spied on them in their male bastion in the back of the school yard and had seen them playing the tag game just for fun. Mildred was very athletic, generally preferring to play with boys rather than girls, so she was fairly confident she could beat any of them at this game as she did frequently on the ball field or at any running race.

Arnold reached up into the rafters and pulled the two three-foot-long sticks from their hiding place and handed one to Mildred.

The two children walked to opposite sides of the small hut and a third boy – the referee – stepped in between them. Arnold and Mildred brought the tips of their sticks together and the referee held them in place, checking with each opponent for the requisite nod that they were ready to start.

"One. Two. Three," he said and let go of the sticks as he quickly stepped back and out of the way.

Seven ∾

Beep, beep, beep.

A horn was heard repeatedly honking outside the Stratemeyer home until Edna peered out the window in the parlor to see who was making all the racket.

"Oh my gosh! That's Daddy!" Edna called out. She ran to the front door and outside to the edge of the porch, staring at her father who was standing with one leg in and one leg out of a very stylish motorcar.

"Want to go for a drive?" Edward yelled to his daughter, the look of excitement evident on his face.

"Is that ours?" Edna asked in amazement.

"It is indeed. Go get your mother and your sister and we'll take it for a spin."

Maddie and Harriet walked out into the yard and just stood staring at the car. It was maroon-colored except for the polished gold around the windshield, the oil lamps next to the windshield, and the headlights perched on rods on the front of the car. The spoked metal wheels were painted the same color as the body and were rimmed with a thin, narrow tire.

Edna stepped around to the front of the car and put her hands on her hips. "I think it's smiling at me," she said with amusement.

Edna was looking at the two large, gas-powered headlights set like eyes in front of the radiator. They were a good six inches in diameter and wide awake, though not turned on. Edward came around to the front of the car and put his arm around his daughter's shoulders. "By Jove, I think you're right, Edna."

"See here," he said, pointing to the word "Cadillac" in shiny metal script attached to the front of the radiator. "It's a 1909 Model 30 because of the 30 horsepower engine," Edward said with pride.

Edward moved back to the side of the vehicle. "It comes out of Springfield, Mass. Isn't she a beauty?" he said, caressing the wide, black fender as if he were petting the family dog. He could tell his wife was yet to be swayed by his purchase, but he knew over time she would come to enjoy it as he already did.

"It's a touring car." He stepped back and opened the small back half-door. "It has a back seat so we can all go riding together," he said with a grin. "We can take it to the beach, on our weekend outings to the hills, or you could take it down to the market for the weekly supplies. Think how convenient that will be, Maddie."

Maddie didn't move or say a thing, she just stared at the metal contraption, her arms folded across her chest.

"Let's take it for a drive, shall we?"

Edna readily complied, jumping in the back seat, followed not far behind by Harriet. They both sat examining the quilted, black-leather bench seat.

Edward walked up to his wife and gave her his small mustached smile that often softened her heart. Maddie dropped her arms and shook her head in defeat. She looked past her husband and called to the girls. "Harriet, get my gloves and hat, the one with the stout scarf attached, and you each get a nice sturdy hat for yourselves."

Edward beamed with satisfaction as he put out his arm to ceremoniously walk his wife to the vehicle and help her step inside.

The front of the car had two bucket type seats with the same black, quilted upholstery as the back, so Maddie felt a small sense of security as she sat down inside the metal contraption, though she wished the front had the same doors as the back to close her just a bit more safely inside this infernal contraption. Edward stood in front of the car and waited for the girls to return.

Harriet handed her mother her hat, put on her own, and sat in the back with her sister.

Maddie peered at her husband, a look of distress on her face. "Aren't you going to drive?"

"You start the car from here," Edward yelled out to her. "It's got a crank," he said as he bent down and turned the

L-shaped lever until the engine started up, jiggling the car to life.

Edward climbed in next to his wife, touching her gloved hand that held tightly to the edge of her seat. They all coughed until the dark gray smoke from the engine cleared from the motorcar's interior. Edward wiped his brow with a handkerchief and put on his bowler hat. He turned to smile at his girls then released the brake. He moved the levers attached to the center of the steering wheel, putting the car in reverse, then turning to back the car out of the driveway.

The car jerked twice then died. "I'm just getting the hang of this clutch," he said, unfazed by the incident. He put the car back into neutral, put the emergency brake back on, and handed his wife his hat. He stepped around to the front of the car once more and cranked the engine back to life.

This time they made it out the driveway and into the street, where they were jostled into first gear and finally more smoothly into second, then third. They were traveling at a brisk twenty-five miles per hour before Edward felt comfortable enough to look over at his wife. The look of fear in her eyes made him drop the car back down into second and a geriatric fifteen mile-per-hour pace.

"Thank you," she said without taking her eyes off the road.

After they left the city limits and were out into the countryside, Maddie relaxed enough to sit back into her seat. "Will you be taking this into your new office in Manhattan each day?" she said over the loud engine.

"I don't think so. There isn't a good place to park a car

in the city, and even though it's last year's model, I don't want to leave it on the street to get hit by some careless delivery truck. I want to have it around for you and the girls to use."

"I won't be driving this thing!" Maddie said with conviction.

"Then I'll teach Hattie and Edna to drive."

Harriet leaned forward and grasped her father's shoulder. "Really, Father! You mean it?" she said with relish.

"Of course. No good reason why women can't drive."

This proclamation surprised all of the women in the car. As much as society was changing and allowing women more freedoms such as going out unescorted – though rarely alone – or seeking out more manly pursuits such as higher education and working outside the home – as long as they were unmarried – and as free and adventuresome as Edward's new female book characters, Dorothy Dale or the Motor Girls were in his books, the women of the Stratemeyer family knew his more liberal thoughts about women rarely pertained to them. It was understood that even though Harriet was going off to college, finding a husband and getting married was to be her first priorities once she had completed her coursework. So Edward's proclamation of teaching Harriet and Edna to drive a car was quite a surprise to them all.

"I'm off to school in just two weeks though, Father."

"Well then, we better get started right off. Who knows, it might come in handy."

Maddie looked at Edward with a cross expression. "Where is Hattie going to come upon a car?"

"Perhaps…in some emergency. One never knows."

Maddie shook her head in disagreement but knew better than to argue the point. Once Edward had his mind set on something, there was little that could dissuade him. In fact, Maddie was surprised it had taken him this long to purchase a motor car. He had been talking about it for over a year now.

Harriet leaned toward her father again. "Are we going to use the car to take me to Wellesley?"

"That's part of the reason why I decided to purchase it," he called back to his daughter. "That and they're finally starting to get all the bugs worked out of these things. I'd like to take it out west to do some book research this fall."

Maddie turned sharply to her husband. "With you and Edna coming along as well, of course," he said to his wife, though he would be surprised if his wife would be up for the long drive.

Edward had put the car back into second after his wife had started to relax, but he had to shift back down into first as the ruts in the road were starting to rattle the teeth out of their heads.

"I think maybe we should turn back around," Edward said, as much to change the topic of conversation as to get them off the unmanicured roadway.

Edward slowed until he found a farmer's field road and he turned the car around, heading back toward home.

Harriet's first year at Wellesley went by quickly, and when she was back at school the following fall, she was ready to jump back into campus life with both feet. She had already submitted an article or two to the school newspaper her freshman year, but Harriet had a taste for writing much like her father and wanted to do more.

The Wellesley Press Board was created that same year and with her other non-academic pursuits: tennis, field hockey, and softball, with a swim in the large lake on campus – Lake Waban – or a trail ride on one of the school nags when she could squeeze it in, keeping up with her studies was a constant challenge. But Harriet felt she wanted to make more of a contribution to the school she was coming to know and love, so joining an organization like the Press Board, that protected the stories that came out of the school, felt like a logical next step. And by Harriet's junior year she had become the Press Board president.

Harriet was also a suffragette. Fresh from a tour of a Boston garment factory and adjoining housing project, compliments of her economics professor, Harriet was left with enduring memories of the squalor and deplorable working conditions these women were subjected to. She had renewed conviction that these and other women needed to be able to speak to the atrocities that they and their families endured.

Harriet sat on the bed in her room, an expansive space she shared with two other women on the second floor of Miss Lawrence's boarding house. The house was just across from the main gates of Wellesley's girls' college, on the corner of Dover and Washington Streets. Miss Lawrence's was the closest housing arrangement to campus her father could find for Harriet her freshman year, since all the residence halls on campus were full. Harriet had made some close friends that first year that she was loath to change. In fact the group of girls had formed a de facto family named the McNutts. There were even men in this factitious family, played by women, of course – as was the tradition at the all-girls school. This family was a running play of sorts that the girls of Harriet's house kept up all four years they were at the school, even when some of them moved into the schools dormitories as Harriet did her senior year. The girls were named after Biblical figures, faculty they particularly admired, or staff they wanted to impersonate because of some odd trait or quirk of character. So coming back to Miss Lawrence's was an easy choice.

Harriet had on her gloves and hat and sat under a blanket as she tried to open her letter from Edna; Miss Lawrence preferred not to turn up the heat on cold days. She had a fireplace in her own room, so she feigned ignorance when any of the girls complained about the temperature in the rest of the house. The women on the second floor were a bit luckier than those on the first level, since heat traveled up in the drafty, old, Colonial brick home. The girls in the attic room rarely had to put on extra layers. But Harriet had just walked back from morning services and she hadn't quite warmed up yet.

As Harriet rubbed her hands together, in an attempt to warm them by mere friction, she heard Chopin's prelude in E minor floating effortlessly over the frozen campus. It was a Wellesleian tradition for the head of the music department, Mr. Hamilton Macdougall, to perform a brief organ recital to serenade the students for fifteen minutes after chapel during mid-year exams. It was piped out from Chapel Hall on speakers and could be heard for miles in the cold morning air, despite the hilly, mostly wooded campus.

Harriet took off one glove, opened the letter, then put her glove immediately back on again.

February 1st, 1913

Dearest Sister,

I don't know if you've heard, but the Suffragists are walking to Washington to try and disrupt Wilson's inauguration and they're walking right through New Jersey! Isn't that marvelous! Are you a Suffragette? I am!

They will be walking through Newark at 9:30 or 10 next Wednesday, and Mrs. Harris, from the local NAWSA office, has invited me along. Can you imagine! I think I'll have to sneak out of the house so Father doesn't know I am going. He really doesn't see what all the fuss is about. But since Wilson won out over our wonderful Teddy, we need to make sure both Wilson and Taft put The Vote foremost on their agenda by our show of support! I do so wish you could be here!

All the exclamation points in her sister's letter amused Harriet. Since one of Harriet's majors was English composition – the other being music – she had numerous English classes each semester, and the overuse of such a literary ejaculation

(handwritten in margin: real letter?)

would be highly frowned upon by Miss Hart, the professor of her current English Comp II course. That and the overuse of the comma; two things that would cause red marks to erupt all over the page.

Actually, Harriet was now a member of the Wellesley Equal Suffrage League. The group had brought in well known, though sometimes controversial, speakers such as Alice Stone Blackwell, a Boston University graduate and editor on her parents' newspaper, *The Women's Journal*, and Mrs. Park, the president of the Massachusetts Suffrage League. The Wellesley League had even heard the prestigious president of the NAWSA (the National American Women's Suffrage Association), Carrie Chapman Catt, just this last spring. Listening to Mrs. Catt's stirring speech in preparation for the February march on Washington was what convinced Harriet to join the Wellesley League in the first place. After finding out that only six states had ratified a woman's right to vote, Harriet was determined to get involved. She didn't agree with some of her classmates, who thought the vote would only cause discord in their as-yet-to-be-formed marriages. Harriet made it known that she would never marry a man who thought her opinions were only worth sharing in private company.

Unfortunately for Harriet, she was not able to join the marchers along any of the route. She had already been told by her father that she needed to concentrate more on her schoolwork and less on women's suffrage in a response to a letter she had sent her parents on the subject. And from Edna's letter, he must have shared a similar sentiment with her. Harriet was learning to keep her opinions to herself and trying to keep her nose in her books, at least for now.

>   *I'll write and tell you all about it.*
>   *I hope your classes are going well. Personally,*
> *I'm getting tired of the cold and snow.*
>   *Your best sister,*
>   *Edna*

> *P.S. Have you heard from Russell? He sure seemed interested in learning when you were coming home for Christmas. I'll be sure to let you know if I learn more!*

Harriet's major contribution to the school, and that of many other Wellseley girls, would come in March of her senior year.

Harriet woke with her roommate and the rest of her dorm at the sound of a fire alarm. She turned to look at her desk clock. It was 4:45 a.m.

"This is an odd time for a fire alarm," Harriet said.

But both girls got up as they had practiced during previous drills, put on their robes and their slippers, and shuffled still half asleep out of the building along with all the other girls.

Once outside, they could see the reason for the alarm. Bright flames engulfed the windows of College Hall and lit the pre-dawn hours with a warm, otherwise comforting glow.

The girls immediately gave up the prescribed roll call and ran to give any support they could.

As faculty and students alike stood and watched the building being engulfed in flames, one of the professors suddenly exclaimed, "The records!"

"And the schools antiques," another remembered.

Harriet heard their distress and followed them into the building.

Miss Bates turned to Harriet and the other students behind her. "We need help!" she said. "If we form a chain..."

"Yes!" Harriet agreed. "Bridget, you organize it in here. I'll go out and get the girls lined up outside.

Harriet ran out of the building and yelled to those standing a ways off, keeping clear of the flames. Long ago Harriet had taken the school's motto to heart "Non Ministrari Sed Ministrare" – Not to be ministered unto but to minister to – and she didn't think twice when there was a call for help.

"We need to form a line," Harriet yelled. "We need to save Wellesley history!"

Harriet started grabbing girls and placing them in line, as stacks of folders, vases, even the occasional ornamental chair or table traveled out of the burning building hand to hand. The girls formed a line all the way to the library building next door. When a girl needed a rest or became too cold, Harriet found a substitute or filled in herself. They had little more than a quarter of an hour, then all involved had to leave the building to watch it collapse in on itself as large plumes of smoke and brilliant swirls of ash filled the graying sky of dawn. The fire department did arrive, but they could do little to help other than keep adjacent buildings from erupting into flames.

During commencement week in early June, the class of 1914 had an extra reason to celebrate. There were no casualties during the fire and many, including Edward Stratemeyer, contributed money or equipment to the Fire Fund, since the Zoology lab was housed in College Hall and everything that the girls hadn't taken out, had been lost.

Edward, Maddie, and Edna all participated in the weeklong festivities, which included a senior class play, a garden party, and various concerts. Harriet accompanied the choir on the piano during one of the concerts, her parents beaming with pride at her skill. Even Russell Adams made it to the commencement exercises and joined Harriet and her family for the luncheon afterword.

"It is so good of you to join us, Russell," Edward said, pulling the folded, white napkin from his plate and arranging it on his lap. "We are so proud of our Harriet, aren't we, Mother."

"We are indeed," Maddie replied as she squeezed her daughter's hand.

"And she's had three job offers already," Edna added, "one at the *New Jersey News*, one for the *Boston Globe*, and another position as a pianist for a church in Boston! Just imagine, Hattie writing for a newspaper!" She was also proud of her big sister, even though Edna had decided college was not for her.

The color rose in Harriet's cheeks from all the talk of her accomplishments, not because she was not proud of them, but because of her father's thoughts in the matter. Harriet and Edward had a heated argument on the subject just two days earlier. It was the first time Harriet had stood her ground during an argument with her father. They had shared some intense discussions about various state and national topics during her summer's home from college, but no other subject had quite the same impact on Harriet's own life. So she was inclined to agree to disagree with her father on topics such as women's suffrage and temperance, among others, but the subject of Harriet's employment was another matter. It was Edward's opinion that a woman working outside the home, as some of his own female writers did, was fine if the need of employment meant taking care of one's self or one's family. But when a woman, like Harriet, had the wealth of a family at her disposal or her own means by way of inheritance, work for that woman was unnecessary and unbecoming. Besides, it would place the family name in an unflattering light if others found out his daughter was working for a living.

Harriet realized how little she knew of the world of working women when she received her first paycheck from articles she had submitted to the *Globe*. She had pasted it into her memory book as something informational. She was embarrassed into recognizing the piece of paper for what it actually was when a friend asked why she couldn't contribute to a social event on campus when she was getting paid by the newspapers: the *Boston Globe*, the *Newark*

Evening News, and the *Newark Sunday Call.* Harriet went to her scrapbook, pulled out the check, and promptly took it to a bank to cash it. She left the blank space and notation in her memory book as a reminder of the ignorance privilege could sometimes perpetrate.

Edward cleared his throat. "Well, I think Harriet deserves a much needed rest. She's got a celebratory trip to Maine with her father planned, after all, then she'll come home to her family and we will all see things better from there," he said with finality, dancing around the touchy subject.

"But what have you been up to, Russell? My sources tell me that you have ventured into investment banking and are doing quite well."

"I am, sir. It has been not quite two years, but I've been working for the Merchant Bank in New York. I'm learning new things every day and expect to make junior partner in two or three years."

Edward clapped Russell on the back. "Wonderful, my good man. Wonderful. What does the investment community think of all the goings on over in Europe?"

"Yes! Hattie and Father were to take a trip to France and Germany but had to cancel because of tensions in the Balkans," Edna supplied.

"That's unfortunate," Russell said.

"We'll have a fine time in Maine, won't we Hattie?"

Harriet nodded her head obediently.

"I tried to convince her to take a berth on the Endurance with Sir Ernest Shackleton, but an Antarctic expedition was not what Hattie had in mind for a vacation," Edward said with a chuckle.

"Thank goodness," Maddie said. She knew her husband was jesting, but she also knew he would don the fur mitts and boots without so much as a blink of an eye to be one of Shackleton's crew if given the chance.

"We'll visit Portland first off, take in a performance at the new Merrill Auditorium. I hear it's quite grand. Hattie wants to see the Whitmore home in Brunswick, where Harriet Beecher Stowe wrote *Uncle Tom's Cabin*. I hope to make it up to Fort Knox in Bucksport. I don't know if it is open to the public, but such historic sites are always an interest to me."

"Always looking for book ideas, my Edward," Maddie said and playfully patted him on the hand.

"At any rate, you'll have to come by the house when we're back from our vacation, Russell," Edward said. "Harriet can fill you in on all our exploits. And I have yet to hear how you two fared at the senior dance. I remember seeing a bill for a ball gown pass my desk, but I know little else of the affair."

Harriet blushed and passed the sandwiches to her father, hoping to distract him into eating more and talking less, a herculean task at best.

Eight ∾

Harriet set the application down on her father's desk. As usual, he hadn't heard her knock or walk up the stairwell into his writing sanctuary.

"Well, hello, sweetheart. What's this?" Edward picked up the paper and examined it.

"It's an application to the Newark YMCA, for a practical nursing course."

"Practical nursing? Why on earth would you want to take a practical nursing course?"

Harriet squared her shoulders. She had rehearsed her reasoning numerous times, even passing it by Edna just moments ago. Harriet was bored. After all the activity and constant studying of college, being home again was losing its appeal. Initially, being able to sleep in, meet up with old friends, and read until all hours of the night was very satisfying. But it had been three months, and other than her now semi-regular evening dates with Russell and helping Edna take care of their mother, Harriet was getting restless. She thought she had a sound argument in her desire to take a job at the local Home of Incurables, but Edna had suggested a different opening statement to her father, which Harriet agreed was a wise move, so she decided she'd play it out.

"I thought it might come in handy for helping mother. With her new heart diagnosis, I thought it would be wise."

Edward stared at his daughter a moment before he spoke. They had argued numerous times since their return from Maine. Each time it was the same thing: Harriet wanted to use the education she worked so hard to attain, and Edward didn't see the need; he could take care of her perfectly well. But the idea of a nursing course might be just what Harriet needed. It would take her mind off her friends, who were working or getting married, and give her something to do.

Edward stood and grasped his daughter's hand. "I think this is a wonderful idea." He kissed her on the cheek then sat down and signed his name to the bottom of the application, agreeing to pay the fee for the month-long training. When it came to actually working at the Home, the most Edward would agree to was allowing Harriet to volunteer her time. The situation didn't appease Harriet for very long, however. And two months later, when she approached her father again on the topic of employment, she thought she had found another way through.

Harriet was again in her father's study. "This is ridiculous, Father. I have degrees in both English and music.

I had offers from three different very reputable organizations, all without my solicitation, mind you. If papers in New Jersey and Boston both thought I was competent enough to work for them, why don't you believe in me?"

Edward put down his pencil and turned completely to face his daughter. "Hattie, darling, I don't doubt your competence; not one iota. I know you could do anything you set your mind to. It's not that at all."

Harriet saw her opening, so she took it. "Then let me work for you," she said quickly. "I could be another ghostwriter, and you wouldn't even have to pay me. Consider it compensation for my room and board."

Edward stood and started pacing the room, agitated by his daughter's insistence in this matter. "Room and board? That is ridiculous. You have a place in our home as long as you need one," he said, a bit perturbed by the suggestion. "We have gone over this before, Harriet. I will not have a daughter of mine take on the menial tasks of employment as long as I am able to care for her and that is that," he said emphatically, then he sat back down in his chair.

With the use of her given name, Harriet knew her father was serious about his declaration, so she decided to take another tack. "Then do it for my sake," Harriet pleaded, kneeling down next to her father in supplication. "I'm going crazy, Father. Edna and Fran mostly take care of mother, Russell is busy with his own work…I'm left with two hours, twice a week at the Home, which is all well and good but does nothing to stimulate my mind."

Edward understood his daughter's frustration; Harriet

was an intelligent young woman with nothing substantial to occupy her time. Russell and Harriet had seen more of each other since she had been home, but after numerous dinner invitations, he and Maddie felt they had nurtured that relationship as much as they should; it was up to Russell to do the rest. And Edward had to admit it, since moving to his new office at 17 Madison Avenue, he and his secretary Harriet Otis Smith – Edward called her H. so as not to confuse her with his daughter – were up to their ears in work. He had started fourteen new series since Tom Swift – five of which, Edward was proud to say, were written exclusively for girls. And even with the help of his new ghostwriters, St. George Rathborne and W. Bert Foster, he still had trouble keeping up. Besides, his daughter's preoccupation with being employed was beginning to put a strain on their relationship, and that was too precious for him to lose.

"All right. All right," he said, putting up a hand in resignation. "You can work for me."

"Oh, Father!" Harriet stood and kissed him on the cheek.

"But…but you start by editing manuscripts and proofing galleys." Harriet bounced on her tiptoes, squeezing his arm in her excitement. "Then we'll go from there."

It was enough, enough to keep Harriet busy and occupy her time until six months later when Russell finally offered her a proposal of marriage. The happy couple was joined as husband and wife in a ceremony at the Stratemeyer home that next October.

The paper's society column described the wedding as an intimate affair with approximately one hundred guests, who were serenaded by a string orchestra as they strolled among the large bouquets of fresh flowers and potted plants scattered throughout the Stratemeyer home and yard, along with seemingly every delicacy that could be bought or sold. The bride was in a white lace and satin gown with a large train and flared stiff collar, with her bridesmaids in pink and blue. And if Harriet ever felt a need to connect with her family, all she had to do was look down at the ring that was on her finger. The gold band had been formed from a nugget of gold that Julius Stratemeyer had mined in California in 1849. But Harriet would not need this precious metal to bind her to her family; circumstance would supply its own glue.

"Billie!" Margaret said, her arms open wide, ready to engulf her good friend. Harriet accepted the familiar greeting and vigorous hug from her fellow Wellesley sister with a broad smile, though with some physical difficulty. Betty, another "sister," stood next the Margaret awaiting her turn.

"You're as big as a bus!" Betty teased.

"That's usually the state of things when one is seven months pregnant," Harriet shot back.

"And that's why we've come to visit you, Billie dear," Margaret said, taking Harriet by the arm and ushering her out of the smelly, dark train tunnel of Grand Central Station. Harriet didn't flinch at the use of her school nickname. Harriet was Bildad the Shuhite Tufts McNutt in their fictitious campus family, or Billie for short

"You never did say what this visit was all about. You said that some of the McNutts had gotten together and come up with a project for me," Harriet said with suspicion.

"Is there a coffee house, or better yet, pastry shop we could sit in to chat?" Betty asked.

The women walked up the sloped ramp of the station and onto the noisy, dirty streets of the city. Carriages and delivery wagons pulled by horses mixed with the smoky, loud cars and truck engines to make a cacophony of sounds and smells trapped among the tall buildings.

"There's The Happy Baker just up Park Avenue," Harriet said.

"Well, if the baker is happy, then I'm happy too," Margaret said and started across the street.

Harriet had to grab her friend by the arm to stop her from getting hit by a passing car, horn honking at her audacity to assume the right of way. "This isn't Cheshire, Maggie. Buggies and cars don't stop for pedestrians in New York."

The women walked up the boulevard talking happily, catching up on each other's lives since their graduation together not quite two years ago. They had all exchanged a letter or two, but it had been many months since any of them had corresponded with each other.

They could smell the bakery before they could see it, and when they opened the front door, the warm, sweet smell of flaky pastry crust and sugar frosting overtook them like a childhood dream. They squeezed into a small table and ordered coffee and treats all around.

"All right. Now what do you girls have up your sleeves?"

Harriet said, knowing if what they came to talk to her about wasn't important, they would have just written to her rather than taking a trip into the city.

"What do you think about starting the first New York based Wellesley Club," Betsy said with excitement.

"We know what a good organizer you are," Margaret said, "and you have such a way with words, so you were the logical choice."

Harriet hesitated. "I'm not sure, ladies. I just started a newsletter for the Maplewood Women's Club. That takes up a good share of my time, writing articles, gathering submissions from others in the club, and I have yet to find a printer to even print the thing."

"Oh, come on, Billie. We need you," Betty said, looking as pitiful as she could.

Harriet stared at the women and shook her head, a strained smile on her face.

"Great!" Margaret said, grasping Harriet's arm. "I knew you'd do it."

(1914)

"Dearest, you must read this," Maddie said as she entered the parlor where the two had just moments ago been enjoying a quiet evening together. The servants had been excused for the evening so Maddie had gotten up to get the door herself when it rang. *An odd hour in the evening for company,* Maddie had thought. Edna was still living at home but out with friends, as was typical.

Maddie held out the weekly New York magazine, *The Outlook*, to her husband. It was already open to an editorial page with the headline: "Blowing Out the Boy's Brains."

"That's quite the title," Edward said.

"Marion just dropped that off, you know, my friend from two doors down. She thought you would want to read it. It's written by the chief Boy Scout librarian, Franklin Mathiews. She said Mr. Mathiews lambasts clothbound fifty cent novels, saying that they are harmful for boys to read. Imagine that!"

Edward read the beginning of the article.

"What 1,500 School Children Did Between Friday and the Following Monday," and "The Hobbies of 993 Boys" were the captions of two charts that captured universal attention at the Rochester, New York, Child Welfare Exhibit recently held. In both cases reading claimed the largest percentage of time.

"That's wonderful news! I knew, if you could only create the right story, boys would want to read, just like girls."

"But that's not the point of the article, dearest. Read here, on the second page," Maddie said, turning the page and pointing to a section that Mrs. Miller had underlined.

Because these cheap books do not create criminals or lead boys, except very occasionally, to seek the Wild West, parents who buy such books think they do their boys no harm. The fact is, however, that the harm done is simply incalculable. I wish I could label each of these books: *"Explosives! Guaranteed to Blow Your Boy's Brains Out."*

"I think he meant to use the plural possessive of Boys, but then I could be wrong."

"Ed, be serious," Maddie chided. "Because Mr. Mathiews wrote the article, the Boy Scouts of America are recommending it to their boys' parents. That's how Marion came across it. Both her sons are Boy Scouts."

Edward walked back into the parlor and sat down in his wingback chair by the fireplace. Maddie followed close behind, sitting on the edge of her matching chair just opposite.

"This isn't the first time my stories have been criticized by the so-called well educated. Do you remember what happened when the Newark Public Library decided to take all of my books out of circulation, along with Horatio's books and William Adam's Oliver Optic stories?"

"That was over fifteen years ago, Edward. I can hardly remember what I had for breakfast yesterday; how can I remember back that far?"

"I remember. We were so worried that without access to my books, the local boys would lose interest and move onto other stories."

"Yes?"

"Well, they didn't. In fact, sales in New Jersey increased threefold! Because the boys no longer had access to the library editions, they had to purchase copies of their own."

"Don't worry, dear. You know how children are. When the Scouts find out that their parents have been instructed to stop purchasing our novels, the boys will make a concerted effort to purchase them themselves. Children seem to take devilish pleasure in doing just the opposite of what their parents prefer. I know our girls were fairly obedient, but they did have their moments."

"I suppose you're right."

"And I still get stopped by the local boys asking me about my stories. Why, just the other day, a lad stopped me on the street and asked for a replacement dust jacket for his Dave Porter novel. It was a favorite of his and his brother, so much so that they had worn out the cover. I assured him, anytime he needed a new dust jacket, I'd be happy to supply it."

"That's heartwarming, Teddie. Do you still get all that fan mail?"

"Every day! Mostly they want information from the author about what is going to happen to their favorite characters, or they are arguing with their friends if there really is a town that is described in a particular book and want me to confirm or deny its existence. They may even be looking for the author's autograph, which I readily supply for them, of course ,with my own. I have even had a few industrious young girls and boys make suggestions to me for future books. It is inspiring, it truly is."

Edward picked up the article and continued to read, chuckling to himself at various passages. When he was finished, he closed the magazine and looked back up to his wife. "Do you think Mrs. Miller would mind if I kept this?" Edward asked, holding up the magazine. "I must show it to

Garis at the baseball game on Saturday. I know he'll get a kick out of it."

"Yes, Marion said we could keep it. She thinks it's a lot of hogwash, anyway. Anything that gets her boys reading is all right by her."

"Well said, my dear. Well said."

"H. can you come in here, please," Edward said from the door of his small office. Space being a premium in Manhattan, and consequently almost paid for by the inch and not the foot, the Syndicate office consisted of two small rooms, one being Edward's office – only large enough to house a regular size desk, two wooden chairs, and a tall bookshelf. The other was Mrs. Smith's office space and combined reception area – it had three of the same wooden chairs, Harriet's desk, a typewriter and stand, and two filing cabinets.

"Yes, sir." Mrs. Smith stood and pulled her notepad out of her desk drawer and headed into Mr. Stratemeyer's office. She sat down in her usual straight-back chair directly in front of him and readied herself to take notes. Mrs. Smith had been working for Mr. Stratemeyer for over five years now, and the one thing she knew for sure was that she never knew what new idea she would be asked to implement or investigate practically each and every day.

"How are the Dorothy Dale books selling this month?"

"I would need to check my figures from Cupples and Leon."

Mrs. Smith left Edward's office and returned a few minutes later with an open ledger in her hand. She handed it to Edward.

"July's total is on the right side," she said, pointing to the page.

"Down again. That's what I suspected. Ever since we married Dorothy off, sales have been down."

"Well, I suspect the girls think that that is the end of Dorothy's adventures." Mrs. Smith hesitated before she continued. She knew her employer's views on the subject of marriage, and she didn't want to say something he would not appreciate. As busy as she was working for Mr. Stratemeyer, she did appreciate having a job, and Edward was such an agreeable gentleman to work for, she didn't want to jeopardize her position; she could hardly ask for a better employer. "Marriage would tend to...*narrow* a woman's prospects for adventure, and I imagine these young girls recognize that."

"I suppose you're right. It's a bit disappointing, nonetheless. Dorothy was my first girls' series, you know."

"I do," Mrs. Smith replied.

When Harriet Smith started working for the Syndicate, she had no idea, like most others, how many books Edward Stratemeyer actually penned, since he had long ago stopped putting his name down as author of any of his books. She had to learn the details of all of his works in order to keep the meticulous sales records that her employer required. And that took some doing. Edward had come out with thirteen new series since she started with him in 1913. And with each new story came a three page outline for the growing list of ghostwriters that filled out Edward's ideas into a twenty-five chapter book. He had it all down to a science. She was required to type the outlines for him from his new-fangled dictation machine. H. much preferred taking dictation by hand, but she discovered that Mr. Stratemeyer was one for innovations, and dictation was the wave of the future, in his eyes. And if he was writing the story himself, there was typing up his multiple drafts and finally the manuscript itself that would then be sent off to the publisher of choice. If it was a ghostwriter doing the story, Mrs. Smith typed it up after Edward's edits, which he did right on the manuscript with his infamous blue pencil. And on occasion he would send out a letter or two, mostly to the newer Syndicate writers, who just didn't understand his stringent requirements. Harriet had typed up one such letter just that morning to Lillian Garis in relation to one of her Motor Girls stories. Lillian did well with Edward's Bobbsey Twins stories, but she had overstepped her bounds with her latest submission for the Motor Girls, adding in the death of one of the characters – a protagonist, of course, but it was something Mr. Stratemeyer didn't allow.

I have never permitted a murder to occur in any of our boys' books and naturally would not permit that sort of thing in a book meant for girls from ten to fifteen years of age. Nothing is said of such a thing in the outline given for the story.

Mrs. Smith had learned that every story was to be filled with action words and a plethora of exclamation points, though it was to lack any overt violence. The writing needed to be concise, not long and flowery depictions of events or landscapes. If there was any extra fluff, Edward would bring out his blue pencil, cutting fifty descriptive words to a judicious "CRASH!" or a "Suddenly, he fell overboard." The characters themselves were to have plenty of "pluck and vigor" and always overcome their foes against all odds, everyone involved getting their just desserts. Lastly, but certainly not least, the child was to be "hooked" on the first page, and the last page necessitated the description of the next book adventure to come. It was all a tried and true recipe that Edward had honed over the years, starting from his days as editor at Street and Smith. Mrs. Smith had learned it all well when, out of necessity, Mr. Stratemeyer had asked her to start editing manuscripts herself.

Working for the Syndicate also meant keeping track of four different publishers: Lothrop, Lee and Shepard; Cupples and Leon; Merrian Company; and Grosset & Dunlap. That meant knowing what each required for the different series that they published. Plus, Edward was always on the lookout for a better publishing deal. Since he sold only the stories themselves to the publishers – retaining all right to the works – he could take his stories to whomever gave him the best rate, something the publishers knew all too well.

Edward stood from his desk and started to unconsciously measure out the room with his strides. It took him a moment to speak.

"I want to put out a slightly different sales catalog this quarter. I want to highlight all the books we currently have going that are written for girls; remind the young women and their parents of the different options they have to choose from. I want them all there: the Motor Girls, Outdoor Girls, Amy Bell Marlow, Girls of Central High, Moving Picture Girls, Bunny Brown, Nan Sherwood, and of course, Ruth Fielding, though she hardly needs the advertising. I think Lillian Garis is doing a wonderful job with the Ruth books since she took that over, don't you agree?"

"She has continued your wonderful work, Mr. Stratemeyer."

"We have to remind parents that girls need to read girl type stories, good, wholesome girl stories. These young ladies are just not ready to jump into the world of regular, adult novels. Their minds are not sufficiently developed to know what is appropriate among the *best sellers* that are waved before their eyes by book sellers eager for a sale. Don't you agree?"

"Of course, Mr. Stratemeyer. Children need to be guided and so do their parents."

"Right you are!" he said with enthusiasm. "And with the sensible, and might I add auspicious, Child Labor Act that was recently adopted, children are not allowed to work until they turn fifteen. This ensures that more children of all backgrounds have added time on their hands and many of them are young ladies. I am glad Cupples agreed with my request to change the books' cost to fifty cents. It's much easier for children to save up fifty pennies versus the previous dollar, and it's been born out year after year with increased sales." Edward sat back down behind his desk. "I think we need an introductory paragraph in the girl's section of the catalog that illustrates these points to the parent and the publishers alike."

Edward rested his elbows on his desk, putting the tips of his fingers together and tapping them lightly against each other in thought. It wasn't a minute before he dropped his arms and sat up straight.

"Do you mind if I forgo the dictaphone?" he said, "I want to get this down while it is fresh in my mind."

"No, indeed!" Mrs. Smith said with relish and picked up her notepad once more.

"Oh, and before I forget. Did you get the mailing list together for advertising to the Camp Fire Girls? I want to add them to our current list, especially for this catalog."

"I was able to talk with a lovely woman by the name of Charlotte Gulick. She and her husband have a camp on Lake Sebago in Maine for the Camp Fire Girls. She said there are currently over 80,000 Camp Fire Girls nationwide, and they had started just five years ago. Illustrates how young women like the outdoors as much as young men."

"I didn't know that organization even existed until one of the girls showed up on our doorstep selling war bonds, of all things. She was the dearest little thing, though her size maligned her abilities; she was quite the salesman."

"They'll give the Girl Scouts a run for their money."

"If they are at all like the feisty one that visited our doorstep, I think they might."

Nine ∾

(July 4th, 1918. Ladora, Iowa)

This last piece was not going to be easy to play. It wasn't that she didn't know the song; she had played it at every Memorial Day and Fourth of July event she had been at since she was ten. Mildred was part of the Ladora City Band, her primary instrument being the xylophone, though she also played the trombone when it was called for.

Mildred put her trombone up to her lips and blew out the patriotic *God Bless America* with the other members of the band, tears escaping down the corners of her eyes as she forced out the last few notes. The young girl was not one to cry at Patriotic tunes as the older people watching tended to do, but today was different. The band had gathered at the train depot to help see off the young men of Ladora who had signed up for the war over in Europe. From reading the newspapers,

Mildred knew that France and England were taking a beating, which was why her brother Melville, and a group of his friends, had signed up to fight after Woodrow Wilson declared war on April 6th the year before. Melville had completed his basic training and was home to say goodbye to his family, with the other young men of the Iowa Infantry Regiment.

Mildred wiped her tears away with her sleeve, took her trombone apart, and hurriedly put it in its case. She had to find Melville before he boarded the train.

She took off running but had to turn back. "I almost forgot!" She grabbed her going-away gift from underneath her trombone case and ran to find her brother.

Mildred found him standing with the rest of her family huddled around him, saying their goodbyes. He turned to his little sister when she approached. Mildred thrust out the book she had brought him, a book she thought Melville might appreciate: *Dave Dashaway and His Hydroplane; or Daring Adventures Over the Great Lake.* "I thought it was something you could read on the boat," she said.

"Thanks, squirt," he said, rustling her curly bobbed hair. "I have something for you, too."

Melville reached in his canvas shoulder bag and pulled out a wrapped package. Mildred could tell by the shape that it was also a book. She pulled off the string and uncovered a hardbound copy of *Ruth Fielding in the Moving Pictures.* The dust jacket had a large picture of the indomitable Ruth Fielding, her short wavy bob neatly in place. She was surrounded by smaller depictions of Ruth directing a movie with cameras rolling nearby.

→ reflect changing hairstyles of the time

"I know how much you like <u>Lillian Gish</u>, so I thought you'd like to read a bit about someone who makes movies, even if it's a fiction story."

Mildred held the book close to her chest. "It's swell, Melville."

"Oh, and I almost forgot." He pulled out two cardboard-covered composition notebooks. "I had a couple extra of these left from school, and since I won't be using them for a while..."

Mildred took the notebooks as if he were handing her a pair of glass slippers. Writing was her new passion, and she had been doing it incessantly. In fact, Melville had encouraged her to submit a couple of her short stories to the story papers, which Mildred thought was a brilliant idea. Her parents didn't read her stories, but they gave her the stamps to mail off her submissions. She had yet to have any accepted, but she knew it was just a matter of time.

"Write me a really good story, would ya, squirt. I want to brag to my buddies about my sister the author."

Mildred wrapped her arms around her brother, pinning his arms to his sides, the unaccustomed contact immobilizing him further. Mildred only let go when she needed to use her handkerchief.

The train whistle blew and all heads turned toward the train cars.

Mr. Augustine thrust out his hand to Melville. "Take care, son," he said, squeezing his son's shoulder.

Lillian grasped him around the neck for one last hug. "Write when you can," she said through her tears.

Less than a year after Melville joined the Brits and French in the trenches in France, Mildred received her first literary success.

"Look, Mother!" Mildred said, thrusting the children's story magazine *St. Nicholas* in front of her. It was the June edition, 1919.

"It's on page five."

Lillian flipped through the onion-thin pages to the announcement of the June Short Story Winner: Mildred Augustine. At the top of the page was an illustration of a graduate and bride, created by a young contributor with the notation: "a fitting introduction to the month of roses, and weddings, and glad (or tearful) farewells to school or college!" After the picture was Mildred's story: *The Courtesy*.

> *Mrs. Gardner sat gazing out of the window. In her lap lay a letter. The door opened and her daughter Andrea entered the room. Mrs. Gardner, smiling faintly, said, "I have received a letter from Aunt Jane, who will arrive next week to spend the winter with us." For a moment Andrea was too surprised to speak. Then she burst into tears.*
>
> *A week later Aunt Jane arrived, parrot, umbrella, baggage and all. She was even worse than Andrea had imagined. She breakfasted in bed, grumbled at everything, was courteous to no one, and was, in short, as Andrea declared, "a perfect grouch."*

117

As time passed, matters grew worse. The parrot screeched incessantly, and the house was in a constant uproar.

Several weeks after her arrival, Aunt Jane overheard a conversation that caused her much thought. Coming noiselessly past Andrea's room, she heard Andrea clearly say: "Aunt Jane thinks that we should do nothing but wait on her and show her every courtesy, while she just bosses and grumbles. If only she were pleasant, it would be much easier for us to be courteous to her."

Aunt Jane silently entered her room.

Next morning the Gardners were surprised to find Aunt Jane down for breakfast. Later, she helped wash the dishes without even grumbling.

Weeks passed. Aunt Jane became so helpful and cheerful it was a pleasure to have her around.

When spring came, the Gardners wanted her to remain, but, declining, she announced her intention of traveling, providing Andrea would accompany her. Andrea – not from courtesy, but because she really liked Aunt Jane – accepted.

No one except Aunt Jane knew, and she never told, that it was Andrea who had first shown her the need for true courtesy.

"That is wonderful, dear. I'll show your father when he gets in from the clinic." Lillian put her arm around her daughter. "Keep up the good work."

"I plan on it."

Mildred stood at the podium, a small sea of eager faces looking up at her from the movie house seats, where the 1922 Ladora High School graduation ceremony was taking place. Graduation day had finally arrived and none too soon, as far as Mildred was concerned. High school in Ladora was fine as small town schools go, but Mildred was ready to move on to other things. In fact, she had taken summer classes in Iowa City so she could graduate a year early. And as if to bring home the point, the four students in Mildred's graduating class had a hard time stirring up much excitement the week of their graduation. How much trouble can four people get into in a farming community of three hundred? Mildred took it as a sign, to forget Ladora and move on to bigger and better things. For Mildred, it was the State University of Iowa, where she was set to go to school in the fall at the tender age of seventeen.

"The time has finally arrived when we say goodbye to faithful Ladora High," Mildred began, but no sooner had she started her speech than a group of "hang-abouts" outside the theater started honking their horns. Mildred hesitated, waiting for a teacher or perhaps her father to take care of the disruption, but when no one moved a muscle, she continued her well-rehearsed and painstakingly written speech. Unfortunately, no one heard a word. The incident convinced Mildred further of her need to move away from her prosaic town.

Fortunately for Mildred, Iowa City and the University of Iowa was a far cry from Ladora, despite the short forty miles that separated the two towns. In 1855 the University of Iowa was the first public university in the United States to admit women as well as men and was just the progressive institution Mildred was looking for.

With WWI well behind them, the students at U of I, like many others, were ready to move on to bigger and better things. The coeds felt particularly liberated, with the recent spread of birth control from Europe to the United States, and women finally gaining the right to vote in 1920. Skirts to the knee, hair cut short, dates without a chaperone, a one-thirty a.m. curfew for undergrads, the diversity of the mixed race and ethnically diverse six thousand-plus student campus... Mildred was ready to take advantage of it all. She had already signed up to be a part of the school orchestra, accomplished women xylophone players being a rarity, but Mildred didn't want to stop there. So when the Iowa campus Women's Association held its first meeting for undergraduates to introduce the new women on campus to all that U of Iowa had to offer, Mildred and her new roommate, Bernice, from the new Currier Hall, made sure to attend.

A lovely girl in a hip-waisted, teal-green dress greeted them at the entrance to the Memorial Union conference room. She was wearing a gold and black "Women Hawks" button on her chest. Mildred eyed her expertly applied makeup and wavy brunette hair, which was plastered meticulously to her head, with a twinge of envy. Mildred had managed to convince her mother to cut her hair even shorter than it had been to mirror the times, but her curls refused to be tamed in the September heat and humidity. Mildred subconsciously pressed her hand down the side of her head and made a mental note to find out what the girl had used on her hair to create the manicured affect. Mildred and Bernice mingled with the other freshman until another fashionably dressed woman in a light tan dress stood in front of the room and clapped her hands to get their attention.

"Welcome, ladies. If you would please sit down, we'll begin the presentations."

The chatter in the room increased until each young woman found a seat in the rows of wooden folding chairs at the front of the room.

"Hello, ladies. My name is Eloise Naple. I'm the president of the Iowa Women's Association, and on behalf of the women of the University of Iowa, I welcome you to campus."

There was a polite round of applause before Eloise continued with her speech.

"The reason we have invited you-all to this little gatherin' is to make sure you learn all that U of I has to offer its women. There are a wide array of clubs and organizations that you'll be hearin' from today includin' our Cosmopolitan Club that promotes international solidarity, our Women's Athletic Association, for those, unlike myself, who are more physically inclined, and of course, the numerous Greek organizations on campus just to name a few. I'll be speakin' about a club dear to my heart, the Athena Literary Society.

"But first, I'd like to introduce Genevieve Worth, president of the Women's Athletic Association."

Again, there was polite applause as a very brown-skinned, trim woman in a short-sleeved sailor dress stepped up to the podium.

"Hello, ladies. Welcome to U of Iowa. I'm here to discuss all the opportunities we have for you as far as athletics. Let me assure you, this is not your mother's school. U of I has a very strong women's athletic department, allowing you to reach your full potential not only on the field but also off.

"I'd like to highlight some of our offerings, especially the renowned Lady Seals, our much touted women's swimming and diving club. Our girl swimmers regularly compete with the Eels, our men's equivalent, and it's definitely a lively competition. There is no kowtowing to the men in these races, ladies; it's about showing them, and all of U of I, what women can do."

Mildred's eyes were riveted on the fit-looking woman as she spoke passionately about the sport. She wasn't surprised to find out later that Genevieve was the captain of the Lady Seals. The toned muscles in her arms and the bronze color of her skin should have given her away, if Mildred had put two and two together.

Mildred was most comfortable when competing against men, so she decided this group might be the one for her. She had little access to water in Ladora, but when she did get to swim in a local pond or on rare trips to the Iowa River with her father, she was not unlike the family dog; it was hard for her father to pull her out of the water.

Mildred listened politely as Genevieve talked about the women's basketball, baseball, soccer, volleyball, and track teams, but Genevieve talked so passionately about the women Seals, that Mildred signed up for the group the minute all the other women were done speaking. She would have to audition for a spot in the club, but Mildred was confident in her ability and didn't give it a second thought. Genevieve also convinced Mildred to try the new women's soccer team. Practice had already started, but Genevieve touted the sport as a good primer for swimming relays, mentioning that she was also on the team. And since Mildred was majoring in journalism, she thought she should sign up for the Literary Society, as well.

Since this was Mildred's first year in college, coupled with the fact that she was at least a year younger than most of the girls in the room, Mildred decided that being in the university orchestra, a member of the Seals, the Literary Society, and the women's soccer team would be a good enough to start to college life. But by the time the presidents of the Cosmopolitan Club and the Greek journalism sorority, Theta Sigma Phi, had finished talking, she had put those on her list, too. Mildred was caught up in the moment and wasn't thinking of the time she would need to keep up with her math, science, and English composition classes, along with her history of American journalism. And she certainly wasn't thinking about any of that during her first exhibition swim relay that spring at The Big Dipper – the Iowa City municipal pool.

"All right, ladies, caps on," Genevieve said to her partners in the relay.

The women had taken a break after their exhibition dives and were waiting for the finale of the evening, the coed 200-yard relay.

Genevieve walked up close to Mildred so she wasn't overheard by the young men standing close by. "Ok, Millie, you're in our anchor position, so if we're behind, you've got to make up for the rest of us. You think you can do it?"

Mildred unconsciously pulled down on the short legs of her swim suit as she listened. She had long gotten used to the tight fit, scoop neck, and bare arms of these new suits – they were a real asset to making extra time in the water – but the legs were even shorter than the wide-legged, short jumpers that she had worn playing baseball, so she always felt conspicuous wearing them.

"You'll be swimming against McCullough…"

"Their captain!" Mildred said, straightening to stare Genevieve in the eyes.

Genevieve put her arm around Mildred's shoulder and drew her in close. "We have faith in you, Mildred, or we wouldn't have put you in this position."

Mildred made a few quick nods, then adjusted the swim cap on her head. She looked over at the four young men as they stretched and shook their arms and legs to get ready for the event. She paid particular attention to Erin McCullough. The junior had his hair cropped short and was as muscled as his teammates, but Erin was a good inch taller than all of them. This was a public exhibition, but winning was a matter of pride for both the Seals and Eels, the men determined not to let the women outswim them; it would be too humiliating. And the women wanted to show the men, and everyone else, that they could compete, even with the opposite sex. It was irksome to the Seals that they were relegated to the old, cramped school pool while the men were able to use the brand-new facility, which included high diving boards that the women didn't have. This in spite of their ever-growing numbers and their ability to continuously beat school swim records; there were over thirty women in the Seals when Mildred had joined her freshman year. Mildred had run an anonymous editorial in the school newspaper – the *Daily Iowan* – that bemoaned their situation: "If Iowa women cannot have more room in which to exercise their ambitious limbs, if they cannot have high diving boards – then at least they should be praised for the progress they have made in spite of [these] handicap[s]."

"Take your marks," was heard above the din of the crowd in the stands.

Helen was first in the relay. She stepped up to the side of the pool and took her place, ignoring the young man bent over beside her. The starting gun cracked, and the two bodies hardly made a splash as they sliced into the water's surface to come up twenty feet away from where they had started, immediately reaching with their arms and kicking with their legs to propel themselves forward. The loud cheering of the crowd was just a hum in the swimmers' ears.

The two turned the corner with just a foot between them. Sharon took her place on the edge of the pool, and the minute Helen touched the side, she was off, just a second before her male counterpart, making up the small distance the women were lacking. Sharon wasn't able to keep up the pace, however, and by the time she completed her two laps and touched the side of the pool, the women were a good two feet back.

Genevieve was the penultimate swimmer in the relay, and she jumped in with vigor, determined to make up the distance. In the return lap, she was able to narrow the distance to just one foot before Mildred leaped from the side of the pool and effortlessly parted the now agitated surface. Mildred's advantage was her trim frame and the endurance she had for long distances. She had the body of a petite fashion model but the strength similar to that of women who worked on neighboring farms lifting bales of hay or wrangling large farm animals, though she had never done either. Those attributes coupled with her amazing stamina, and the young woman was hard to beat. Neither Erin nor Mildred saw the crowd rise to their feet or heard the roar that went up as they raced down their final lap to the end of the pool. The *Daily Iowan* called the race this way: "The feature event of the evening was the exhibitions given by Captain McCullough of the University 1923-24 team... In a mixed relay with a man swimming against a woman, Mildred Augustine touched the wall a few seconds before McCullough did."

The rest of the women Seals jumped in the pool to join Mildred in her celebration.

Ten ∽

(1923)

"Sunny, Patty, leave the baby alone," Harriet said from the doorway to the nursery as her oldest child Russell – seven years of age – and her first daughter Patricia – just two – pushed the wheeled, wicker baby bassinette back and forth between them.

"But Camilla likes it," Russell said, looking up from the baby's bed. "How come you're all dressed up?" he asked.

Patricia walked over to her mother to touch the shimmering black fabric of her dress.

"Your father and I have a fundraiser dinner to go to. Now it's time for you to eat." Harriet walked over to her son and took hold of his hand. "Mabel made a wonderful roast and it's getting cold."

Russell pulled away from his mother. "I'm not hungry,"

he said, crossing his arms across his chest and putting on his best stern face.

"But Grampa Ed and Grandma Maddie are coming to watch you, and if you don't eat your dinner, they won't come," Harriet lied.

Both children brightened at the mention of their grandparents. Patricia clapped her small hands together with glee. "Bumpa!" she squealed.

"Yes, Bumpa and Grandma," Harriet said.

Harriet ushered the children out of the room and toward the dining room.

"Will Grandpa tell us a story?" Russell asked.

"If you eat all your dinner, Grandpa will tell you a story," Harriet said, knowing his father would make up a story at the drop of a hat, just as he did for her and her sister when they were young, whether they ate their dinner or not.

(March, 1925)
"Settle down. Settle down," Mr. Maulsby said from the front of the small classroom.

William Maulsby was a favorite of the journalism students because he was considered the "real McCoy"; he had been a journalist in the trenches of WWI and was easily distracted into telling his sometimes gruesome overseas adventures.

Everyone took their seats, a few of the young men lingering at the front of the room eagerly examining the walnut-colored box on the front table. They obviously knew what it was. Most of the other students in the room, including Mildred, did not.

"All right, fellas, I'll let you play with it after class," said Maulsby as he stepped between the box and the young men, turning them toward their seats.

Maulsby sat next to the box and rested his arm on top of it. It was about twice the size of a bread box and longer than it was tall. There were three squat, diamond-shaped, gold metal pieces affixed to the front of the box with three smaller versions of the same thing just below. Each metal piece had a black dial running horizontally through its center. In between these six dials were two small round dials. Mildred wasn't sure what it had to do with Maulsby's Reporting and Correspondence class, but she was about to find out.

"I won't insult your intelligence, and mine, and tell you why today is significant. But what you may or may not know is that for the first time in history, the inauguration of a president will be broadcast live via AM radio." Mr. Maulsby tapped the top of the large radio next to him with a smile.

The students in the class started to chat with one another at the astounding news. Radios had slowly crept back into use after being banned during the Great War, but programming was minimal and reception was typically lousy. When Calvin Coolidge was elected president in 1925, they were a rarity in most households, owned mostly by men who liked to tinker with the finicky contraptions.

"As you can imagine, reporters live for days like today.

But since we can't be in our nation's capital to report on this noteworthy event, I thought I'd bring Washington to you."

The professor turned to face the large box and turned one of the small round dials, sending a staticky squeal into the room. Maulsby kneeled down in front of the radio and quickly turned one of the larger dials to change the squeal to a quiet whine.

"Sorry about that."

Maulsby played with more of the dials, his head leaning into the box so he could hear. "The university has installed an antenna on the roof of Close Hall, so we should get pretty good reception," he explained as he moved his hand from one dial to another in seemingly random order.

Squawks and screeches emanated from the box until finally a far off voice was heard.

"Got it!"

The professor turned up the volume so everyone in the class could hear the gravelly sound of a male voice.

There are dignitaries from every state and many different countries with us today, along with our radio listeners, a first for a presidential inauguration.

The students applauded. Maulsby turned the volume down on the radio until the voice of the announcer was a mere whisper and unintelligible to the students. He sat on the table next to the radio and leaned back onto the top.

"Does anyone know what other first will be happening at Coolidge's inauguration?"

There was a lot of talk among the students, but no one was brave enough to venture a guess.

"I'll give you a hint. A rather noteworthy figure, our current Chief Justice of the Supreme Court, will be administering the oath of office."

Mildred's hand shot up. "President Taft!"

"Exactly, Miss Augustine. Nice job."

Mildred leaned over to her friend, Laurel, and whispered, "I only knew that because old man Baker made us list out the presidents this morning in history class. He told us that Taft was now a chief justice."

Laurel gave Mildred a co-conspiratorial wink. In her junior year, there were a total of four females out of twenty-six students in the newly-formed school of journalism. Most of the professors didn't seem to take notice of the girls' gender, but oftentimes the locals in Iowa City gave the girls strange looks when they were in town getting details for a story for the school paper, the *Daily Iowan*. So the two girls were very close and always celebrated even small instances where they were able to show up their male counterparts.

"Now, I didn't bring this here just so you could be in on this small piece of history, though I agree, that would be a good enough reason in my book. But you, or your parents, have paid a goodly amount to attend this college, so I want to give you your money's worth. I've got an assignment for each of you."

There was a group groan and a general slouching in the chairs around the room.

"What is this? Are you reporters or just bystanders here to listen to a good speech?"

Mildred looked over at Laurel. Both women opened up their notebooks and pulled a pencil out of their purses.

"Since the *Iowan* has recently become a member of the Associated Press, we'll be getting their stories on the inauguration for the paper, no doubt, so what I want you to do is compare what you come up with for copy versus the Associate Press pieces."

There was a general grumbling in the class at the request. "I know, I know," Maulsby said, putting up his hand to quell the protest. "This is only your fourth week in class, but most of you are second-year students, so I think you can handle it. And unlike real copy for the *Iowan* that Professor Gallup will edit, I'll be editing these pieces, and you know what a softy I am compared to George."

The students chuckled. Most had seen a fair amount of blue correction marks on pieces they submitted for the school paper. It was always a learning experience giving copy to Professor Gallup to edit, but most knew it was just part of being in his class and they appreciated the feedback. It wasn't going to be any different working on a real paper once they graduated; it was a part of the job. Mildred had learned a lot already in her first two years at Iowa. She had stayed in Iowa City and taken summer school classes with the goal of graduating early, as she had done with high school. And she continued to send off stories to children's magazines, somewhat as a diversion from class work but also with the continued desire to see her name in print. It was a thrill she continued to aspire to. She wrote series stories about Midget, the same girl she had written about in high school.

Maulsby turned to the radio again and turned up the volume. Students toward the back of the room moved their chairs closer to make sure they didn't miss a detail.

Mildred stood outside William Maulsby's office, nervous about knocking, though she wasn't sure why. It wasn't so much that she didn't think he would help her, it was more related to what her request was about. Mildred pursed her lips and knocked. She heard a muffled "Come in" from the other side of the door, so she opened the door and walked in.

"Hello, Mildred! How are you this fine day?" Maulsby said, pushing his chair away from his desk to allow him to rest one ankle across his knee. "Excited about graduation? One more class this summer and you'll be done."

"I am, Mr. Maulsby. I really am!"

"That's quite the accomplishment, graduating in three years," he said. He picked up the pipe from his desk and started filling it. "Better than most of the fellows in your class."

"Well, I'm kind of anxious to get out in the real world, get a job, get my own apartment, maybe do a little traveling… you know?"

"You mean you're *eager*," he said, correcting her.

Mildred rolled her eyes – *always editing, these professors*. "Yeah…I mean eager. Anyway, that's why I'm

133

here. I am applying to a few papers, and I wondered if you'd be willing to write me a letter of recommendation?"

Maulsby flipped open his lighter and lit his pipe, puffing out blue-gray clouds of sweet smelling smoke. "I'd be happy to, Mildred." He leaned back again, the springs in his chair groaning from the pressure. "But have you heard the rumors about the new Master of Journalism program?"

"I have, but I wasn't sure they were true."

"Well, I can't say for sure, but it looks to me like it's going to happen, and I'd like to see you apply."

Mildred hesitated a moment before replying, her face slowly softened as she thought about the prospect. "I'd like that, Mr. Maulsby, that would be wonderful, but..."

"But...?"

"I need a job, and I'd like to get a job in a bigger city. I mean a really big city like New York."

"Is that where you're applying?"

"There and for a journalism position at the *Clinton Herald*." Mildred looked down at the ground, embarrassed to be applying at such a small town paper. But she decided with all her experience writing for the school newspaper, if the position in New York didn't pan out, they would surely take her at the *Herald*. Any job in journalism was better than no job in journalism. She wasn't in college to get a husband, like some girls she knew. She wanted to make a difference in the world or at a least be a part of the world, not just a decoration on some man's arm.

"Good to keep your options open," Maulsby said.

"Remember, sometimes that first job isn't the job of your dreams, but getting experience behind that news desk is what's important. Don't forget that."

Mildred looked up and smiled. "I won't."

"Wherever you end up, make sure you contact the school next spring to confirm my suspicions. I'll look for your application and see if I can help get you a good professor to work with," he said with a wink.

Mildred reached out her hand. Mr. Maulsby took the pipe out of his mouth and leaned forward toward Mildred. "Thanks, Mr. Maulsby. I really enjoyed your classes."

"Thanks, Mildred. I'll be looking for your name in the bylines."

Mildred grinned and left the room, off to her next adventure.

Eleven

(1925)

"H…" Edward handed Harriet Smith a typed piece of paper as she sat at her desk. "I'd like this to go out in the April edition of the *Editor*."

Harriet took the paper and read it over.

The Stratemeyer Syndicate, Edward Stratemeyer, proprietor, of Newark, N.J. and New York City, can use the services of several additional writers in the preparation of the Syndicate's books for boys, books for girls, and rapid-fire detective stories. These stories are all written for the Syndicate on its own titles and outlines and we buy all rights in this material for cash upon acceptance. Rate of payment depends entirely upon the amount of work actually done by a writer and the quality of same. All stories are issued under established trademarked pen names unless otherwise agreed upon...We are particularly anxious to get hold of the younger writers, with fresh ideas in the treatment of stories for boys and girls.

Harriet Smith put down the paper after she had finished reading it.

"I just can't keep up with all the work. We're keeping four ghostwriters busy and we still can't keep up," Edward said. "And I think Maddie is getting irritated with me spending so much time at work, and rightfully so."

Harriet nodded her head, her eyes wide with anticipation. She was hoping Mr. Stratemeyer would finally look for more help since the busier he was, the busier she was. And her husband was also starting to complain about all the extra time she was spending at the office. Their kids were all grown and out of the house, and they had both envisioned taking long weekends to the mountains or trips down the coast. But with Harriet's hours, that was an impossibility. The Syndicate was juggling twenty-three different series books, and that meant one to two books in each series per year. That was a lot of outlining, editing, rewriting, and corresponding with publishers as well as with the writers. They had sold three to four million books in 1924, so they had the funds for additional help. And it wasn't that Mr. Stratemeyer didn't compensate her well. He was very generous and even made sure she got a bonus at the holidays, but there comes a point when living and breathing your job gets tiring, and Mrs. Smith was no spring chicken.

"I'll make sure they get in right away, Mr. S.," she said, pulling out her index card address file.

"Put one in the *Editor and Publisher*, as well. Something smaller, perhaps: Experienced fiction writer wanted to work from Publisher's outline or something like that."

"Right away," Harriet said, writing down his request verbatim so she wouldn't forget.

"By the way, how is Magdalene doing?"

Edward leaned on the doorjamb between her office and his. "Her headaches have improved some since Harriet's latest baby was born. She has trouble keeping up with the older two, but she really likes those little ones."

"Oh! That reminds me." Harriet opened her bottom drawer and pulled out a small box tied with a soft-blue ribbon. "I made this for the little fellow," she said, handing the gift to Edward. "It's a knit hat and mittens."

"Well, how nice of you, H. That wasn't necessary."

"How is that new baby doing?"

"Fine, just fine," Edward beamed.

Harriet noted his obvious pleasure at just the thought of the boy. "How nice of Harriet and Russell to name him after his grandfather."

"It is, isn't it. And when the little tike gets old enough to get into mischief, he can blame it on his Grandpa Edward," he said with a smile, then retired into his office.

Many writers responded to the Syndicate ad, but only a few would live up to Edward's standards.

It was one o'clock, a whole hour before Leslie McFarlane needed to be behind his desk at the Springfield, Massachusetts newspaper, the *Republican*. But he had seen an ad in the *Editor and Publisher* while he was stirring his oatmeal in the rooming house he had rented on Pearl Street. The only appliance he was allowed in his room was a hot plate, and without refrigeration he wasn't afforded many options for meals until the cold weather set in and he could store some milk and meat on the windowsill between his window and storm.

Leslie had the hotel beat at the paper, which basically meant the Hotel Kimball, the only large hotel in town. It was a prized job at the paper for the younger journalists on staff since the Kimball was the place where local business' or service clubs held their banquets or club luncheons. Someone on staff needed to report on these social events, so the reporter on this beat was sure to make out with at least three free meals per week, if not more.

April 26, 1926

To Whom it May Concern,
I saw your ad in the Editor and Publisher *and I'd like to find out more about the kind of writer you're*

139

looking for. I have written for the Cobalt Daily Nugget, *the* Sudbury Star, *two Canadian newspapers, then for the* Ottawa Journal *and the* Montreal Herald *plus I've written numerous fictional stories for magazines including the* Adventure. *My current employment is at the* Springfield Republican *in Massachusetts. I have sent along one of my more recent stories for you to review.*

I look forward to hearing from you,
Sincerely,
Leslie McFarlane

Leslie pulled his letter out of the typewriter and looked it over. He took it over to the desk of fellow writer, Buddy Brook, who had his feet up on the desk and was reading the paper, cigarette smoke dancing lazily above his head. Leslie flicked at the worn sole of his shoe. Buddy dropped his paper.

"This is my reply to an ad looking for a fiction writer," Leslie said, handing the letter to Buddy. "Tell me what you think."

Buddy took it without question and looked it over. Buddy, like most of the writers on the *Republican,* had higher aspirations than writing for a newspaper all his life. Buddy's dream was to be a song writer, so Leslie knew he wouldn't have to explain his passion for writing stories.

"I don't want the guy to know I'm a twenty-three-year-old high school graduate."

Buddy handed it back to him. "Looks good to me. I'd run with it," he said, cigarette bobbing in his mouth as he spoke.

"Where's the writing job?"

"It doesn't say. It just gives a P.O. box number."

"Worth a shot," he said and returned to reading the paper.

Leslie picked up the copy of his 20,000 word magazine story, *Impostor*, gave it a good luck kiss, and put it in the large envelope with his letter. His reply came in less than a week.

May 4, 1926

Dear Mr. McFarlane,

We received your response to our advertisement and would like to move further with the process of considering you as a writer for the Syndicate. But first, I would like to explain a little about our company. We prepare manuscripts for publishers with an emphasis on serial books for juvenile readers.

I have penned many of these books myself but as of late, I have had to concentrate on plotting out the books and planning new books. This has precipitated the need for other writers, such as yourself, to flesh out the stories for me. You must know that all the writers who work for the Syndicate do so under complete anonymity; it is something that I insist upon. If you are chosen to be a Syndicate writer, I would pay you a flat rate of $100 per story. You also give up all future rights to the stories and their characters.

I will be sending you two books for your perusal. One is from the "Nat Ridley Rapid Fire Detective" series, which chronicles the exploits of a clever and daring young detective. There are fifteen volumes in this series to date. The second is from the "Dave Fearless" series and tells of the adventures of a young deep-sea diver and underwater explorer. There are just six volumes in this series so far. I think you would be suited for either series, but look them over and pick one that you might like to start with. Once you have decided which young man suits you best, I'll send you an outline for two chapters of the next book in the series that I would like expanded to approximately 2,000 words. I cannot pay you for this initial exercise, but if you pass muster, as they say, you will be guaranteed full payment as described above.

I think you might be a good fit for the Syndicate, Mr. McFarlane, and I look forward to seeing what you can do for my stories.

Yours truly,
Edward Stratemeyer

Two days later, two paperback books appeared in the post. After reading through both, Leslie decided Dave Fearless was the boy he wanted to work with, if not just because of his name. Leslie McFarlane was going to be the next Roy Rockwood. He sent off a letter to Mr. Stratemeyer indicating his preference and waited impatiently for the outline. It came back as a three page outline for twenty-three chapters. Leslie was cautiously optimistic that Stratemeyer changed his mind and wanted more than the first two chapters until he read the enclosed letter.

May 14, 1926

Dear Mr. McFarlane,

I have sent along the outline of the next installment in the Dave Fearless series for you as a trial run, so to speak. I ask that you follow it closely. I also want to impress upon you that none of my characters commit or are involved in violent acts: No character should die or be grievously injured in any of my stories. Keep in mind the young minds you will be writing for; there should be no foul language and I prefer no romantic involvement with the main protagonist. You will note, as per the sample volumes you have read, that there is much action in these stories particularly in the first few pages. The reader needs to be hooked on the first page. As you will also note in the outline, chapter one includes a reminder of what has happened to the main characters in the previous volumes. Please flesh out the first two chapters and send them back to me for review.

Remember, this is an unpaid exercise, but if what you send me meets the Syndicate standard, you may fill in the rest of the story. Upon completion of the manuscript, you will be sent a check for $100.

Yours truly,

Edward Stratemeyer

That night, after the newsroom had shut down for the

evening, Leslie put a clean sheet of paper in his typewriter, ratcheted it in place, and began to write.

Dave Fearless Under the Ocean,
or the Treasure of the Lost Submarine.

Chapter 1
The Menace From the Mist

Leslie hesitated a moment then began again, tapping steadily on the keys.

Dave Fearless looked out over the rolling waves and frowned as he saw a greasy cloud rolling in from the horizon.

"There's a fog coming up, Bob."

"Looks like it. Do you think we had better turn back?"

"Perhaps we should," agreed Dave. "We want to be back at Quanatack in time for supper."

The two chums, Dave Fearless, young deep-sea diver, and Bob Vilett, marine engineer, were cruising off the coast of Long Island in Dave's motor boat, the Amos. Now, as Dave remarked, a fog was rising and they were a long way from home.

"We can't depend on the weather at this time of year," said Dave Fearless.

Hardly had he spoken when the steady throbbing of the engine became slower. It coughed jerkily for a moment and died.

"I thought something would happen," said Bob

Leslie was on a roll. He completed both chapters in less than two hours. With only a few typos to fix, Leslie collected the four sheets of paper and mailed them back to Mr. Stratemeyer, then headed home to throw something in a pan for dinner.

It took about a week to hear back.

May 24, 1926

Dear Mr. McFarlane,

I have reviewed your start of the Dave Fearless story and found it satisfactory. Please continue with the rest of the book. After you send the completed manuscript back to me for editing, you will receive your check.

Yours truly,
Edward Stratemeyer

P.S. Please sign the attached agreement and send it along immediately. Thank you.

"Satisfactory? That's less than glowing," Leslie said. He read through the second page.

```
Leslie McFarlane. (672)
            Newark, N.J., May 24, 1926
```

For and in consideration of the sum of

One Hundred Dollars, ($100)

the receipt of which is hereby acknowledged, I hereby sell, transfer and set aside to Edward Stratemeyer, Literary Agent, xxxxx xxxx xxxxxxxxx, his heirs and assigns, all my right, title and interest in a certain story written by me on a title and outline furnished by said Edward Stratemeyer and named

Dave Fearless Under the Ocean

In making this transfer I hereby affirm that my work on the story is absolutely new, and I hereby grant to Edward Stratemeyer full permission to print the story under any trade-mark pen name that may be his business property, and I further agree that I will not use such pen name in any manner whatsoever.

"Well, here goes nothing."

Leslie picked up his pen, dipped it in the ink well, and signed the bottom of the contract.

$\mathbb{T}$ welve ⌒

Leslie wasn't the only one to see the Stratemeyer advertisement. There had been a steady stream of letters since Harriet had placed the ads just a week before. Edward had assigned Harriet to look over the letters and give him only the ones she thought he would approve. Edward pulled another letter from the steadily growing pile. Envelopes had return addresses from Waynesboro, Virginia; Framingham, Massachusetts and Washington, D.C.; as well as Fertile, Minnesota and Cuyahoga Falls, Ohio. The one he held in his hand was from Clinton, Iowa.

April 17, 1926

Dear Sirs,
    I understand that the Stratemeyer Syndicate can

147

use the services of writers in preparation of books for boys and girls and also in the short story field. Will you kindly furnish me with information concerning this work and your terms?

I have sold twenty-eight stories in the past two years to St. Nicholas Magazine, Lutheran Young Folks, Young People, Youth's Comrade, *and similar magazines and papers. In addition, I have sold a number of articles, feature stories and fiction, and have turned out about six hundred printed inches of newspaper material each week for the last year.*

In September I am planning to change my location to New York City.

Yours very truly,

Mildred Augustine

Edward nodded his head in satisfaction. "H., can you come here a minute?"

Harriet Smith entered Mr. Stratemeyer's office and stood in front of his desk. He handed her Mildred's letter. "Read this one."

Harriet read over the letter. "I thought that was promising, as well. And she's a woman, too. You haven't gotten letters from many women, especially ones with her education and experience."

"I agree."

Harriet handed the letter back.

Edward pulled out a piece of paper from his desk drawer and opened his ink well. "I'm going to write this young woman and ask her to send me some of her stories. We'll see how strong her writing skills are, then move on to step two."

May 21, 1926

Dear Miss Augustine,

I received your stories and have looked them over with a great deal of interest, and it is just possible that in the future I may be able to use your services, provided we can come to terms that are agreeable to both parties involved. I will contact you when something comes up that might be appropriate for your skills.

Yours truly,
Edward Stratemeyer

(July, 1926)
Mildred stood outside the Madison Square Park office building on 25th Street in Manhattan and looked up. It was a tall, concrete building that had too many floors to count. She held onto her new hat from Paris so it didn't land on the pavement and get mussed. Mildred was returning from a weeklong trip to Europe where she took in as many sites as the train schedules would allow. It was the trip she gave herself before she was to re-enter the hallowed halls of the

149

University of Iowa in the fall, this time in the new Master of Journalism program. She had taken a ship out of Le Havre, France, so Paris was the penultimate stop on her whirlwind trip through Germany, France, and England.

The building in front of her was where the Stratemeyer Syndicate had its office and since Mildred was in town for two days checking up on job postings, she decided it was as good a time as any to stop by and introduce herself to Edward Stratemeyer, even if she didn't have an appointment.

Mildred swallowed hard. *He did say he was interested in working with me at some point,* Mildred reassured herself as she stared at the front doors to the building, contemplating whether she should really go in uninvited. *And if he was serious, he'd want to meet me in person, if he could, right? Besides, if I'm going to try to move to New York, I'd have to get a job in New York, so this is important.*

Mildred set her mouth, squared her shoulders, and walked through the heavy metal and glass front doors of the building.

It so happened that Mildred didn't end up getting the job she had been looking for from the Syndicate, or anyone else in the city for that matter, but her visit with Edward Stratemeyer was impressive enough for him to send a letter to Mildred soon after her move back home – she was staying there for the summer before her return to school.

September 20th, 1926

Dear Miss Augustine,

> *I am pleased to tell you something has transpired*
> *that will allow me to offer you a position as a writer for*
> *the Syndicate. As I have mentioned in our unexpected,*
> *though pleasant, meeting in New York a few weeks*
> *back, all my writers work under pen names. The name*
> *and books that I need a new writer for is Alice B.*
> *Emerson of the Ruth Fielding series.*

Mildred dropped the letter into her lap. "I can't believe this," she said out loud.

Her old school chum, Jennifer, turned around from the book she was reading on Mildred's porch. "Believe what?"

"The Stratemeyer Syndicate wants me to be the next Alice Emerson," Mildred said in disbelief.

"Who's Alice Emerson, and what's the Stratemeyer Syndicate?"

Mildred picked up the letter again to make sure it was her name on the letterhead. "Alice Emerson is the name, the pseudonym really, for the author of the Ruth Fielding novels." Mildred's voice was starting to rise an octave or two as the significance of the moment began to sink in.

Jennifer's mouth dropped open, and she rose to her feet. She grasped Mildred's hands and pulled her to standing, then proceeded to pump her arms and turn Mildred in circles, ratcheting up the excitement further. Mildred readily complied, and soon the two were giggling and jumping like grade school girls on their last day of school.

Mildred couldn't believe her luck. She had grown up right along with Ruth Fielding, which was first published in

1913. In fact, Mildred still had many of Ruth's stories up in her room. Ruth was an amateur sleuth who had started out cracking small crimes at her boarding school, eventually becoming a famous Hollywood producer solving big time mysteries. She was every girl's idol. Of course, Mildred had not kept up with the series of late, but in his letter Mr. Stratemeyer had promised to send her the last two books in the series so she could be brought up to speed. Mildred, in the leave-no-stone-unturned style she had been known for at the *Herald*, was already planning to read more of the series, to ensure she was fully prepared for the job.

When the girls were done dancing, Mildred finished Mr. Stratemeyer's letter and the accompanying two-and-a-half-page outline. The new story was titled: *Ruth Fielding and Her Great Scenario; or Striving for the Motion Picture Prize.* Edward had written a synopsis at the top of the outline.

> *In this volume a bitter rival has learned that Ruth was writing a prize scenario* [script] *and laid a plot to rob the girl of the rewards of her labor.*

He also gave away the titillating news that Ruth and Tom, her long time beau, were tying the knot. Mildred was rather displeased with this turn of events for Ruth. Mildred and her fellow female classmates at the University of Iowa worked very hard to get where they were, and Mildred didn't like the idea that young girls who read the Ruth Fielding series would be encouraged to think that marriage was the ultimate goal of every woman. Mildred knew this sentiment was not the norm, but Ruth Fielding wasn't your ordinary woman; she was a successful, independent business woman. Mildred was pleased when Mr. Stratemeyer made the comment in his letter, "...we do not desire too much love-making in these books for girls." Writing about romance wasn't Mildred's strong suits, so it was an easy decision to keep Ruth's independence, even after she got married. Besides, it would make for a more exciting series. How many mysteries can a housewife come across while cleaning her home and shopping at the local market with the kids?

The outline was not unexpected. Edward had mentioned during their meeting in New York how writers worked within the Syndicate. That was when she also learned of the writers' lack of rights to the works they helped create. She wasn't sure she agreed with that part of the partnership, but she found it hard to give up the chance to get a book in print, even if it wasn't fully hers. Mildred's first love was juvenile fiction, so she took immense pleasure in creating stories for young readers, even if this time she was only filling in an outline. She also realized, at $125 per story, it would be a good way to help pay for her master's program and could even continue once she returned to the working world.

Mildred worked steadily, though with some difficulty, on the story the rest of the summer and had completed the first six chapters just before heading back to school. Part of the difficulty was her lack of knowledge of the film industry and her unfamiliarity with writing a romance. Ruth and Tom's love affair was a subplot to *Her Great Scenario*, but she wanted it to be authentic, nonetheless. Mildred sent off the first chapters to Mr. Stratemeyer for comments while she continued writing, hopeful of his approval. His reply was short and succinct.

September 29th, 1926

Dear Miss Augustine,

I have sent back the chapters with my edits. You will notice some consistent items that need correcting as you continue. I have also attached a letter that explains the basic guidelines to follow when writing any Syndicate story for juvenile readers. Rework these pages and send me three to four additional chapters.

I want to tell you not to be discouraged; it takes most of my new writers some time to learn how my stories need to be constructed. I think you can do this work when you catch the idea of just what is wanted.

Yours truly,

Edward Stratemeyer

During the first term of her master's program, Mildred spent all of her free time doing her rewrites on the story, then wrote the Syndicate owner her response.

October 6th, 1926

Dear Mr. Stratemeyer,

I regret that the chapters of the Ruth Fielding serial were not satisfactory. I have attempted to rebuild the story, and appreciate your criticism. In the first chapter I have changed a number of speeches and have entirely rewritten the second and third chapters. I have the first eighteen chapters finished when I received your criticism, but if you find the enclosed ten chapters suitable, I can polish it up, and place the entire manuscript in your hands within a few days. I eagerly await your response.

Yours truly,
Mildred Augustine

By the end of October Edward Stratemeyer was doing the final edits on the completed story of *Ruth Fielding and Her Great Scenario.* After he had handed it off to H. to type for the publisher, he started putting in place a series he had been thinking about for some time. It was another juvenile serial, but this time there would be two protagonists, two brothers to be exact, and they would be amateur detectives. And Edward knew just the person for the job.

October 10th, 1926

Dear Mr. McFarlane,
I have sent along the outline for that new series I had mentioned to you of late. As you may or may not have noticed, detective stories such as the works of S.S. Van Dine, AKA Willard H. Wright, and Agatha

Christie are all the rage. Knowing the reading taste of young boys the way I do, I think they would enjoy something similar, though with protagonists more their age. I have in mind two high-school-age boys whose father is a private investigator. The series title is "The Hardy Boys" with the author's nom de plume of Franklin W. Dixon. These books will be clothbound vs the paperback you have been working on, so your writing payment will increase to $125. I have attached an information sheet with all the initial characters listed and the plot outline per usual.

If you meet my usual expectations with this first volume, then two more volumes will quickly follow.

Yours truly,
Edward Stratemeyer

The information sheet was to the point.

The Tower Treasure

Setting: small city on Barmet Bay called Bayport, somewhere on the Atlantic coast. The boys go to Bayport High.

Characters: Frank Hardy - sixteen

 Joe Hardy - fifteen

 Laura Hardy - the mother

 Carson Hardy - the father, private detective

Chums: Chet Morton - chubby farm boy and

      fun-loving lad

 Biff Hooper - athletic, good to have around in

      a fight

Tony Prito - Italian friend
Iola Morton - Chet's sister, is partial to Joe
Callie Shaw - is partial to Frank
Hurd Applegate - eccentric stamp collector
Adelia Applegate - Hurd's sister, lived with Hurd
Chief Collig - local police chief
Detective Smuff - local police detective
Con Riley - town constable
Rocco - Italian fruit stand owner
Ike Harrity - ticket seller
Henry Robinson - Applegate's caretaker
Mrs. Robinson - Henry's wife
Perry Robinson - Henry's son, school chum of the Hardy Boys
Red Jackley - ex-convict, burglar by trade

   Story Synopsis: Hurd Applegate is robbed of $40,000 worth of jewels and securities. Just before he dies, Red Jackley confesses he stole the items and hid them in "the old tower," but they can't be found because everyone is looking in the wrong towers – Applegate's mansion towers. Henry is a suspect so he is arrested for the crime. Frank and Joe finally find the actual "old tower" – the old water tower – and find the loot. Henry goes free.

   Leslie put a piece of paper in his typewriter, pondered a moment, then began to tap on the white keys. It took Leslie three weeks to take the boys from the treacherous Shore Road motorcycle ride to accepting the whopping reward check of $1000 ($500 for each boy) and a meal that would have any boy supposing he had died and gone to his maker. Then Frank and Joe were sent off to the Syndicate for approval. Stratemeyer's usual subdued approval came in the form of two more outlines: *The House on the Cliff* and *The Secret of the Old Mill*, the next two volumes in the Hardy series and what Leslie found out later was the completion of the breeder books that had come to be the hallmark of the Syndicate. If these three books, all published at the same time, sold well, MacFarlane would be authoring more volumes of the two fun-loving detectives. He had no idea of what was to come.

Thirteen ∼

It took over a year for Edward to come up with a female counterpart to the Hardy Boys. When the idea had solidified in his mind, he went looking for a publisher.

July 27, 1927

Suggestions for a new series of girls books.

From Edward Stratemeyer. Confidential. Please return.

These suggestions for a new series for girls verging on novels. 224 pages, to retail at fifty cents.

I have called this line the "Stella Strong Stories," but they might also be called "Diana Drew Stories", "Diana Dare Stories", "Nan Nelson Stories", "Nan Drew Stories" or "Helen Hale Stories."

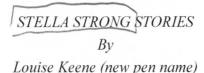

STELLA STRONG STORIES
By
Louise Keene (new pen name)

Stella Strong, a girl of sixteen, is the daughter of a District Attorney of many years standing. He's a widower and often talks over his affairs with Stella and the girl was present during many interviews her father had with noted detectives and at the solving of many intricate mysteries. Then, quite unexpectedly, Stella plunged into some mysteries of her own and found herself wound up in a series of exciting situations. An up-to-date American girl at her best, bright, clever, resourceful, and full of energy.

STELLA STRONG AT MYSTERY TOWERS
(or, The Secret of Twin Towers or, Stella Strong at the House of Mystery)
How Stella visited the old Tower House and met the rich and eccentric maiden ladies, Patricia and Hildegarde Forshyne, who were much disturbed by many unusual happenings about the place. She learns that some relatives are trying to get possession of the Forshyne fortune. Stella was once made a prisoner, but turned the table and made a most startling exposure.

THE MYSTERY AT SHADOW RANCH
(or, The Mystery at Shadow Valley)
A thrilling tale of mysterious doings at various places in the valley. Many thought that robberies of rich homes were contemplated. It remained for Stella Strong to clear up the perplexities.

THE DISAPPEARANCE OF NELLIE RAY
(or, The Disappearance of Martha Brown)
In this tale either a rich girl or an eccentric rich lady disappears under most puzzling circumstances. The authorities were at their wits' end to locate her. Stella Strong unearths one clue after another and follows up a perilous trail to triumph.

THE MISSING BOX OF DIAMONDS
Stella arrives at a summer hotel to find great excitement because of the disappearance of a box containing some famous diamond jewelry. Stella gets mixed up in the affair, but finally manages to clear herself and find the valuables.

THE SECRET OF THE OLD CLOCK
A large estate remains unsettled because of a missing will. Some domineering rich folks claim the entire estate. But Stella Strong thinks it should go to two deserving poor girls. A letter is found stating that the location of the will is described in a paper secreted in the old family clock. The clock has disappeared and

efforts to find it had been in vain until Stella hears that it had been taken to a summer camp miles away. She arrives at this camp to find that the place has been looted and the clock is gone. How the old timepiece was finally recovered and how this led to the finding of the will makes interesting reading.

L. F. Leed, a Grosset & Dunlap editor, sent Edward their thoughts in return.

Dear Mr. Stratemeyer,

We liked the outlines of your new series but prefer one of your other suggested names: Nan Drew, or perhaps Nancy Drew. This, of course, would precipitate a name change of the series as well. While the titles get the basic point across, we feel some changes in this area are needed as well. We very much like your title THE SECRET OF THE OLD CLOCK, and the other titles suggested are: THE HIDDEN STAIRCASE, THE HOUSE OF MYSTERY, THE MISSING JEWELS, THE MYSTERIOUS GUEST, THE SEVEN BLACK PEARS. If these titles are acceptable, the stories can be written in some consecutive order around them and we shall be very glad to have them worked out along these lines.

It took Edward another couple years to put his idea in place. In the meantime, Mildred was adding to her family, as well, though her characters weren't fictional.

no wedding dress?

Mildred stood uncomfortably in a light-blue suit and short, white veil alongside her brother, Melville, on cement steps under the arched entrance of the Fourth Presbyterian Church on Chicago's Michigan Avenue. The large, gothic-looking structure, with its single bell tower, loomed above them, quite out of place among the modern shops that the street was quickly becoming famous for. Mildred hadn't had time to purchase anything from any of the stores, even if she had the money to do so. She and her family had arrived in town just that morning since no one wanted to spend the money for an expensive hotel in downtown Chicago. Chicago was a compromise for Mildred's fiancé's parents, who lived in Ohio, and Mildred's family, who still lived in Ladora. The church was to appease Mildred's mother, who had stopped hinting at her desire for her daughter to take up the faith but wanted, at a minimum, for Mildred to get married in a Presbyterian church. It was a lovely church. Finished in 1914, it was one of the oldest buildings on Michigan Avenue; the other was the Old Water Tower, which was just a couple blocks south.

"So you ready for this, squirt?" Melville asked. Her brother had noticed Mildred's subdued mood and wanted to find out what was bothering her. "I know the whole church thing was Mom's idea, but it's just a few of us. How bad can it be?"

Mildred stared at the bouquet of white lilies in her hand.

Her romance with Asa Wirt had been a whirlwind affair. They had met when she was completing her master's at the University of Iowa. Asa was working for the *Associated Press* in Iowa City, and since the school newspaper, the *Iowan*, used AP articles, it was just a matter of time before they stumbled upon each other. Their first encounter was when Mildred had gone to the AP office to get some clarification on an AP article the school was running. It turned out that Asa was taking some technical classes at the university, so Mildred, trying to be friendly to the new student, invited him to one of the graduate students' football parties. It didn't hurt that the young man was easy on the eyes. A romance soon blossomed, and before Mildred knew it, Asa had proposed and they were heading for Ohio and Asa's new job – a promotion within the *Associated Press*.

Mildred finally looked up at her brother. "I can handle the wedding, it's the move to Cleveland I'm not so sure about."

"It's a sight bigger than Iowa City. I'd think you'd like that."

"I do. I do. But it's…it's so far from you and Elaine, plus there's mom and dad. They're not getting any younger, ya know."

"You can't stay in Iowa forever, Millie. I'll look after the folks for us."

Mildred gave Melville a skeptical look.

"Okay, okay…Elaine will help me look after the folks."

Her skepticism turned into a satisfied smile.

"The other thing that worries me is I haven't gotten a job

yet. We'll be fine on Asa's salary at the AP office, of course, but you of all people know that's not why I work."

"I know. You're the most ambitious women I know." Melville pulled the collar up on his suit jacket as a cool March wind blew off Lake Michigan. Now he knew why Chicago was aptly named the Windy City. Mildred grabbed hold of her small veil to keep it from floating off down East Delaware Place and into the lake.

"I thought you waited on getting a job after finishing your master's last year so you could work on your stories."

"I had, but St. Nicholas can only publish so much of my stuff; they need to feature other writers, too. Besides, after Asa proposed, I didn't want to start somewhere just to quit, knowing Asa was up for a promotion and probable move."

"Aren't you still writing the Ruth Fielding stories for that company in New York?"

"Yeah."

"Well, why don't you see if they have other books you can work on. As popular as you say those are, they gotta have other books they need help with."

Mildred stared at her brother. She had never thought of that. Mildred had learned a thing or two since she started writing for the Syndicate two years ago. Now that she knew about all the different series that Edward Stratemeyer had going, there was bound to be some turnover in ghostwriters, or maybe Mr. Stratemeyer was cooking up other book ideas. She would have to write him right after their return from their honeymoon to Ireland.

Mildred reached up and kissed her brother on the cheek,

startling him. Mildred wasn't the kissing type. "Thanks, Melville. That's the best thing I've heard all day!" Mildred grasped her brother's arm in hers. "Now, let's go get this nonsense over with."

It took over a year for Edward to put his plan in place, but by September of 1929 he filled Mildred in on his new book idea.

Dear Mrs. Wirt,

I have just succeeded in signing up one of our publishers for a new series of books for girls, the same length and make-up as the "Ruth Fielding" books. These will be bright, vigorous stories for older girls having to do with the solving of several mysteries. The publishers would like to have three volumes for publication this spring. Kindly let me know immediately if you could do them in the style of the "Ruth Fielding" and if you could complete each manuscript in about four weeks time. I am now getting out the outline for the first volume and will have to get the series started without delay. The pseudonym I have chosen for this series is Carolyn Keene. Since they will be clothbound as the Ruth series, the writing price will be the same $125/volume.

Trusting that you had a nice vacation and got the bass you were after, I remain,

Yours truly,
Edward Stratemeyer

166

This new series would sell for the same fifty-cent price as the other Syndicate series, giving Stratemeyer a royalty rate of two cents per copy.

Mildred was writing articles for various Cleveland journals, but her love was still juveniles, which she continued to write and submit to children's magazines under A. A. Wirt. In September, when Mildred received the letter from Mr. Stratemeyer about his new project, she readily accepted his offer, not blinking as she signed the accompanying copyright abdication letter. The outline for *The Secret of the Old Clock* appeared a few days later. Mildred could tell by the tone of the letter that Edward had a close attachment to this series, much more than the Ruth Fielding novels; the outline, at three-and-a-half pages, was more detailed than his Fielding outlines had been. Perhaps it was the success of the Hardy Boys series, which Mildred had found out just recently was also written by the Syndicate. She had picked up a copy a few weeks ago, wondering if Franklin W. Dixon was a real person or a pseudonym for a ghostwriter such as herself.

Mildred and Leslie McFarlane would never meet. Even if they had lived in close proximity, it was Edward's wish to keep his ghostwriters from crossing paths. In fact, he would never set up meetings with his local writers unless there was sufficient time in between appointments. This was something Harriet Smith learned early on in her dealings with the Syndicate writers.

Mildred excitedly read the letter that accompanied the outline, ready to get started on the new book.

October 3, 1929

Mrs. A. A. Wirt
1410 Roycroft Ave
Lakewood, Ohio

Dear Mrs. Wirt,

I have your letter of October 2nd and am glad to know you can take up the new girls' series for me. It will be all right if you can get the three volumes done inside of four months, although I would prefer it if you turned in the third manuscript around the middle of January.

With this I am mailing the complete outline for the first "Nancy Drew Mystery Stories" entitled
The Secret of the Old Clock.

As this is a first volume, there is as yet no cast of characters.

I trust that you will give this outline and also the note about it a very careful reading. The places mentioned are of course all fictitious. We would like these stories written very much in the manner of your "Ruth Fielding" books, but with perhaps a little more of the girlish tone. But we do not want these stories to contain too much of purely social affairs, but rather quick action and with a strong holding point at the end of every chapter. The price for these books will be the same as for the "Ruth Fieldings."

In reading over the plot, you will, I am sure, see the advantage of bringing out the disagreeable points of the Topham family and especially the daughters and also the advantage of stressing old Abigail's poverty and then her sickness and also the poverty of the Horner girls. All these things will increase the interest in what Nancy is trying to do.

Kindly acknowledge the receipt of the outline so I shall know that you have got started on these stories.

With best regards and trusting that you will be able to give us a first story that will make all girls want to read more about Nancy Drew, I remain,

Yours truly,

Edward Stratemeyer

Weeks later when Mildred looked at Mr. Stratemeyer's lengthy and encouraging ending salutation, Mildred wondered if Edward had a premonition of what was going to happen two weeks after he had sent her that letter, the day that would come to be known as Black Tuesday. The historic financial crisis actually had started in March of 1929, when there was a significant one day drop in an otherwise very vigorous market. The market rallied that day after bankers had promised to keep lending, but Asa, who kept track of such things, was nervous.

He had wanted to put their money into stocks like everyone else in 1928. It was the talk around the water cooler or in the speakeasy. It just seemed like the thing everyone was doing and everyone seemed to be doing it well. Risk takers even bought stocks "on margin," which allowed all kinds of people to get into the business of investing with as little as 10 to 20 percent of the cost of the stock, taking a loan from a broker for the other 80 to 90 percent. It was risky if the stock went down, but if it went up, as they had been doing fairly steadily, it was just a matter of time before the investor made some money and was able to pay off on his margin loan.

When the stocks took that first dip in March, Asa took much of their money out of the stocks they had invested in and put it in the bank. And when the next big dip occurred on October 24th, when more than double the number of previous stocks that sold in a full day had been sold in just half-a-day's time, Asa was at the bank the very next morning to withdrawal all of their money, not trusting what even the banks could promise. Asa had tried to get it all in big bills, but there was still the question of where to put it. The young couple lived in an apartment in the city, so they didn't have a back yard in which to bury it, and neither thought the old adage of putting one's money in a mattress was a good, or particularly comfortable, thought. That's when Mildred came up with the idea of hiding it in the tubes of her xylophone. Asa agreed with a chuckle and a shake of his head, mostly because he couldn't come up with a better plan.

As the world around them crumbled, Mildred felt even more compelled to finish the Nancy story she had just begun. She had been given only four weeks in which to complete the task and only had two weeks remaining. She was reasonably happy with what she had done so far. Interestingly, the story revolved around a dead man, actually the dead man's substantial fortune and all the people standing in line for a piece of that fortune.

First on the list were the undeserving Tophams. Mildred thought Edward would be happy with the way she "brought about the disagreeable points" of the "well-to-do," "pretentious" Topham family, especially the two sisters, Ada and Isabel. Mildred described the older Isabel as "vapid" and "artificial." Ada was portrayed as untrustworthy and willing to lie to cover her mistakes, such as an incident in a department store in which Ada breaks a vase (purely by accident, mind you) but blames it on the store clerk. Mildred thought it was particularly clever writing, when introducing the sisters to the readers, to have the girls being rude to a store clerk before they even noticed Nancy. This would show that it wasn't just Nancy they disliked, they were disagreeable to almost everyone. And when they finally did see Nancy, they refused to speak to her until Ada bumped into her on their way out. Nancy held her tongue, as a proper young woman would do, when Ada admonished Nancy for not watching where she was going. Nancy even refused to gossip with the store clerk after the Topham girls had left. Everyone in town knew about the Topham's probable inheritance of Josiah Crowley's fortune that Nancy and almost everyone else thought should go to the oh-so-poor – though "plucky" – Grace and Allie Horner and crippled, old, *and* poor Abigail Rowen. Who wouldn't be rooting for these sorry souls over the rich and arrogant Tophams? Mildred thought Edward was laying it on a bit thick when he also added a pair of spinster cousins of Crowley's – Matilda and Edna Turner – and two male cousins, William and Fred Mathews, who had taken care of Josiah after his wife had died. To add a bit of realism to the story, Mrs. Crowley was to have died of influenza after the war, as so many had the year the story was to have taken place, 1918.

Mildred also took pride in her portrayal of Nancy. Of course, per Mr. Stratemeyer's request, she was keeping Nancy on the moral side of any situation. But besides Nancy being smart, an upstanding citizen, defender of the poor, and righter of wrongs, Mildred wanted the young girls who would be reading about Nancy to look up to her and aspire not only to her skills but her brains, as well, of which Edward and Mildred had both given her in fistfuls. Nancy was not only able to take care of herself and her widowed father, Carson Drew, she was able to fix a "puncture" on the new, blue roadster that Carson had given his daughter for her birthday and do a bit of tinkering to get a persnickety boat motor engine running to get her out of yet another jam. And to show Nancy's feminine side, the girl not only wore up-to-date fashions, she was able to bandage old Abigail's ankle so it was feeling better by the time the water on the stove was ready for tea.

But Nancy wasn't just clever, a model citizen, and skilled with her hands, Nancy was strong and athletic; Mildred made sure of that. If she wasn't hiking at the girls' camp on Moon Lake with her friend Helen Corning, she was playing tennis, water polo, or just plain swimming. From Edward's outline Mildred knew Nancy was going to be subdued by robbers at the Topham bungalow where Nancy had been searching for Josiah's old clock, the old clock that held the answer to the location of the most recent Crowley will. It just so happened that the Topham bungalow was on Moon Lake as well. In Mildred's rough draft she had Nancy escaping from a closet the robbers threw her into, after a brief moment of despair, by calming herself so she could reason her way out of the obvious mess she was in. First Nancy tried a hair pin, then finally by using brute strength, she broke the hinges of the door enough to free herself. The black – and drunk – caretaker ended up helping, too, but it was Nancy herself who got out of the seemingly perilous situation, as she would do time and time again.

Of course, everything turned out well in the end, as all Stratemeyer juveniles are designed to do. The will was found, even though Josiah Crowley foolishly put it in a safe deposit box in a nearby town and under another name. Grace and Allie got most of the fortune – the large sum of seventy-five thousand dollars each in addition to all of Josiah's furniture (furniture that the Tophams had taken for their own, of course)! This was quite a hefty sum even before the market crash, but now it would seem out of sight for most of Nancy's readers. Abigail was bequeathed the same amount as the Horner sisters, an obvious affront to the Tophams since Abigail wasn't even related to Josiah. The two sets of cousins received twenty thousand each. And the Tophams? Well, Edward – or was it Mildred – had the Tophams get what everyone by the end of the story wanted them to get: nothing. And to add insult to injury, Richard Topham had his credit reduced at the bank because of his loss of the Crowley fortune and the fact that he had lost heavily in the stock market. So the Topham family was reduced to selling their home and moving into something smaller. Oh, the shame of it all!

Of course, being the upstanding citizen that Nancy was, she refused any reward for capturing the thieves at the Topham bungalow, though Nancy knew the Tophams wouldn't offer a reward anyway, especially if they found out it was Nancy who had recovered their things. The Horner sisters tried to give Nancy something, too, but the only thing that Nancy would accept was the old clock that had started it all. A fitting gift, Mildred surmised.

As requested, at the end of the story Mildred mentioned the next book in the series, *The Hidden Staircase*. After Mildred pulled the last paper out of the typewriter, she sincerely hoped she would be the one writing it.

She heard back from Mr. Stratemeyer less than a week later, after she had gotten back from a fishing trip to Canada with her husband:

Dear Mrs. Wirt,

I received the manuscript for the Old Clock and was overall pleased. I will need to rewrite the first half of the story because it was a bit slow and various incidents are rather too loosely connected, but I can take care of these issues. I think you hit your stride in the later part of the book, however. The last eight chapters were particularly well done so there will be only minor adjustments I will have to make there. I'm sure the publishers will be pleased.

I have attached the outline for The Hidden Staircase *and an accompanying copyright agreement, as per usual. Make sure you write this new volume as you have in the latter chapters of the Old Clock, making your characters as vital as possible.*

I look forward to reading volume two.

Yours truly,

Edward Stratemeyer

Mildred looked over the outline for the new novel. This mystery seemed even more intriguing than the first, with supposed ghosts in a pre-Civil War mansion, cries in the night, and missing valuables when all doors and windows to the mansion were closed and locked. Nancy even brandished a revolver in this volume. Even more interesting were the threatening notes aimed at Nancy herself and the imprisonment of Nancy's father, Carson Drew.

Mildred characterized the villain in this story, Nathan Gombet, as a truly nasty man, appearing as if he was actually going to hit Nancy on their very first meeting. There was also a black character in this story as in the first, an "old negress" this time, who worked for Nathan and was his accomplice in his diabolical plan. When pressed by Nancy and the police, the woman tried to deny her involvement: "How you talk! Crime? What you mean crime? I's just an old culled woman who makes her victuals workin'! You can't bluff me with yo'

Other topic to investigate: ethnic diversity

scary talk." But, of course, the woman broke down and finally admitted her guilt.

Nancy's old housekeeper, Hannah Gruen, appeared a bit more often in this story. We learned she has a sister, when she told Nancy she was going to go with her to the "movie picture show," but Hannah was still not much of a character, in Mildred's eyes.

Nancy eventually found the set of old stone steps mentioned in the title, falling head first down them when she stumbled upon them unexpectedly. They set her on the path to solving the mansion mystery and saving her father. Again Nancy refused the reward from the mansion's owners – elderly, rich spinster sisters – but she took a valuable urn as compensation, a not-so-small memento of the perilous case.

In the end, Mildred had the requisite teaser for book number three and Carson Drew's proclamation of Nancy's skill as a sleuth, promising to give his daughter all of his mystery cases, declaring: "As a detective, you have me backed completely off the map!"

Two weeks before Christmas Mildred received another letter from Mr. Stratemeyer.

Dear Mrs. Wirt,

*I have received the manuscript of "*The Hidden Staircase*" and read it with much satisfaction. It seems to me it ought to interest any girl who likes mystery stories. I shall make only a few changes and those of small importance.*

With this I mail you my check for the MS., with usual receipt to be signed and returned.

I also enclosed a complete outline for the next story in the series to be called

The Bungalow Mystery

With this outline I am sending the outlines also of No. 1 and No. 2 of the series, so you can refer to them if necessary.

I think the new outline will appeal to you, as it is full of action and with many good holding points. Of course, keep the girlish part girlish and don't get the dramatic part too melodramatic. The second story was very well handled in this respect.

Please let me know if I can expect the MS. by the 15th, or 20th of January next.

With regards, I remain,

> *Yours truly,*
> *Edward Stratemeyer*

Mildred immediately got to work on the next Nancy book.

In January Edward came down with pneumonia and remained at home to recover.

With Edward convalescing, Mrs. Smith had even more work to do, and she wasn't always sure how to proceed.

Mildred wrote to Edna in January looking for some guidance. Since Edna still lived at home, she ended up being the nursemaid for not only her mother, who now needed one-on-one care, but for her father, as well. Mrs. Smith didn't feel she could bother Edna's sister, Harriet, since she was busy with her family of four and her many other civic and social activities. Besides, Harriet Adams hadn't been to the office in years and had no idea what her father was up to. At least Edna lived with Maddie and Edward, and now was forced to be the go-between for her father and everyone who wanted to correspond with him. It wasn't until March that Edward made it back to his office.

Fourteen ∾

Once more Mrs. Smith looked at the watch attached to her blouse. It was suspended upside down by a lovely gold pin so that she could read it without stopping what she was doing. It was a Christmas gift from the Stratemeyers, and she admired it greatly. But just now, Harriet wasn't doing much of anything except worrying. Edward had sent her a message that he was returning to the office this very morning, but it was 8:30 and he hadn't yet arrived. If Mr. Stratemeyer was anything, he was punctual, and he expected the same of anyone who worked for him. Writers, who frequently were used to working on only vague timelines – unless they were required to follow newspaper deadlines – tended to amble into meetings with Mr. Stratemeyer at any odd time past the appointed hour. This only happened once, however. Besides not wanting his ghostwriters to meet and compare notes while they sat in the Syndicate's small reception area, Edward was a busy man, and he didn't like to waste time waiting on anyone. Many a writer had been told, in no uncertain terms, that that kind of behavior would not happen under his employ, or they knew where the door was and they were free to use it. Edward himself arrived at eight a.m. on the dot unless there was an odd occurrence with a cable car or some illness of Maddie's that he had to attend to.

Harriet was worried that his illness had gotten the better of him again and a message had yet to reach her from Edna that informed her she would be required to soldier on once more and manage as best she could.

There was really quite a lot to do, so Mrs. Smith turned and placed a piece of paper in her typewriter to ready it for yet another letter to a publisher. This one was to Grosset & Dunlap regarding their Ted Scott flying series. Ever since Lindbergh flew across the Atlantic in 1927, flying had been on everyone's mind. Of course, Edward got right on the bandwagon with Ted Scott along with another flying series, Slim Tyler, that Mr. Stratemeyer had been working on recently. She had typed up the outline for books one and two of the new series before Edward became sick, and she was waiting on outline number three in the breeder set, as Mr. Stratemeyer called them. He had narrowed down the list of ghostwriters for this new story line but, as of yet, had not picked anyone to start the writing, so she needed to ask G & D for more time in getting them the stories. Harriet missed the rattling of the glass door as Edward opened and closed it, walking into the small reception area.

Her glasses almost flew off her face as she turned to face the slim figure that stepped into the room.

"Mr. Stratemeyer!" she said. Harriet stood to walk around her desk and greet him. Harriet stopped short when she got a good look at the stooped, thin man before her. Edward Stratemeyer was always slight in stature but now he was downright gaunt. Mrs. Smith was shocked but tried not to let on. "It's so good to see you, sir!"

Edward clasped Harriet's hand and squeezed. "I'm sorry I'm late, H. I would have been on time if it hadn't been for all the people who stopped me along my way. It was very touching, really. And I didn't have the heart to cut any of them off. I knew that you had things under control here, so I let them ramble on."

"I'm not so sure how much of it is control or just putting up a good front," Harriet said with a chuckle.

"Now, I know that isn't true. I truly appreciate all you have done, H. I really do."

"It was my pleasure, sir."

They dropped hands and Edward started for his office. "What do you have for me this morning?" he said with a grin.

Edward opened his office door to find four neatly stacked piles of papers on the front edge of his desk. Harriet went over to the piles and pointed them out.

"This stack is stories that need editing: the X Bar X Boys, the Hardy Boys, a Ted Scott, and a Jungle Boy, as well, if I'm remembering correctly. I could have done them myself, of course, but since I knew you were coming in today, I left them for you."

Edward stepped behind his desk and gingerly sat down.

Harriet eyed him dubiously, then stepped up to the second pile. "These are correspondence from your publishers. Various things here about marketing, a few pieces of artwork for the Ruth Fielding book to look over, and questions about the new Campfire series that I thought best to leave to you."

She pointed to pile number three. "These are stories that I've edited in the last few days. I wanted you to look them over before we responded to the writers or the publishers." Harriet picked up the first one on the pile and handed it to Edward. "This one is the last Nancy breeder, *The Bungalow Mystery*. I think there are a few things that need changing yet, but Mrs. Wirt is slowly getting the feel for your requirements. I thought you'd want to look at that first thing. G & D has been pressing me hard to get all of our books off to them to print. This depression has the publishers so on edge.

"I think only five or six of our books are selling well enough to keep us afloat," Edward said.

Harriet nodded solemnly. She knew the sales figures as well as Edward, and considering all that was going on in the United States and in the publishing world, she was glad she was still employed. Every day she walked past numerous men, and even families, camped out beside buildings or in the city parks, the men having lost their jobs and ability to pay their rent. Then with Edward getting sick, she thought she would soon be unemployed, as well. Goods were getting harder and harder to come by, and with the scarcity of products came higher prices for food or goods that were now considered luxury items. Harriet wasn't on par with the likes of the

Stratemeyers, whom she suspected were fairly conservative in their investments and probably weathering the storm fairly well, but she knew she was much better off than most, so she kept her mouth shut and her nose to her typewriter.

"Speaking of these trying times, have you had any complaints from the new writers about our lower pay rate? I hated doing that, especially to our seasoned writers, but with times as they are, I really had no choice. We've lost so many readers of late."

"No, sir. I think they know how lucky they are to even have work, as many as there are around town that have been laid off." Harriet stepped up to the last pile. It was the largest of the three. "That said. This stack is personal correspondence: a few get-well wishes that I haven't had time to get off to you at home, but mostly writers looking for work. I've marked a few of the more worthwhile ones with a star." Harriet rustled through the stack and found a letter with a blue star in the corner and set it on top of the pile. "I know you have a few new series you're working on," Harriet said, nodding in the direction of some handwritten outlines to Edward's right, "so I thought I'd start the culling process before you got here, since there are so many to go through."

"I appreciate that," Edward said.

"How many writers have asked for the advance I have been offering?"

"Four since you've been gone, so that makes a total of six, so far. I know it's greatly appreciated, sir, especially for those who have families," Harriet said.

"It's not much, but it's something."

Edward sighed as he looked at the workload ahead of him. He looked tired before he had even begun. Harriet wasn't sure how well her employer was going to manage, but she was too afraid to even contemplate anything else, so she forced her anxiety out of her mind and got about their business. "Shall I get you a cup of coffee, sir?" Harriet asked.

"That would be lovely, H." Edward said and leaned back in his chair with Mildred's manuscript in hand. "And Harriet," Edward said, stopping her before she closed his door, "Thank you again for all you've done. I couldn't have managed without you."

Harriet blushed at the compliment. "You're welcome, Mr. Stratemeyer," she replied and shut the door behind her.

Over the weeks that followed, Edward was not his ambitious self, leaving early each day and taking an hour with a tasks that normally would have taken him half the time, but Mrs. Smith was just glad to have him in the office again. She didn't like being responsible for the workings of such a large firm, and she had started having trouble fending off the ever-increasing questions from the publishers and writers. It took until late March of 1930 for Edward to get Mildred the outline for the fourth Nancy story, *The Mystery at Lilac Inn*.

Much to Mrs. Smith's chagrin, Edward's recovery didn't last long. Come May first he had been relegated to his bed once more and by the 10th, at the age of sixty-seven, Edward

Stratemeyer, the most prolific children's author of his time, lost his battle with pneumonia.

The letters and accolades came pouring in. *The New York Times* wrote two articles about Edward in a week's time.

> *EDWARD STRATEMEYER. Author of Boys' Books*
> *Dies in Newark at Age of 67*
>
> ---------------
>
> *FUNERAL TONIGHT FOR E. STRATEMEYER.*
> *Wrote 'The Rover Boys' Series, Which Had Sales*
> *Exceeding 5,000,000 Copies. --------- 40 OTHER*
> *BOOKS FOR BOYS*

There was even an article in the *Syracuse Herald*.

> *"The Rover Boys" Creator Is Dead. Newark,*
> *N.J., May 10 (AP) —The creator of "The Rover*
> *Boys" died tonight. He was Edward Stratemeyer,*
> *but to millions of American youths who devoured his*
> *narratives, he was "Arthur M. Winfield," or "Captain*
> *Ralph Bonehill."*

Alexander Grosset wrote to Maddie: "He was a 'grand old man' of the Juvenile book world, and his passing will leave a place that will be difficult to fill,"

Leslie McFarlane was as shocked and grieved as many of his fellow ghostwriters.

Although I had never met him personally I felt that I knew him as a real friend by reason of my five years' association...His kindness to Mrs. McFarlane and myself at the time of our marriage and on the occasion of the birth of our daughter betokened a personal interest that we appreciate more than he possibly imagined. I think he must have been a very kindly and warm-hearted man...My work for Mr. Stratemeyer helped me so much in days of my literary apprenticeship that you may be sure this letter is no hollow and conventional expression.

Of course, Mildred wrote condolences to the family, as well, but she had other concerns, particularly about the next book in the Nancy series, *The Mystery at Lilac Inn,* and about her place in the Syndicate. These were concerns she expressed solely to Mrs. Smith so as not to bother the family in their time of mourning. Mildred wasn't even sure how much the family was involved in Edward's business, but she did know Harriet Smith knew what was what, so she started there.

As you requested, I will forward the Nancy Drew volume as soon as completed, which should be sometime this month. As soon as you know what is to be done about future work, I will appreciate being notified.

The family was devastated, of course, and Edward's death put Maddie back in bed for days. But decisions had to be made, and quickly. Many lives would be affected if the Syndicate went under, most notable Edna and Maddie, who relied solely on its income. Harriet's husband had his family of five well taken care of through his work as a broker, but he'd be stretched thin if he had to take on an ailing mother-in-law and spinster sister-in-law. So the daughters set up a quick meeting with the only person who really knew what was going on in the business.

"Thank you for meeting with us at such short notice, Mrs. Smith," Harriet said. Mrs. Smith had brought a waiting room chair into Edward's small office, so the three ladies were sitting almost knee to knee in front of Edward's large, wood desk. Luckily the era of large dresses with multiple layers was gone, replaced by slimmer, knee or calf length one-piece dresses or suits of soft rayon or linen.

"First off, we wanted to let you know that I've talked with Father's lawyer, and he is working on getting the executorship of the company moved from our mother to Edna and myself," Harriet said.

Mrs. Smith relaxed a little in her chair. She wasn't sure who the company had gone to, but it was a relief to know she would be dealing with the daughters instead of Magdalene. It was too big a job for a woman who was easily bedridden, and as far as Mrs. Smith was aware, knew very little about the goings on in the office.

Harriet and Edna looked at each other briefly before Edna spoke next. They had obviously planned this meeting out. "As you may have suspected, we have decided the only logical course of action would be to sell the company outright," Edna said. "Harriet is very busy with her family and her other activities, and I really have no interest in learning the intricacies of the company, let alone trying to run it."

"We suspect, with your vast knowledge of the workings of father's company, that anyone who purchases it would certainly want to keep you on," Harriet quickly added.

"Oh, yes. That would only make sense," Edna said, nodding eagerly, purposely trying to dissuade any thoughts Mrs. Smith might have to the contrary.

"As you may remember, I had helped Father when I first graduated from college, but as it has been so long since I had any dealings with dad's company, it only makes sense to find a buyer."

Edna nodded her agreement.

"We certainly appreciate you handling things since Father's passing," Harriet said, stealing a quick glance at her sister, "and we hope that you can stay on until a final decision has been made."

"Of course. Of course. Your father was too kind to me and my family to think of any other course."

Now it was Edna and Harriet's time to relax. Both knew that if Mrs. Smith decided to leave before a sale could be procured, the company would precipitously decrease in value, something the sisters wanted to avoid at all costs.

"We'll be meeting with Father's lawyer early next week to find out details of the holdings of the company and the specifics of how to move forward with the sale," Harriet explained. "In the meantime, if you have questions, we ask that you direct them to me. Edna is busy with the funeral arrangements, managing the help at home, and helping the nurse with Mother, which is a full time job, of late."

Mrs. Smith looked over to Edna, who didn't speak but continued to nod her agreement.

"I have suspended my activities with my clubs and at church until this is all taken care of. As luck would have it, I've lost another nanny, but I have a line on someone from a friend in the Mayfield Neighborhood Association, so I hope to have someone to free up at least four to five hours of my day, if all goes well."

"I'm so sorry for your troubles, Mrs. Adams, and at this trying time, too" Mrs. Smith said with all sincerity, though a part of her thought about how the lives of these two women were so very different from her own, with worries of nannies and house staff that needed supervision and direction.

"Thank you, Mrs. Smith," Harriet said.

"Now I suppose we should start on more practical matters," Edna said. "To take some of the burden off of you, I would like to take over the paying of the writers' salaries, and of course, your salary, as well."

Mrs. Smith's eyebrows rose. She had no idea the sisters would actually want to help with any of the day to day operations. Paying salaries wasn't much, but it was something, Mrs. Smith thought.

"May I ask, have you spoken to the publishers?" Mrs. Smith asked. "As you can imagine, they are nervous about the turn of events."

"I'm glad you mentioned that," Harriet said. "I will take

on the responsibility of talking to publishers as well as any press who come looking to do a story on Father. And anyone making inquiries about purchasing the company should be directed to me, as well. I will be setting up meetings with the publishers this week. I need to get their input on how to move forward with the sale. I'm sure they'll have some good suggestions."

Harriet handed Mrs. Smith a piece of paper. "Toward that end, I've listed the items I would like you to put together on each of our publishers."

Mrs. Smith looked at the paper. It was a list of basic informational type questions on each company: number of years they had been working with the Syndicate, number of series they handled currently and in the past, plus any other non-series books they published for the company. There was also a column for royalties for each book and the royalty payments for the previous year. Harriet wanted to know where each book stood as far as salability, looking for the good performers she could tout to prospective buyers.

"We will be letting them know that we will be suspending the publication of any of the current series, that is, until a buyer can be found."

Mrs. Smith sucked in her breath. She knew this was logical, but she imagined the faces of the writers and publishers at this startling news, people who had relied on the Syndicate for its steady and prolific output.

"If there is other information that you think might be helpful with my meeting with these companies, please feel free to add that as well," Harriet said.

"Of course. I can start on this right away."

"After that task is complete, I'd like you to start on a listing of the current books and book series that Father has going, plus a list of the books he has in production or at minimum has outlines for..." Harriet stopped herself in mid-thought. "I assume the writers still work off of Father's outlines, don't they?"

"Yes. Yes, of course."

"Splendid. I think that would be a good start in educating us in what we are dealing with."

"Would you like to see the outlines for books that he is... I'm sorry, *was* working on?" Mrs. Smith looked at the empty chair and uncharacteristically clean desktop and blinked her eyes repeatedly, trying to keep her tears from spilling over. "It's still hard to believe he's gone."

Edna reached over and grasped Mrs. Smith's hand. "It is, isn't it? We can hardly believe it ourselves."

"We are just glad his suffering has ended. He will be greatly missed, but he lived a very full and good life," Harriet said, her voice on the verge of breaking.

"The important thing is to do our best for Father by taking care of something that was very important to him: his stories," Edna said.

"Indeed. It's the least we can do for Father," Harriet said, pulling out a handkerchief and dabbing her eyes.

Edna reached for her sister's hand and tried to blink away her own tears. It took a moment for the three women to compose themselves.

"Well, I think we all have our work cut out for us," Edna finally said.

Harriet put her handkerchief in the sleeve of her suit jacket. "Is it possible to have the publisher's information to me by Thursday?" she asked.

"I'll have it done by tomorrow if you like. I can have it sent to your home, to save you a trip into the city."

"That would be lovely."

Harriet stood. Edna and Mrs. Smith followed suit.

"Do you have time to get me the information on the employees? I'd like to work from home, if I can," Edna asked.

"Of course," Mrs. Smith said, walking back into the reception area and up to her filing cabinet.

"I will leave you ladies to your work," Harriet said. She walked over to Mrs. Smith and gave her a polite hug. "Thank you again for staying on. We couldn't do this without you."

"So true," Edna said. "So true."

Harriet put on her rain jacket and left the women to their work.

Unfortunately for all involved, the attempted sale of the company, as tempting as it was for those who knew its worth, was not going well. The depression had narrowed the family's prospects more than anyone had realized, and with a company that ended up being valued at approximately half a million dollars, the list of buyers in that price range were few and far between. Mrs. Smith was getting nervous.

June 21, 1930

Dear Mrs. Adams and Miss Stratemeyer,

I am concerned that things are not progressing with the sale of the company. If the books do not get under way before long the publishers can hardly have them, at least not more than one or two of them, for early spring publication... The greatest danger is that if things drift too long the authors will be immersed in other things and cannot go on with the Syndicate books, for, after all, their needs will continue in spite of the law's delay, and that, just at this time of readjustment, would be perhaps an irreparable loss... Authors cannot be picked out of the gutter at will - or out of a garret, the traditional place for authors to live. Nor have the new authors ever done perfectly satisfactory work until after a preliminary training under your father's methods on some three or four or five books. The first volumes have always had to be written in part, talked over, usually rewritten and then in the end heavily edited...

In this vein, I have taken it upon myself to complete an outline for the Hardy Boys, the Honey Bunch, the Ted Scott Flying Stories and for Nancy Drew. Two had sketches for outlines. The Nancy story was only a brief description your father had sent to G & D for the fifth book in that series. If you approve, I will send these off to the appropriate writer so they can continue these series and hopefully have something to send to the publishers for the usual spring publication.

When their contact in the publishing houses didn't

produce a buyer, the sisters had Mrs. Smith place an ad in *Publishers Weekly* in a last ditch attempt to save the company from closure.

No buyer was found.

The sisters sat down in Edward's office on the third floor of the Stratemeyer home to decide the fate of their father's long-standing company.

"Well, Edna, what do you think we should do?"

Edna stood and walked over to the window turret. She caressed the worn leather back of Edward's favorite chair, envisioning her father sitting there in his usual pose, a stack of papers in one hand and pencil in the other, staring in rapt concentration at the typed words on the page. Eventually she turned back toward Harriet. "I'm really not sure, Hattie. I know what Father would want us to do, but I'm not sure I'm up for it. After meeting with Father's lawyer, I realize how little I know about his business."

Edna sat down in Edward's chair with a flump. "Did you have any idea he was selling movie and radio rights?"

Harriet shook her head. "None whatsoever."

"I would hear father talk about this series or that at the dinner table, but I had no idea how complex the business is. Dad has fourteen books running, and that's not counting the ones he has in production!"

"I know. We'll have to do something about that."

Edna stared at her sister and her brow furrowed. "Do something? We need to sell the company, that's what we need to do," she said emphatically.

"We've tried that. We both agreed that the *Publishers Weekly* advertisement would be our last. We need to decide what to do soon or Father's company won't be worth any more than one of his fifty-cent novels."

Edna dropped her gaze to her lap, pursed her lips, and after a moment of contemplation, looked back up into her sister's expectant face. "Well, it doesn't take a genius to see what you want to do, as much time as you have been spending at Father's office, of late."

Harriet straightened at her sister's attempted slight. "I've been trying to keep the company afloat, Edna. You know that. And yes, I think we can do it, if we work together. I've talked it over with Russell and he agrees we should give it a go."

"But Hattie, little Edward is just five."

"It won't be easy for me, I know that, but Sunny is thirteen and the girls are getting big enough to help the nanny. The children will manage."

"People will talk," Edna said in one last ditch attempt at getting her sister to change her mind.

"People will always talk, Edna. This is important for Father's memory. And besides, if we can't sell the company, what are you and Mother to live on?"

Edna's eyes opened wide. "I'd never thought of that."

"You'd have to get rid of the maid, the chauffeur, the cook, and maybe even this house! That would be taking jobs away from people who have been very loyal to the family for many years, let alone being a significant disturbance to

Mother," Harriet said, trying to convey the import of their decision – in her favor – to her younger sibling.

Harriet let that sink in for a minute or two before she pressed Edna for a decision. "I really don't think we have any choice in the matter, Edna. I really don't."

Edna slowly turned to her sister, a look of resignation across her face. "I suppose you're right," she said with a sigh. "But do you really think we can do it?"

A smile spread across Harriet's face. The prospect of running such a big, complex company was daunting, but it was a task Harriet had never dreamed, as a married woman with four children, would be given to her and one she secretly relished to undertake. After all the battles she had with her father to allow her to work after college, now she was not only going to be returning to the working world at the age of thirty-eight but she would be running an entire company. This was an opportunity she didn't want to pass up.

Harriet knelt down in front of her sister. "I think we can do it, Edna. I do. I've been mulling it over, and I think the logical thing to do is close Father's Manhattan office and move the company to New Jersey, so it is closer to home for both of us," Harriet said, a brightness in her voice hinting at her excitement at the prospects ahead. She stood and started walking the length of the room. "I'll take on most of the tasks, at least initially, since Mother would be upset if you were gone from home too long."

"I suppose," Edna replied with a hint of dismay. She too never envisioned herself a businesswoman, but Harriet was warming her to the idea, and the thought wasn't totally abhorrent to Edna, either. But she knew it would be a lot of work, and her unfamiliarity with it all frightened her. "Do you think Mrs. Smith would be willing to move, as well? She has been such a help, and she knows so much about Father's work, I would hate to lose her."

Harriet stood in front of Edna. "I don't see why not. We've been paying her handsomely for all her extra duties. That, of course, would stop once I'm up to speed on everything. You and I, that is," Harriet said, correcting herself. She started walking the room again.

"First thing we need to do is create new story outlines for the more popular series: the Hardy Boys, the X Boys, the Rovers, the Honey Bunch, and of course for Nancy Drew." Harriet swung to face her sister once more. "How about you start on the Barton Books for Girls and the Honey Bunch? I think those series would suit you just fine."

Edna slumped into her chair. "I haven't read any of Father's stories since I was small," she lamented. "I wouldn't even know where to start."

"Well then, you better start reading!" Harriet said with little sympathy. "They're not difficult reads, Edna. They're children's books, after all. And we'll ask the lovely Mr. Garis for help, too. I'm sure he'd be willing to fill us in on the finer points of how Father did his outlines."

"That's a good idea! He and Lillian have both been writing for father for years," Edna said with a hint of optimism.

"After the new outlines are completed, we need to eliminate some of the less profitable series. We just don't have time to learn all of father's stories, and it makes no sense to do so if they are barely breaking even."

"Wonderful idea," Edna said.

"If you don't mind continuing to pay the hired staff, I'll continue to deal with the publishers, illustrators and the like."

Edna stood and stared up at her sister, a mixture of awe and bewilderment on her face. "Do you really think this is going to work, Hattie?"

Harriet gave Edna a strong, sisterly hug. "I do, Edna. I do. Let's go give Mother the good news."

The sisters clasped hands and left their father's study, where the flower-papered walls were always in bloom, seemingly nourished by years of Edward's unfailing optimism and rich imagination. Traits his daughters would soon be putting to the test.

Mrs. Smith was quite surprised at the sisters' decision, as were many of the publishers. And when she finally got over the shock of it, Mrs. Smith came to the somewhat painful decision to hand in her resignation. It just wouldn't be the same without Mr. Stratemeyer, she thought. She had been his sole office assistant for seventeen years, and she was getting too old to break in a new employer, let alone two *women*, whom she suspected might possibly be harder to work for than their father.

Edna was staggered by the news. Harriet took it in stride. Fortunately Mrs. Smith had agreed to stay on until their planned move to New Jersey.

All three women took to the task at hand. Edna began

reading, Harriet started delving into the files and papers in her father's office with a fine tooth comb, and Mrs. Smith, after ordering new company stationery for the sisters, sent off letters to the current writers to inform them of the change at the helm and to make sure they were still willing to stay on board ship. On July 7th she wrote to Mildred Wirt:

Before Mr. Stratemeyer's death Grosset & Dunlap OK'd a title for a fifth volume in the "Nancy Drew Mystery Stories" for publication in 1931. Mr. Stratemeyer had indicated briefly to the publishers, as he always did, the direction the story was to take. He had not, however, elaborated that nucleus for the author.

The publishers are asking for their manuscripts for their 1931 output, and this morning I wrote out the outline in full for this new "Nancy Drew" tale. Mr. Stratemeyer's heirs, and I as well, hope you will undertake this new volume. Also the publishers are eager to have the author continue with this line.

I should like to hear from you if you think you can undertake this work. The executors, Mrs. Russell V. Adams and Miss Edna C. Stratemeyer, will have to settle the financial part, though I shall offer now on their part the same compensation you have been getting.

Hoping to hear from you soon a favorable reply, and if I do and as soon as I do I will send to you the outline for the new tale.

Mildred held her breath as she read through the entire letter. As favorable as Mr. Stratemeyer had been about her Nancy stories so far, with the captain having abandoned ship – albeit not by choice – Mildred was unsure where the Syndicate would be sailing off to, if it would be sailing at all. Unlike many other writers, Mildred was having some success in finding publishers for her own stories. Cupples and Leon had picked up the first of what Mildred hoped were many Penny Parker mystery stories, and she had her Ruth Darrow flying stories already in print and selling well. But with the times what they were and Nancy being one of her favorite stories to write, she didn't want to lose the Syndicate business. Then there was the Ruth Fielding series Mildred was working on, as well. Being a writer for that series held a sentimental place in her heart, since it was a childhood favorite and her first book with the Syndicate. Mr. Stratemeyer had been so good to her over the years, giving her a Christmas bonus each year, and now the news that she – as all of the Syndicate writers per Edward's will – was to get an amount equal to one-fifth of their Syndicate earnings, astounded her.

Mildred immediately replied to Mrs. Smith in the affirmative. She was finally able to relax when a few days later, the outline for *The Mystery at Shadow Ranch* appeared in her mailbox. She picked up the outline and skimmed through it. It was obvious that someone other than Mr. Stratemeyer had created it, for it was short on detail but had two interesting new additions – tomboy George Fayne and the more ladylike Bess Marvin – that pleased Mildred at the practicality of the idea.

Mildred took the steps up to her apartment two at a time, eager to share the news with Asa before he ran off to work. He was pulling a week of night shifts at the AP office, which meant he left for work soon after dinner. She ran over to her husband, who was sitting in his chair smoking and reading the paper. She kissed him on the forehead, crumpling his newspaper.

"What's all the excitement about?"

"I finally got another Nancy story!" Mildred said and skipped into the kitchen.

"That's wonderful, dear?" Asa went back to his paper when he heard pots and pans clanking in the kitchen. He put his paper down when he remembered that Mr. Stratemeyer had died a few weeks back, and there was some question about his successor and even of the continuation of the Syndicate itself.

"Who did they end up getting to do the outline, then?" he yelled out to his wife.

Mildred stuck her head out of the kitchen door. "What did you say, dear?"

"Have they found someone to run the company already?"

"I don't know."

Mildred opened a cupboard drawer and rummaged through it until she found what she was looking for at the very bottom. She pulled out a brightly-colored, glossy-paged recipe book. The woman on the cover was in pearls and a form-fitting evening dress. She was lighting candles on a besplendered dining room table. Mildred guffawed at the image. The book had been a wedding gift, and even though she hadn't used it very often, it had come in handy a couple months ago when she had to plan a whole meal for a party of six. Asa had surprised her with the announcement that he had invited a few fellows from work over that coming Saturday with their wives. Mildred was in a state at the news until she remembered the long forgotten gift. Up to that point she had managed to find excuses to avoid giving any kind of dinner party for their friends or Asa's colleagues, but she had decided her time had come. She had to step up and show those other women that she could cook too, even though she hardly knew a springform pan from a cookie sheet, and they would all have to eat from their laps, since Mildred and Asa didn't have a table to sit at.

Asa looked at his watch, set down the paper, and walked into the kitchen to stand next to his wife.

"Well, then who wrote the outline for you?" he asked, leaning on the counter.

"Mrs. Smith, I think." Mildred opened the book and paged through the clean pages until she found what she was looking for. "Yes, it *was* Mrs. Smith. She mentioned it in her last letter."

"What are you doing?" he asked.

"I decided to make that dessert you like so well," she said, moving past him and pulling a can of sweetened condensed milk out of the cupboard.

"I'd like to stay for the show, but I've got to get to work," he said and kissed his wife on the cheek.

"You can have it for breakfast," she said with a smile.

Asa shook his head and grabbed his wife around the waist. "I'm going to have you for breakfast," he joked and nuzzled his face into Mildred's neck.

With a half-hearted nudge, Mildred pushed him away. "After work, dear," she said as she directed Asa out the door.

Mildred pulled a saucepan out of the cupboard, filled it partway with water, and put it on the stove to boil. She picked up the can of sweetened milk and looked at her recipe once more. "Yup, that's what is says, 'put can in water and bring to a boil.' "

She set the can in the water and looked around for Mrs. Smith's outline.

"I can get a start on this while that warms," she said to herself. Mildred pulled out her orange crate from the coat closet – the only mobile piece of furniture she had in the their small apartment – and took her typewriter out from inside it. She set it on its end in the kitchen next to the stove and placed the typewriter on top. She took a box that held all her papers from underneath their bed. Mildred pulled out the chair from the bedroom, placed it in front of the crate, slipped a clean piece of paper in the typewriter, and began to plunk on the keys. Mildred got so caught up in what Nancy and her new friends, Bess and George, were doing that she forgot about the can in the pot on the stove.

That was until she heard a loud bang and turned in time to see the condensed milk can drop to the floor beside her with a clunk. It was empty, the top blown clean off.

"Oh dear," Mildred said, afraid of where the insides had gone. Mildred looked over the stove top. There was a smattering of burnt milk here and there but very little that she could see. She forced herself to look in the only other logical place it could be. Mildred gazed upward and found the rest of the contents plastered in a large, dark-brown blob on the ceiling above her head.

"Maybe it's time to move to a bigger apartment," Mildred mused as she stepped back to avoid anything falling on her head.

Fifteen ৵

As Mildred steeped herself in horse hide and horse apples in *The Mystery at Shadow Ranch*, the Stratemeyer sisters were working on their move to East Orange, New Jersey.

Edna,

I have found the best place for the new office! It's in East Orange, no more than fifteen minutes away from either of our homes. Come by my home first thing tomorrow morning and I'll have the realtor take us to the office and show you around. It's considerably more affordable than being in Manhattan, so we can each have our own office space. If you approve, and I'm sure you will, we can sign the papers right then.

Also, I've attached some ideas for the new Doris

Force series we discussed the other day. Look it over and tell me what you think. Letting go of those poorly producing series was a good business move for us and has given us more room to work on books that better fit what is popular at the time.

Since the Nancy books are going like hotcakes, (did I show you the June figures?!) I want you to start Nancy's next adventure: The Secret of Red Gate Farm. *I'll set up a lunch meeting with the Garises so we both can get some help making up these outlines. It will take a little time to get the hang of it (I think Father could do these in his sleep) but we've got Dad's old outlines to look at so that should help, as well. I'll have the Nancy books sent over to you so you can see what she has been up to and get a feel for how Father wants her portrayed. There are only three published so far, the ones Father outlined. Nancy's a little brash for my taste, but the young readers (and the publisher) seem to like her antics, and I don't want to change what is working. As Father would say; if it isn't broke, don't fix it.*

I think things are slowly falling into place, and I am optimistic things will continue in this manner.

Hattie

P.S. I have three secretaries lined up to interview at the Manhattan office, Thursday, 9 a.m. sharp: Doreen Miller, Agnes Pearson, and Susan Moore. I hope you can be there.

The sisters moved into their new office in October.

Harriet showed Edna her new office. "It's so roomy," Edna exclaimed.

"It is, compared to Father's office." Harriet walked over to her plain wooden desk. It seemed to fit well with the two rust-colored, velour chairs she had sitting in front of it. "And look at this," she said, turning a small box next to the phone so Edna could see. "If you push this button here, you can talk directly to Agnes."

Harriet pushed the button and spoke into the box. "Agnes, I'm showing Edna how the intercom works."

Agnes stepped into Edna's office. "I'm sorry, I was helping unpack. Did you need something?"

"No, Agnes, I was just showing Edna the intercom, and you don't have to come into the office when we call you, use the intercom. That's what it's for," Harriet said, a bit irritated.

"I'll be. You're just like Father, Harriet, always getting the newest gadgets."

Harriet smiled with satisfaction at the comment.

"Well, I'll leave you to unpack your things," Harriet said as she started for the door. "But we have to get those letters out to the writers first thing tomorrow."

"They're not going to like getting a cut in pay!" Edna said.

"That may be so, but we're just doing it to the less profitable series, and if they don't like it, there are lots of other writers out there looking for work."

"Father was certainly shrewd when he had them all

write under pseudonyms. They are a lot easier to replace that way."

"They are, indeed," Harriet said with a nod.

It took until early 1931 for Edna to come up with an outline for the next Nancy book, and according to Mildred, it wasn't quite up to par with their father's or even Mrs. Smith's outline.

"Mrs. Adams," Agnes said after she knocked quietly on Harriet's office door. "I have Edna's correspondence here. This one came by express, but Edna didn't get a chance to respond to it before she left on her vacation," Agnes said, pulling out a larger envelop from the pile. "I think it's a manuscript, so I thought you'd want to deal with that first."

"Smart thinking, Agnes. Yes, I'll take them," she said, reaching out her hands for the small pile Agnes was carrying.

Harriet leafed through the various letters then opened the large envelope. It was from Mildred Wirt.

May 11, 1931

Dear Miss Stratemeyer,

 I am submitting "The Secret of Red Gate Farm" today by express and hope that it will fulfill your requirements. I venture to call your attention to the length of the plot which, you will note, is a full page shorter than usual. In the story it was difficult to find chapter endings with sufficient suspense, and the book

*ran some chapters short. To lengthen them out I added
a few incidents but even so it was necessary to dwell
upon the 'cave' scenes a bit too long. I believe that I
would be able to handle the denounement with better
technique if the plots were somewhat longer.*

*I hope this meets with your approval. I look
forward to your reply.*

> *Yours truly,*
> *Mildred Wirt*

"Well, it is Edna's first attempt," Harriet said to herself.
Agnes had already left the room. Harriet sat back in her chair
and brought a finger to her lips. "Good thing Mildred's been
working for Father for so long. Nancy is too good a series for
us to let it slip."

Harriet pulled a piece of paper out of her desk drawer
and picked up her new fountain pen. A Sheaffer salesman had
visited the office just the day before, showing Harriet the new
styles of celluloid plastic pens on the market. Harriet gazed
down at her new, sleek pen before she began writing. She
liked how these new self-inking pens worked, not having to
putz with pen tips and ink wells. And since Agnes was the one
filling the pen, she didn't have to fuss with ink at all. She also
liked the new colors the pens came in of late. The one Harriet
admired in her hand was a lovely marbled green.

May 18, 1931

Dear Mrs. Wirt,

My sister is currently on vacation and wasn't able to answer your letter before she left.

We are sorry that you found the outline short, and, although we have not as yet read the story, we hope that the material which you inserted will hook up well with the story without seeming like intruding insertions. I read a couple of chapters, and up to that point the story is excellent...

Thank you for getting the story back to us so soon. The publishers seem to like Nancy Drew and her adventures and have already been asking for this volume. It is possible that they will request a second one for this year and, if so, we shall communicate with you. We also like what you have done for the Doris Force series and anticipate continuing that series, as well.

As always, thank you for your efforts in this time of transition.

> *Sincerely,*
> *Mrs. Harriet Adams*

Harriet blew on the letter to hasten the ink drying, folded it carefully, put it in an envelope, and scribbled Mildred's address on the front.

Come that fall, outlines had improved somewhat but sales

had not. Edna entered Harriet's office, a dour look on her face knowing that they were to discuss finances, her least favorite aspect of the business and one she left mostly to Harriet.

"I wanted you to see this letter from Altenius Publishing about the sales in July for the Doris Force stories," Harriet said, handing the paper to Edna.

"Oh, my. This isn't good."

"No. I agree. I think we finally have to ask Mr. McFarlane and Mrs. Wirt to decrease what we pay them for their stories as we have the others," Harriet suggested.

"I would have to agree. I just hope they will want to stay on. Remember what Elizabeth Ward told us when she quit? She said that the going price for stories is $175. And we have only been paying our writers $125, before the cuts, that is. We lost Mr. Duffield over the same issue," Edna lamented. "The Hardy and Nancy books are our best sellers."

"I'm well aware of that, but we have to cut corners somewhere. We already stopped giving out Father's little gifts at Christmas and for weddings or births. I'm not sure what else we can do," Harriet said while she nervously played with her new fountain pen. "And Mother has no problem spending money or giving it away to the help."

"I've repeatedly talked to her regarding that, Hattie, but I'm not sure I can do anything about it," Edna said in a defensive tone. "The help has started going behind my back when they don't like something I've told them, and Mother tries to appease them by giving them money. I'm not sure what else you want me to do," she said, crossing her arms. "She has her own money from her family and from Daddy's estate."

"Well, we'll both be supporting her when it all runs out," Harriet said, obviously upset about the matter.

"Isn't Mildred working on a Nancy and Doris Force story now?" Edna asked, trying to change the subject.

"We'll have to wait until those two are completed before we let her know of the change. Maybe to cushion the blow, we'll give her the next two Ruth Fielding outlines at one time and another Nancy story. That should be harder to turn down, even at twenty-five dollars less for each."

Edna sat on the edge of her chair. "Wonderful idea, Hattie! You do have a good business sense, I must say."

Harriet smiled back at her sister in satisfaction, the current rift easily forgotten.

Sixteen ∾

Mildred and Asa sat across from each other at their new kitchen table in their slightly larger apartment in Cleveland. After the condensed milk incident, Asa agreed that maybe Mildred needed her own dedicated work space where, when she was writing, she could concentrate on writing – and not try to cook at the same time. Their new apartment had a living room large enough to house a work desk, a kitchen large enough to put in a small table for two, and one bedroom. It wasn't much better than their apartment on Marvin Place, but it gave Mildred room to spread out her work, so she had easier access to it when she had time to write. That was between the swimming classes she taught, the meals she made, and the research she did for the stories she was writing.

Mildred was opening the mail as Asa sat reading. She bypassed the bills and opened the letter from the Syndicate.

Her face flushed the farther she read. Asa had his face in the *Cleveland Post* and didn't notice his wife's consternation.

"I can't believe this," Mildred said in a huff.

"Can't believe what, dear?" Asa said, not putting his paper down.

"They want to start paying me $100 per story!"

Hearing the distress in his wife's voice, Asa put down his paper. "Who?"

"The Stratemeyer sisters. They claim they're not selling as many books, so they can't pay me the same rate."

"I would suspect that's true."

"That might be, but I don't have to accept it. I've got enough writing experience to ask for even more than the $125 they normally pay. Plus with my new Ruth Darrow series going, I don't have to keep working for those old maids."

"I thought Harriet was married."

"She is. And you're splitting hairs," Mildred said, exasperated.

Asa looked contrite and went back to the topic at hand. "Well maybe you should remind them about your experience and how you do have other work you could be doing. They are new to the business, after all."

Mildred stood. "I should, shouldn't I?"

She started walking out of the room but stopped and turned back to her husband.

"I had considered quitting after Mr. S. died, as bad as the outlines they were sending me were, but I thought I might as well stick it out since I know the Nancy and Ruth characters so well. It's not really all that much work to piece together a volume."

"Go write your letter."

Mildred nodded in agreement and went to her desk in the living room. She put a piece of paper in her typewriter and began to compose her letter.

I...am sorry to learn that the business has not been as good as before with the syndicate. I have always tried to cooperate in every way possible, but I feel that I cannot take less than one hundred and twenty-five dollars for each manuscript - an average of about one-fourth cent a word...At the time I started to work for the syndicate, about five years ago, I believe, I accepted this rate, for at that time I had not had a great deal of experience in book writing. I have never requested a raise although my work has improved, as you will note by comparing it with my earlier volumes. Then, too, after the first year, Mr. Stratemeyer always gave me a bonus, which helped out. As the rate now stands I am receiving less than I did when I first became associated with the Syndicate.

I realize what difficult times we are passing through and would have been willing to accept some reduction were the amount paid not already as low as I feel I could accept with justice to myself. I have recently signed for a new girls' series and have other work in prospect. In my negotiations with the

*publisher I reserve time for syndicate work but unless
I hear from you soon I must fill up this vacancy.*

Mildred pulled the letter out of the typewriter and took it to her husband to read. He handed it back to his wife. "Point well made, dear, but maybe you should soften the ending a bit. You are trying to get them to change their mind, after all."

Mildred read it over again. "I suppose you're right."

She went back to the typewriter and added two more lines.

I trust that the future will produce happier circumstances which will permit a resumption of our relations.

With best personal regard and kind wishes for the continued success of the Stratemeyer Syndicate, I remain,

> *Yours truly,*
> *Mildred Wirt*

Harriet's response wasn't exactly what Mildred was hoping for.

September 28, 1931

My dear Mrs. Wirt,
Of course, we were disappointed that you felt you were unable to acede [sic] to our request in regard to the writing for certain books, but we are really

delighted to hear that your are making out so well with your own stories. As we do not want to hold up any of your own work, we thought it best to write you that we have been able to place the writing of the Doris Force books with someone else. As the Nancy Drew story would not have to be decided upon immediately, we are reserving our decision on this matter. If we should decide that we would like you to do it we will communicate with you at a little later date. We would, however, like you to continue with the Ruth Fielding series. Since we are currently only publishing one of those per year, we hope that is something that can fit into your busy schedule.

We wish you every success with your new girls' series.

Sincerely,

Mrs. Harriet Adams

Harriet and Edna felt confident in their decision to put Mildred on hold in relation to the Nancy series. They had *The Clue in the Diary* in hand and a new writer already working on their Doris Force series. Someone they felt could take on the new Nancy Drew, as well.

Seventeen

(1933)

Miss Pearson entered Harriet's office and stood just inside the doorway. Harriet looked up when her door opened. "Miss Edna Yost has arrived."

Harriet put down her editing pen and moved the manuscript she had been working on to one side of her otherwise immaculate desktop. Edna Yost was a newspaper woman and despite the glowing comments she had written in the June edition of *Publishers Weekly* about their Nancy, Harriet didn't trust the press. She had been part of that world in college, and from her experience, she knew they often were looking for the next big scoop. She had planned for this meeting to be brief.

A young, well-dressed women with short bobbed hair, a dark wool skirt, and white blouse walked into the room. She

218

had on a matching jacket topped off with a small brimmed hat perched on her head at a jaunty angle. Harriet stared a minute, not having expected someone employed by a newspaper to be able to afford the latest style.

Harriet stood when the woman entered the room. Miss Yost held out her hand to Harriet. "I'm very pleased to finally meet the most prestigious businesswoman in the New York metropolitan area," she said, shaking Harriet's hand with vigor.

Harriet instantly beamed.

"Please, have a seat," Harriet said, motioning to the two velour upholstered chairs in front of her desk. "Can I get you some coffee or tea?"

Miss Yost's complementary opening was having the effect she had wanted. "Tea would be nice," Edna replied.

Harriet bent down toward her intercom and pressed a button.

Miss Pearson's muffled, distorted voice boomed into the quiet room, "Yes, Mrs. Adams?"

"Miss Yost and I would like some tea, please."

"Right away," Agnes said and was gone.

"Intercom. Impressive. All I get from my editor is 'Yost' at the top of his lungs," Edna said with a chuckle.

Harriet laughed along with her then sat down.

"How may I help you, Miss Yost?"

Edna scooted to the edge of her chair. "After the last article I ran in PW, *Publisher's Weekly*, about popular children' series, my editor wanted me to do a feature piece on the writers of the various books I spoke about, so naturally, the Syndicate, the creators of the most popular of the series, was on my A list."

Harriet relaxed back in her chair with a smile. *Maybe I don't have to worry about this one*, Harriet thought.

"I was meeting with Mr. Arthur Leon, of Cupples and Leon, the other day, asking him about Carolyn Keene, Roy Rockwood, and Franklin Dixon and he referred me to you. I'd like your permission to interview these writers."

Harriet chuckled lightly and leaned forward on her desk. "Well, I'd be happy to oblige, but these people don't actually exist."

Edna's cocked her head, as if she hadn't heard correctly. "You mean they're all pseudonyms, every last one of them?"

"Every last one of them."

Miss Yost sat up even straighter, bringing her pen up to her notepad. "Well that changes things. I'm sure our readers would love to know that fact. Can you tell me more? Why the pseudonyms? How many actual writers do you have?" she said, rattling off her questions in quick succession.

Harriet put up her hand to try to squelch the young women's enthusiasm. "Miss Yost. You must understand, if this information were to get out to our young readership, they would all be disappointed. To them, and frankly to us, as well, these writers do exist. In fact, my sister and I have built up biographies for these writers, so we are consistent when answering the fan mail of these impressionable readers."

Edna's pen fell with an audible plop. She sat speechless, trying to think how she could resurrect a writing assignment that presently seemed to be dead in the water. She knew she could do it, but at the moment she wasn't sure how. She'd have to go back to the office to regroup. She closed her notepad. "Well, thank you for your time, Mrs. Adams," Edna said, standing and extending her hand.

Harriet took it. "My pleasure. It was nice to meet you. I like to meet other women who work in non-traditional occupations," she said.

Miss Yost nodded and left Harriet's office, already forming a plan in her mind for her article. She'd have to pass it by her editor, but she hoped he would accept it. She surmised that if she talked about all the different writers in the children's book industry who wrote under pseudonyms not just the Syndicate writers, it might go over better with Mrs. Adams. It would certainly be a scoop as far as the Syndicate was concerned, and not something they would necessarily appreciate.

"Have you seen this?" Edna stepped into her sister's office without knocking. She was waving a copy of *Publishers Weekly* in front of her.

Harriet put down her pen. "I have. I'm working on a response right now."

Edna plopped herself down in a chair in front of Harriet's desk and opened the paper, looking at the article. "She told everyone that our writers are working under pseudonyms! Now everyone knows!"

"What I can't abide is what she said about Father."

"I hadn't seen that."

Harriet looked down at her open copy of the small weekly. "Page 1596. Just keep reading from where you left off."

Edna found the page and read the section her sister pointed out. "Well, I never. Our process is 'devoid...of literary sincerity or literary merit!' The gall!"

"Indeed."

"I hope you plan on addressing that. Such slander! Do you think we could sue?"

"Calm down, Edna. I think the appropriate course of action is send an open letter to the editor. In that way we get our point across to everyone – the paper as well as the readership."

A smile spread across Edna's face. "Very wise, sister. Very wise." She shut the weekly and turned to leave the room. "I almost forgot," she said, turning around again. "Have you read the latest Ruth Fielding volume?"

"I just haven't had time. I assumed you were keeping tabs on that series."

"I am, and I'm not happy with what Mr. Karig is doing with it." Edna pursed her lips, apprehensive to continue. She stepped closer to her sister. "What would you think of asking Mildred Wirt to do the next volume? We might have to agree to the $100 fee we paid her on the last Dana Girls book."

Harriet stared at her sister before responding. Ruth had been a popular series and one that her father had started, so she hated to see it go downhill. Besides, there was the potential for lost revenue if the kids didn't like it and sales went down.

"I don't think we can afford it, Edna, though the idea of staying with Mr. Karig does go against my grain."

"Is there an issue with his Nancy stories?" Edna asked.

"I'm afraid so. They need so much rewriting that I practically have to write the whole thing over."

Edna sat back down. "Well, once we check out the next Ruth story, we could ask Mildred to restart Nancy again." She hesitated, knowing her sister didn't like paying writers more than the now standard $85 per book. "Do you think she'd take the lower rate?"

"I have no idea, but we won't know if we don't ask. First make sure she hasn't lost her touch when you read over the Ruth Fielding story, then go ahead and offer her the next Nancy: *The Clue of the Broken Locket*."

"Have you started on the outline?"

Harriet dropped her pen. "It's not due until the spring of '43, Edna."

"Yes. Yes, of course." she said, a bit embarrassed at her presumption. She knew her sister was busy with the business as well as keeping up with the sporting events and recitals of her four children, which she went to, as well. She really didn't know how her sister managed it all. "I'll get right on that letter."

"You do that," Harriet said and went back to her own letter.

Even though Mildred agreed to write the next two books in

the Ruth Fielding series, Edna's plan for Ruth's marriage didn't sit well with her fans. After Mildred wrote *Ruth Fielding and Her Greatest Triumph* and *Ruth Fielding and Her Crowning Victory*, the series was canceled by its publisher because of lagging sales. Edna then posed the question to Mildred about writing Nancy again.

Eighteen ∿

Mildred opened the large envelope, hoping it was what she thought it was. She pulled out a letter penned by Edna Stratemeyer, skimmed through it, and flipped to the book outline. Mildred had agreed to restart Nancy, admitting to the sisters that she had been a favorite of hers and, despite the lower $85 book fee, she was willing to write the next book in the series.

Mildred looked through the character list, making sure they hadn't gotten rid of Bess or George, Mildred being particularly partial to George. She liked George's tomboy spirit and can-do attitude that complimented Nancy so well. Mildred thought George was the more practical version of what she wanted to portray for young female readers. Mildred liked Nancy, of course, but Nancy lived such a charmed life. She was a good character for young girls to dream about, but

George was a bit more true to life. Mildred was also pleased to see that Ned was still in the series, as well, though she noted Edna's specific instructions not to make him a significant part of the book. She wanted him as "filler" only.

"Guess they learned from Ruth that marriage kills an independent character like Nancy or Ruth," Mildred said to herself.

Mildred paged through the remainder of the outline. "They've gotten more detailed in their outlines," Mildred noted. "But at least it's work."

Mildred had lost her own Madge Sterling series a year ago and Ruth Fielding had been dropped by the publisher, so she was happy for the new work.

Mildred sat down at her desk and began her now very familiar process. It felt good to reacquaint herself with the characters again, and once she had a couple of chapters down on paper, the rest came fairly easily. Five weeks later, she sent in the completed manuscript for *The Clue of the Broken Locket*. She thought she had done a good job jumping back into the series after being away for two years, so she was surprised when Edna wrote her a letter pointing out the things they had to change. Mildred immediately sent a response back.

April 30th, 1934

Dear Miss Stratemeyer,

I am sorry you did not like the way I handled George Fayne, but in the early volumes of the series she was the 'slangy' type, and thinking that her character had been changed in the latter volumes, I tried to represent her as she was in the beginning.

Mildred didn't like the sisters' desire to "soften the boyish glibness and swagger of George..." as Edna had explained in her letter.

"Either these women don't know the past volumes as I do or they don't care about the incongruity of the change," Mildred said out loud. "But I need to work, so I better watch my tongue."

Mildred ended her letter in a softer tone and kept on writing for the Syndicate.

"Agnes, can you come in here, please. I'd like to dictate a letter," Harriet said into her intercom.

Miss Pearson acknowledged the page and entered Harriet's office, notepad in hand. It had been Harriet's habit, since taking over the Syndicate, to keep her mother, and sometimes even her sister, up on what was going on in her family by letter. Harriet didn't always have the time to go to the family home and spend time at her mother's side. Magdalene was now bedbound, having more frequent issues with her heart. Two days ago had been the fifth anniversary of their father's passing, so she had been thinking more of her family of late. She and Russell made their yearly pilgrimage to the gravesite to lay flowers, and so Harriet could have a private conversation with her father. Harriet wanted to tell him about the new Dana Girls and Kay Tracey series she and Edna had started. She was particularly proud of these series because they were their own invention, modeled after what Edward had done with other girls' series, but it was still done without their father's guidance, and both series had been doing fairly well. She knew he would have approved. She also knew her mother would be thinking about the anniversary, as well, so she wanted to give her something to distract her thoughts, if only for a short time.

Miss Pearson sat down in front of Harriet and readied herself for the dictation.

Harriet set down her pen and leaned back into her chair. "Dearest Mother, the children still have a month or so left of school but you know what that means: I've gotten out the seed catalogs and I'm making my list of things to plant. I know you always said to wait until after Memorial Day, so I'm trying to be good and follow your instructions, but I know I can start putting potatoes in the ground even if we get a late freeze. I've got your favorite, sugar snap peas on my list, but you must let me know if there is there anything else you would like my gardeners to plant for you and Edna."

Harriet's letter was interrupted by Miss Pearson's phone. Agnes hesitated, looking at Harriet for a clue as to what she should do.

"Go ahead and answer it," she said. "This letter can wait."

Miss Pearson rushed out of the room and picked up the phone. Harriet went back to editing the manuscript that she had been working on, but when she heard the "Oh my!"

coming from the other room, she set her work down and listened more intently.

"I'm so very sorry, Miss Stratemeyer. Yes, I'll tell her immediately."

At those words Harriet rose, a tight feeling in her chest.

Miss Pearson rushed back into the room and stood to stare at her employer, her face flushed and bewildered.

"That was Edna?"

"Yes."

"Is something wrong with Mother?" Harriet asked, slowly coming around her desk.

"Yes."

"She's dead, isn't she," Harriet said.

Agnes stepped forward, thinking she might reach out to Harriet and embrace her but then she thought better of it. "I'm so sorry."

Harriet sat down hard on the edge of her desk. "She's with Papa now," she said softly and mostly to herself.

Despite the significant blow to the family with the loss of Magdalene, the book business kept on moving; in fact, it seemed to be prospering. That next year the sisters asked Mildred to take on the Dana Girls Mysteries in addition to Kay Tracey and her Nancy stories. And things kept on moving for Mildred, as well.

Nineteen ∾

(1936)

Mildred walked out to the mailbox at their new, two-bedroom home on the outskirts of Cleveland. The couple had done well enough and had been saving long enough to afford the small dwelling in the quiet, tree-lined neighborhood. It was Saturday, and Saturdays were Asa's days to fix breakfast, so Mildred woke a bit later than normal and took her time getting dressed and ready for the day. It was March and still cool in the early morning, so Mildred had a hat and coat on when she went out to get the mail. She riffled through the letters as she strolled up their short driveway to their front door. She stopped and sat on the small bench just outside their door to open the letter from the publishers Cupples and Leon, too excited to wait even a minute to open it and read its contents. Mildred had sent them a manuscript for a new

230

mystery story she had written, *The Clue at Crooked Lane*, and she was very anxious to see what they thought of it. Mildred covered her mouth and squealed in delight.

She burst through the front door and ran into the kitchen. "They're going to publish it! They're going to publish it!" Mildred said excitingly, waving the letter in front of her husband's face.

"Who's going to publish what, dearest?" Asa asked, guiding his wife away from the stove, so neither of them would catch on fire in his wife's excitement.

"Cupples and Leon. They want to publish that mystery I sent them. Can you believe it? Then with my Penny Nichols book, and Dana, and Nancy…"

Asa looked at his wife's face getting paler as she spoke. "Mildred, I think you should have a seat." He sat his wife in a kitchen chair and handed her the glass of orange juice he had sitting on the table. Mildred drank it down without thinking. Two seconds later Mildred was leaning over the sink, orange slime dripping from her mouth and nose; the juice had come back up as fast as it went down. Asa stood next to her patting her gently on the back.

"Wow, sweetie. You need to calm down a bit here. It's just a book."

Mildred turned on the faucet and doused her face in the cool running water, then blindly reached out for a towel.

"Oh. Yes." Asa scrabbled for the towel hanging from the oven handle and handed it to Mildred.

Mildred sat back down and looked at the empty juice

glass with consternation. "I'm not that excited," she said, bewildered. "And I feel perfectly fine."

Mildred felt her stomach when it rumbled an audible complaint, then she looked up at her husband. It took her a minute, but it finally dawned on her. A smile slowly slid across her face.

"What?" Asa asked, totally confused by Mildred's reaction to their own little mystery.

Mildred grasped her husband's hand. "Mr. Asa Wirt. I think you're going to be a father."

Mildred didn't let the sisters know of her pregnancy or her child, Margaret Joan, until two months after she was born. The sisters were happy for Mildred and her husband, of course, and quite astonished that they had no clue that anything was happening with their Cleveland writer since Mildred met all of her deadlines with no indication of any change in her lifestyle. So in 1937 the sisters hesitated when they asked Mildred if she was interested in being the new Helen Louise Thorndyke, author of the Honey Bunch Books. Mildred didn't respond to the sisters right away. There had been the small issue regarding Mildred's choice of words in some of her recent Nancy and Kay Tracy stories. They thought that the "heroines [were] being too officious..." or going "beyond the bound of respectfulness for their elders." Edna felt that Mildred's characters were using language that was "decidedly abrupt and not youthful" when Mildred used terms such as "she informed" as a dialogue attribution, in addition to having a "boyish ring throughout."

In her letter of acceptance of the Honey Bunch authorship, Mildred felt compelled to mention the sisters' verbal slap on the wrist.

In accepting this new book series, I feel compelled to address your concerns of the Nancy and Kay characters being disrespectful of their elders. I am not, at least in the case of Nancy Drew, only following what I have done in the past with this series but also keeping Nancy the smart and independent young lady that she has been portrayed through the years. In addition, it never occurred to me that the use of 'she informed' was brusque or unusual...and there are perhaps other expressions of mine which could be altered to meet your wishes, if I know just what they are.

The sisters took Mildred's explanations in stride, but it did not change their desire for more ladylike behavior for their heroines.

The Adams and Stratemeyer families had their own changes to deal with. Harriet's oldest son Russell, was at Princeton after graduating cum laude from his preparatory school that spring, and her oldest girl Patricia or Patsy as everyone called her – just fifteen – had started to work outside the home; Harriet, obviously going out of her way to ensure that Patsy wouldn't have the same work restriction that her grandfather had imposed on his daughters. And Edna, at the ripe age of forty-two, had her own wedding to plan.

As their busy lives progressed, one of their old ghostwriters and Edna Yost of *Publishers Weekly* were stirring up a bee's nest that the sisters thought they had long ago calmed.

"Mr. Karig, welcome," Edna Yost said, shaking Walter's hand. "Sit down."

Edna pointed to a straight chair next to her desk, then sat down in her own. She pulled out a notepad and flipped it to a clean page.

"So you have some information for me about the Stratemeyer Syndicate?" Edna asked. Miss Yost had not given up on finding out more about the Syndicate after her interview and subsequent article about the company three years earlier. It had garnered much interest from the *Publishers Weekly* readers and even a rebuttal from Harriet Adams herself on how Miss Yost's characterization of Edward Stratemeyer was "unjust" and even "libelous." In Miss Yost's mind, Harriet forgot to mention the word 'true.' Negative or not, it was all good press and better yet, her editor was behind her one hundred percent.

"I heard you were still digging for information, so I thought I'd see how much it was worth to you."

Edna eyed Mr. Karig with a twinge of surprise. "I don't know what you've heard, Mr. Karig, but we don't pay for information."

Walter absently turned his hat in circles by its brim. "Well, that's unfortunate, because I have concrete proof that the famous Nancy Drew stories were written by someone other than Carolyn Keene. And I know who that someone is!"

Edna leaned in toward Walter. "And who might that be?"

Walter looked around the room, then back to Miss Yost. "Me."

Edna's eyebrows shot up in surprise. She picked up her pencil and readied herself to get down the details.

"Listen, Mr. Karig. I know we can't pay you, but I would guess the publicity of such a statement in PW would be worth a month of new book orders for you, at least."

Walter thought about Edna's assertion a moment then sat back in his chair.

"All right then," he said, and he pulled out a folded piece of paper from his jacket pocket and tossed it in front of Miss Yost.

She opened it and scanned over the document. "So this is from the actual Library of Congress?"

"It's on their letter head, isn't it?"

"I just wanted to make sure. If we publish this, it will be quite a blow to the Syndicate. They want to keep this kind of information a secret."

Walter slammed his fist down on Edna's desk. "Listen. I'm tired of those two biddies telling me what I can and can't say! I wrote those stories and that piece of paper proves it!"

"Mr. Karig, calm down." Edna looked around the open office at all the faces that were now pointed in their direction. "I'll be happy to set the record straight. I just want to make sure you know what you're getting yourself into. The Syndicate may be run by two women, but it is run by two very wealthy and connected women."

"I'm not afraid of those two. I can handle them."

"All right," Edna said, picking up her pencil again. "So give me some details."

(1937)

"I don't mean to mix business with pleasure, Edna, but we need to talk," Harriet said, pulling her sister out of the family living room and into the front hallway. Harriet looked up at the second story landing, recalling how, not so long ago, it was Edna who was leading the family up those stairs and around the house the day their father had brought the family here in hopes that Magdalene would like it as much as he did. It seemed like just yesterday to Harriet. Yet both their parents were dead, and it was Harriet who was seeing her sister off on a honeymoon that neither thought would ever take place. Where had all the time gone?

Edna stared at her sister as Harriet gazed off in the distance. "Harriet. Harriet. What did you want?"

"Oh, yes. I'm sorry. Just reminiscing."

Edna smiled at her sister and grasped her hands. "It is a bit funny, isn't it? It was so long ago that we were young girls in this house."

"I was thinking how it seemed like just yesterday."

Edna squeezed her sister's hand. "Is that what you wanted to talk to me about?"

Harriet shook the cobwebs out of her head and looked directly at her sister. "No. No. I hadn't heard back from you about the Karig issue, and I needed to make sure you agreed with my plan on how to deal with him."

"Yes, I'm sorry. With the wedding and getting ready for our honeymoon, I just haven't had time," Edna said. "Yes, go ahead and see if you can get that changed at the Library of Congress. It's not true, so I can't see why they wouldn't change the author listing back to Carolyn Keene."

"And then there is the small matter of selling the movie picture rights to Nancy to Warner Brothers for the movies they want to produce."

Edna's face brightened at the mention of the deal Harriet had been working on with the film production company. She had no idea such a thing could happen and was glad Harriet was going to be around to finalize the sale.

"What are they offering?"

"Five thousand five hundred dollars, but I think we should ask for at least $6500."

"I agree," Edna said without hesitation. "Never give them what they're asking. Mother taught us that much," she said with a grin.

"And I've got the new release forms ready for the writers to sign," Harriet added. "With this Mr. Karig problem and the film proposal in the works, I think it's prudent to make sure all our writers understand they have no claim to anything related to the stories they write for us. They are paid for the work they do and should be happy with that," Harriet said with conviction.

"Agreed," Edna said, squeezing her sister's arm.

A loud, boisterous laugh in the next room turned both women to look in that direction. "Now, enough about this nonsense," Edna said. "Wesley sounds like he's having too much fun in there without me."

Harriet pulled her sister close for a demure kiss on the cheek. "I'm so happy for you, Edna. I really am. Mrs. Wesley Squier, I can hardly believe it."

"Thanks, Hattie. I can hardly believe it myself."

And the sisters walked arm in arm back into the party.

Edna and Wesley were not able to honeymoon in Europe, as Edna had wished. With Hitler having signed a pact with Italy and Japan – a country chest deep in its own invasion of China – and the Spanish Civil War going full tilt, the family felt it was not a safe place to visit. And when things only escalated, it meant that in 1940 Nancy Drew's plans to travel to England in the *The Mystery of the Brass Bound Trunk* had to change, a book that Mildred had penned the year before.

"Thank you for coming, Mrs. Adams, but I think, under the circumstances it's rather important that we meet," Mr. Grosset said to Harriet from behind his desk.

"Of course, Mr. Grosset. You said it was something

about the last Nancy volume we sent you. Is there something wrong with the writing?"

The publisher clasped his hands in front of him, laying them on the top of his desk. "No. No, not the writing per se. It's the setting, really. With what is going on currently in Europe, we think it would be best to move Nancy's adventure to a more...politically neutral location," he said, trying to keep his voice relaxed. Harriet Adams was an excitable woman, at least when it came to her books and Nancy Drew in particular. But Nancy was their top children's book seller, so he wanted this meeting to go well. Harriet had never hinted at taking her publishing business elsewhere, but he didn't want to take any chances.

"I see," was all Harriet said. Harriet was thinking of all the research and rewriting it would take to pull off such a switch; Harriet was as much a stickler for truth within their fiction as her father was. It would mean either paying Mildred to do the research to relocate Nancy and her chums to a new location, or she would have to undertake it herself. Edna was spending less and less time in the office with a new one year old at home taking up more of her time. Her sister didn't seem to have the ability – or was it desire – to juggle her family and her work as Harriet herself had done all those years, and with a much larger family on top of it.

But what could be done? The expansion of Germany into Poland, the Netherlands, Belgium and parts of France was the main topic of conversation in most homes, church functions, or barrooms, always accompanied by the question: Were we going to be able to stay out of the conflict? Roosevelt talked of isolation, but Harriet, like most, doubted the United States' ability to do so. It only seemed logical to avoid the whole topic of England in Nancy's story. And at any rate, Nancy could hardly be solving a mystery with air-raid sirens going off around her.

"You're right, Mr. Grosset. Of course. Do you care where Nancy travels to?"

Mr. Grosset's face relaxed, pleased that Mrs. Adams understood the need for a change without arguing the point. Harriet might have been a woman, but she was as stubborn as any man when it came to negotiating for the Syndicate.

"It's entirely up to you, Mrs. Adams. It just needs to be in a location that is presently not involved in the conflict. Mexico, perhaps, or Buenos Aires."

"I'll confer with my sister and take care of it," Harriet said, then stood. "Thank you for your time, Mr. Grossett," she said, holding out her hand for him to shake. "I appreciate you looking out for our interests."

"My pleasure, Mrs. Adams, as always," he said with a smile. "Oh, and congratulations on your Nancy books being printed in Braille. You must be very proud of that."

"Thank you. I am." Harriet strode out of the publishers office with her head high, knowing it was her hard work that was keeping her father's company going and, in fact, taking it places Edward had only dreamed of.

But the conflict in Europe quickly escalated, from Germany's invasion of Poland in 1939 to the bombing of London in the Blitz of 1940-1941, prompting Franklin Roosevelt to institute a peacetime draft. Harriet's oldest son joined the Air Corps and was a training pilot at an air base in Florida. Patsy was in her second year at Wellesley College. Harriet couldn't have been more proud of both of her children. But while Harriet and others were worrying about their husbands and sons, Mildred had family worries of her own.

(1940)

Mildred looked at her husband across the dinner table and frowned. "Is the meatloaf not sitting well, Asa?" Mildred said with some concern. Her husband had stopped eating and was just pushing the meat and potatoes around on his plate.

"Something at the new office bothering you? Maybe you can ask to be sent back to Cleveland. Toledo is no paradise, and with my new Penny Parker series into its second volume, I'm sure we'd manage."

Peggy, in her highchair, reached for her mother's plate. "I want more meat," she said decisively.

"Sure, sweetie. Here you go." Mildred cut off three-quarters of the remaining piece of meatloaf on her plate and put it on the wooden tray in front of her daughter, cutting it into pieces a three year old could manage.

"It's not the office, dear. I'm still the new kid on the block, but I can handle the office politics just fine," he said with a forced smile. Asa reached over and rubbed his left arm, looking at it as if he didn't recognize his own limb.

Then he looked up at his wife and blinked hard, twice.

"I thus don...don kno..." his voice trailed off in a slurred mumble as he leaned on the table and stared at his plate.

Mildred's heart started pounding in her chest at the sight. She stood and shook Asa's arm. "Asa. Asa! What's the matter?"

Asa stared up into his wife's face with a blank expression, as if he didn't know who he was looking at.

"I'm going to call the doctor," Mildred said, rushing to the phone. She picked up the receiver and realized she and Asa didn't have a physician in Toledo yet. They had moved to town four months ago – another promotion with the Associated Press for Asa – and Mildred had not gotten around to finding a new doctor for either of them. She had found one for Peggy, but hadn't seen a need to find one for her or Asa. They were rarely sick and there were so many other things to do living in a new city. "Damn it!" she said. She looked back over at her husband, who had his head in his right hand, his left arm hanging oddly limp at his side. "I'll call Peggy's doctor. He'll know what to do."

Mildred glanced at the number taped to the wall above the phone and dialed as tears ran down her cheeks.

Twenty ∾

The spry little Camilla wiggled on her Aunt Harriet's lap as her seventeen-year-old cousin, and namesake, sat at the piano in the Adams' living room, entertaining the family after a Sunday dinner. Two days earlier was the tenth anniversary of the death of the family patriarch, and Harriet liked to have everyone close by to help keep her mind occupied. Camilla's ever-doting mother sat by their side.

"So what shall we do to celebrate Nancy's anniversary?" Harriet asked her sister. "It was ten years on April 28th when the first volume came out, and we've since sold two and a half million copies. That's certainly something to celebrate."

Edna took her daughter's hand and swung it to the music as Harriet bounced Camilla lightly on her knees. The elder Camilla was playing a swing tune, a bit harsh for after dinner entertainment, Harriet thought, but it did have a catchy rhythm. Harriet preferred crooners such as Bing Crosby and Kate Smith or the melodious tones of the Mills Brothers, not caring that they *were* a colored group. In the evenings, with their new console radio, if one of the children didn't have a recital or a sporting event, the family would tune into almost anyone they wanted to hear. Harriet and Russell Sr. preferred listening to the New York Philharmonic or the Guy Lombardo Show. Edward, the youngest at fifteen, preferred the likes of Dick Tracy and the Green Hornet, or more recently, Abbott and Costello.

"I would say we bring out a special volume but with Mildred's husband so ill, I don't think that would be wise to put that kind of pressure on the poor girl. How old is her little one now, anyway?" Harriet asked.

"She's three. Just a year older than Camilla."

"I can't imagine taking care of a three year old and a sick husband on top of all the writing she is doing."

Harriet's daughter finished her song and her young cousin wiggled off her aunt's lap to give the older Camilla a hug.

"I was thinking about that. I think the next few outlines we send should be filled out a bit more than our previous ones. I know she generally bristles at our long outlines, but I think under the circumstances, she would appreciate the gesture."

Camilla ran back to her mother's side. "Millie said it's time for dessert," she said, grasping her mother's hand and pulling her toward the dining room.

"Just a minute, Camilla. Aunt Hattie and I are talking."

But Camilla was not to be dissuaded and continued to pull even harder on her mother's arm. "Wesley. Wesley, would you take Camilla to the dining room. I'll be right along."

Camilla instantly dropped her mother's hand when she saw her father turn toward her. She reached her arms up to him, and he swept her up onto his hip. "You're too big for Daddy to carry, Camilla," her mother scolded, pulling at Camilla's dress so it lay more modestly over her legs.

"Not for my big, strong Daddy," she said with a grin as she patted Wesley's cheek. Wesley shrugged his shoulders at his wife and took their daughter into the other room for her dessert.

Edna leaned in toward Harriet and lowered her voice. "Before we go in, I wanted to hear what was happening with Nancy's book in Norway. Just when we get her in our first foreign market, she gets shut down. What happened?"

"Well, the war happened," Harriet said, shaking her head in disgust. "The publisher was working on translating volume seven and the Nazis stopped production.

"I had no idea they were in Norway."

"They invaded in early April. I read in the paper just today that they entered Belgium and the Netherlands on the 10th. They are all over the place."

Harriet took a deep breath. "It worries me, Edna. I know Roosevelt said he won't send our boys over there, but we're giving them so much aid, the troops can't be far behind, or why would he have instituted a peacetime draft?"

Edna grasped her sister's hand and squeezed. Now with a child of her own, she had a better sense of the agony Harriet must have been going through with her son in the service. She had no words to comfort her sister. Nor would she know what to say when Harriet and Russell's worst fear came true. Two years later the Adams family received a knock on their door. Harriet was called from her office and Russell was paged at the stock exchange; they were needed home immediately. Harriet, working only ten minutes from home, arrived first. When she walked into the parlor and two well-dressed young men in Air Corps uniforms stood to greet her, Harriet's eyes rolled back in her head and she collapsed to the floor. She was revived with smelling salts by her husband, whose red rimmed eyes told her what she already knew: Russell Jr. was dead. He had been killed in a flight accident in Florida.

After the tragedy at Pearl Harbor just three months earlier and the United States entrance into the conflict with Germany and Japan, Harriet was sure Sunny would be sent off to the Pacific, a prospect she was proud to support around the Ladies Aid Circle at her church but would keep her up well into the night when the lights were turned off and she was left to her own thoughts and fears. But Sunny never got the chance.

Edna closed the Syndicate for several days until she felt it was prudent to go back to work. She wanted to explain to the publishers and writers about the tragic event in the Adams' home and assure them that she would be handling things until such time as Harriet felt well enough to return. It took Harriet two months to make it back into the office.

Twenty-one ❧

(1942)

Edna walked into Camilla's bedroom, her daughter at her side. The younger Camilla ran over to her cousin, who was standing in her closet, rummaging through her clothes.

"Hey, sweetie! How are you?" she said to her namesake as she bent down to take her in her arms.

Harriet looked up from behind the pile of clothes she was folding and stared at her sister. "What are you doing here, Edna?"

"I thought you could use some help packing Millie's things," she said. "Can't a sister help her niece pack for her first trip to college?" Edna said in mock disappointment. She walked over to her niece and gave her a hug and kiss. "I'm so excited for you, sweetheart. And Wellesley, too. Your mother must be so proud."

Harriet watched Edna, still perplexed by her sister's appearance. Edna bent down to her daughter. "Camilla, you keep Millie company while your Aunt Hattie and I have a little chat, won't you?"

Camilla nodded her head with excitement, eager to spend time with a cousin who loved to spoil her.

"I need to take a break anyway, Camilla. How 'bout we go to the kitchen and see what Fannie has baking." The older girl bent down to the younger and whispered in a conspiratorial tone, "I think she's baking me some cookies for my trip!"

The little girl clapped her hands together and raced out of the room, Millie following close behind.

"All right, Edna," Harriet said, dropping the pair of slacks she had in her hands. "Why the unexpected visit?"

"You always could see right through me, Hattie," Edna said with some embarrassment. She moved a hat box off the chair of Camilla's dressing table and sat down. "I have some exciting news!" she said with glee. Then looking at her sister's solemn face she tempered her excitement. "Well, it's exciting for my family, and I hope you'll be excited for me too, Hattie."

"I can't be excited if you don't tell me what it is."

"Yes. Well...Wesley and I have decided to move to Florida. Isn't that wonderful! We're not getting any younger, and with Mother gone...well, we just want to live somewhere where it's warm for most of the year, and we want to move before Camilla starts school; she so loves it on the beach when we vacation there. Plus we don't want her to start to make friends up here and then yank her away from them in a year or two. It would be cruel."

"And the Syndicate?!" Harriet responded, quite unprepared for Edna's news.

Edna shifted uncomfortably on her chair. "Yes. Well…I plan on helping out as much as I can from my new location. You can write to me about decisions that have to be made jointly, and I can write back. We can call and talk if we need to. And for the story outlines, I thought it would be best if you hired someone to do that." Edna looked down at her hands, unsure of how her sister would take to the idea. "You were always better at that than I was, anyway, Hattie."

"So you want to maintain equal shares in the company but you want me to do most of the work?"

"Yes! I mean, no!" Edna said, a flustered look on her face. "I…I want us to hire someone to take my place, and I would decrease my share to say…forty percent?"

Harriet just looked at her sister and didn't say anything. Edna walked over to Harriet and sat on the bed next to the pile of clothes Harriet had been folding. "I know this is a surprise, Hattie. I didn't mean to spring it on you, but I just didn't know how to tell you other than to come right out with it. You know that the company means more to you than it ever did to me. You and dad were the writers in the family. Gosh, you'd have been working on a newspaper after college if Father hadn't put the kibosh on the idea."

Harriet let out a big sigh, which Edna took as a small sign of submission. "Can't you be happy for us?" Edna asked.

"Of course I'm happy for you, Edna. It is just such a big change."

Edna stood and took one of Harriet's hands. "So then you'll agree?"

Harriet gave her sister a weak smile. "I can't very well see how I can do anything else," she said with a chuckle.

"Oh, thank you, Hattie," Edna said, leaning down and giving her sister a small hug. "I knew you'd understand."

Edna turned and started out of the room.

"Oh, I did send off those letters to the writers about trying to watch the use of gasoline or other non-patriotic consumption by characters in their stories, though I reiterated the need to avoid any direct mention of the war in their plot development. I agree that the children don't need to worry about such things. Many are going to be affected enough by the rationing or they might even have family members who don't end up coming back; we don't need their favorite book characters bringing up such sore subjects."

"Thanks," Harriet said and started back on her folding. "When are you planning on leaving?"

Edna looked a bit sheepish. "Next month."

Harriet's eyebrows shot up in surprise, and it took her a moment to respond. "All right then. We'll have to meet first thing Monday morning, and you can start filling me in on where you are with things at the office."

"Of course. Wonderful idea. I'll see you Monday, then," Edna said and started out of the room again.

"You're not going to stick around and help us pack?" Harriet asked.

Edna spun on her heel and looked surprised at her sister's question. It took her a minute but when Harriet cracked half a smile, Edna smiled too. "Oh, you're such a tease," she said and left Harriet alone amidst the trunks, suitcases, and stacks of clothes.

Harriet thought she had let her sister off fairly easy with her sudden decision to leave the business primarily in her hands. She was quite sure it wasn't a sixty-forty split of responsibility, but Russell still had a very good job at the brokerage firm and the Syndicate was doing quite well, so Harriet didn't see a need to belabor the point. She didn't let up quite so easily on Mildred, despite Asa's continual inability to work, though her remonstration was politely veiled as a compliment.

December 8th, 1942

Dear Mrs. Wirt,

In commenting on your manuscript, I am going to make a very unusual criticism. You work too hard! We find English too perfect for a little girls' book. The sentences seem to be long and full of big words. Since we intend to simplify the manuscript a good bit, we are sorry that you went to so much trouble to make it such a perfect specimen from the point of view of synonyms and descriptive phraseology.

I do appreciate getting the manuscript to us so

*promptly and under such trying conditions. I am sorry
about the delay in getting the check to you, but I have
been working literally nights and days to keep up with
our schedule since Edna has left for Florida.*

*I do have to say thank you for the wonderful
magazine serial for the* Calling All Girls *magazine.
That was one of Edna's last outlines before she left
us. They really wanted "Carolyn Keene" to write the
serial mystery, so we knew just the person to ask to
flesh it out for us. We feel honored that the subscribers
of the magazine voted Miss Keene as their favorite
author, beating out Louise May Alcott of all people,
and you should feel honored as well.*

*I hope your writing is going well, and may 1943
hold good things in store for you.*

Yours truly,

Mrs. Harriet Adams

(1943)

Mildred took the criticism in stride. She really had little
choice. She needed to do freelance work so she could stay
home and take care of little Peggy and Asa, who had another
small stroke.

To keep Asa up on the goings on of their modest home
in Toledo, Mildred opened their mail at Asa's bedside. She
knew what a struggle it was for him to watch her working so
hard while all he could do was lie in bed or sit on the couch.

primary
breadwinner

Occasionally he would keep an eye on Peggy, who was now five and able to entertain herself with her doll or with coloring next to her father's side while her mother was in the other room tapping away feverishly at her typewriter.

Mildred was opening a large envelope from the Syndicate when Asa tapped his wife's shoulder to get her attention. "It's big," he said his speech somewhat slurred. He stretched out his right arm in a one-armed "big" sign. Asa had taken to using hand gestures to make himself understood. It was too frustrating to try to talk most days.

"I know," Mildred nodded. "They still send the detailed outlines. I've tried to tell her it would be easier for me to write from a more streamlined outline, but Harriet can't seem to give it up. You would think with her sister gone, she would want to ease up a bit, though she said that she's hired more office staff to help her."

Asa nodded his agreement.

Mildred returned to reading Harriet's attached letter and chuckled. She touched her husband's hand and laughed. "Oh, you'll get a laugh out of this, Asa. She's disappointed in Nancy's romantic life in the *The Secret in the Old Attic*, the last story I sent them. She said she's consulted her daughters on this and they agree that Nancy's notions of romance are a bit dated. I guess her youngest is dating an ensign in the Navy." Mildred looked at her husband, her eyes bright with amusement. "Amazing! The woman who was the first to get a Masters in Journalism at University of Iowa, who started working way before it was something women had to do, is old-fashioned."

Asa added a half-smile to his wife's mirth and tapped her arm in encouragement.

Mildred's humor turned sour when she thought about actually writing some romance into Nancy's story. She knew it wasn't her strong suit; Nancy, Dana, Peggy, and Kay were all unmarried, independent young women, and up to this point, the Syndicate had been very content with that fact.

She sighed and smiled back at her husband. It might be a bit of challenge, but Mildred was accustomed to challenges.

Twenty-two ❧

"Ok," Mildred said, pulling a brush through her hair before putting on her lipstick. It had been so long since she had had to dress to go to work, eighteen years, in fact when she worked at the *Clinton Harold* in Iowa. The excitement of her new position as a reporter for the *Toledo Times* almost equaled her anxiety. "Peggy still likes her night-light, so please leave the hall light on for her," she said to her mother, who had moved to Toledo to watch her grandchild while her only daughter went back to work. "And she'll tell you I don't make her eat broccoli, but don't believe her," Mildred said, looking at her stockingless legs in the mirror with some dismay. She was doing her part for the war effort by not wearing stockings, but she felt totally naked without them, though not enough to draw a faux stocking seam with a marker down the back of her legs like some women did.

Mildred was on the late shift at the *Times*, working until eleven at night, though for Mildred it would end up usually being until one-thirty or two in the morning; she was always trying to find ways to make herself indispensable.

Mildred frantically rustled through her purse. "I can't find my glasses!" she said in a panic as she ran to her desk to shuffle papers and open drawers in an attempt to find her glasses, a necessity for her at the age of thirty-four.

Lillian tapped her gently on the shoulder. Mildred swung around in surprise. Her mother handed Mildred her glasses. "Oh, thank you!"

"You need to relax, Millie. You're going to be fine," Lillian said as Mildred took one last look at herself in the mirror.

"It's important I do this right, Mom. My editor told me in no uncertain terms, the minute this war is over, I'm out of a job." Mildred turned to her mother. "And I have to show them from the get-go that that would be a mistake."

Lillian shook her head and smiled. "How 'bout you start the job, first. Worry about the end of the war when it comes," her mother said, then crossed herself. The Americans were finally out of South Africa and had just entered Rome in early June, in addition to the continued battles in the Pacific against the Japanese. The Russians were starting to make some headway on the Eastern front, but it still didn't look like any of it was going to end any time soon. Lillian was selfishly relieved her son, who had done his part in WWI, was too old to be drafted for this horrible war and her grandchildren were too young. But she felt for the mothers and fathers who were losing sons every day; the list in the paper of the dead or the missing never seemed to get any shorter.

Lillian pushed her daughter out of the bathroom. "Now go kiss your husband goodbye and get going."

"Is he up?" Mildred whispered. After Asa had suffered three additional stokes, he no longer got out of bed and, subsequently, slept most of his day away. It was part of the way she consoled herself when she tried to justify her reasons for getting this job. She had done well working as a publicity writer for the *Toledo Community Chest* but this job at the *Times* was the job she had always dreamed of. Having her mother willing to take care of Peggy had tipped the scales, and she decided she couldn't pass up the opportunity. She didn't care that she got the job mostly because the newspaper was desperate for staff, seeing that they were losing more and more male reporters as the war trudged on.

And things were looking up at the Syndicate, as well. After much back and forth with Harriet, she had finally agreed to let Mildred work off of shorter outlines, more like the ones Edward used to send her. Harriet was pleased enough with how the latest Dana girl volume had turned out under the new arrangement, that she had sent Mildred the same skeletal outline for the next Nancy Drew story, *The Mystery of the Tolling Bell* in January of 1945.

Now Mildred had a new routine. After she slept her now usual four to five hours, she would set up her typewriter next to her husband's bed, placing Peggy on the floor next to her as she began her story writing. She was exhausted, but she couldn't give up either her books or her position at the *Times*. Neither her ego nor her circumstances would allow it.

It was a very pleasant surprise that, after some wrangling with Edna, who was getting more and more difficult when it came to the company finances, Edna finally agreed with Harriet to give Mildred a bonus check of $1000. Since she had left for a warmer climate, she had stuck up for Mildred whenever Harriet complained to her about the trouble she was having with Mrs. Wirt, be it the length of book outlines or how Nancy and her chums should be portrayed. But when it came to a choice between loyalties or Edna's pocketbook, the pocketbook won out every time, so this was quite a turn of events for Edna. Both women had grown up knowing little want, and maintaining that lifestyle took some effort on Edna's part, now that she had her own family and household to pay for and maintain. In this case Harriet was buoyed by the fact that the war was finally over and that, after reviewing the Syndicate income for the last fifteen years – at Edna's insistence – they had indeed done quite well through it all and in particular because of Nancy. Harriet thought it was a well-deserved reward, even though she had yet to give herself a raise in the three years since she had taken over the majority of the work of the business. Harriet would leave that fight – and a few others that were building between the sisters – for another day.

Miss Walters knocked gently on Harriet's office door. Donna

Walters had started with the Syndicate soon after Edna had left. She was an aspiring editor, having graduated from Wellesley the year Harriet had advertised for assistance. What better place to learn about editing than at the company that put out the likes of the Rover and Hardy Boys and her personal favorite, Nancy Drew. She had grown up with Nancy, as many girls her age had done, and upon joining the firm, she was shocked to find out who the real Caroline Keene actually was. After a year of typing up Harriet's edits, checking grammar and punctuation on stories, and writing cover jacket blurbs, she had finally been given the job of first edits on The Bobbsey Twins, the Honey Bunch, and her beloved Nancy Drew. Of course, Harriet checked her edits before Miss Pearson typed them up to send to the publisher, but it was a big step for Harriet to give up any amount of control over her stories, especially her precious Nancy.

"I'm sorry to bother you, Mrs. Adams, but I just had to show you something." Donna walked over to her desk, handed a manuscript to Harriet, and perched herself on the edge of one of the chairs in front of Harriet's desk.

Harriet paged halfway through the document then looked up to Donna, confusion on her face. "You stopped editing partway through."

"It was just terrible. I didn't see a reason to continue."

Harriet looked closer through the manuscript, checking out the blue marks and notations that Donna had made on the page. Comments such as: "This doesn't sound like Nancy" after some dialogue Nancy was having with Ned, or "I can't tell Bess from George in this conversation" as

Nancy's chums were discussing how they were going to help Nancy out of a bind.

"I know you've had to do more rewriting on the last few Nancy stories, but this is worse than usual," Donna said in a matter-of-fact tone. Harriet had shared with Donna that Mrs. Wirt was having some trouble at home, though she didn't go into the details as she felt was only proper. This meant Miss Walters had no idea of the multitude of stresses Mildred was under, and as a young, unmarried, twenty-something with no real experience of her own, she couldn't even imagine what Mildred was trying to juggle. "I didn't know if you wanted to send it back to Mrs. Wirt for her to rewrite or not. This would take a lot of effort on your part to fix."

Harriet took a deep breath as she gazed at the typed pages, blue marks coloring the page like doodles on a school girl's notebook. Maybe now was her chance. She had been trying to convince her sister that Mildred, as good as she had been for the Syndicate in the past, was just becoming a liability. Donna was correct, Harriet had to do more rewrites on both of Mildred's last Nancy and Dana stories, and she didn't have time to do even that much. She had made an exception because of Mildred's history with the organization and her present situation at home. As a working mother herself, Harriet knew some of what Mildred was dealing with, but she was willing to do only so much and had been mulling over different ways to convince Edna it was time to let Mildred go. This manuscript was just the ticket. Harriet leaned on her desk, staring at the young, eager face in front of her and smiled.

"I need to discuss this situation with my sister before I make a final decision. But why don't you take a stab at the rewrite yourself, then give it to me and I'll finish it up. How does that sound?"

Donna practically jumped off the edge of her chair, but she held herself in check, wanting to maintain a professional demeanor with the very proper Mrs. Adams. "That would be wonderful, Mrs. Adams!"

Harriet handed the manuscript back the Donna.

"You won't regret it, Mrs. Adams. I promise!" she said and practically skipped out of the room.

Unfortunately for Harriet, Edna didn't agree on how to proceed with Mildred. In fact, she questioned Harriet's assessment of Mildred's work by asking to see the outline that Harriet had sent Mildred to work from. This incident was another item of late that grated on Harriet in relation to her sister. A year earlier, Harriet had proposed starting a new baseball book series. At the beginning of the year Edna had traveled back home for the christening of Camilla's first child, a beautiful baby girl, and Harriet had tried to talk to her sister about the series at that event. Edna had put her off, not wanting to talk about work at such a joyous occasion. But when Edna did not respond to two subsequent letters on the subject, Harriet had had enough, and told her sister so in a letter she wrote her in January of 1947.

I was rather amazed at your recent reply to my letter about what you wish to do concerning the new series. I wrote to you nearly a year ago about this, and

261

again some months later, so it seems to me that you had a long time in which to get the "expert advice" you mentioned. I had hoped to have the whole matter settled for Income Tax purposes, and also for [a] contract with the publishers. At the end of the week I shall deliver the second baseball story to Cupples and Leon and I dislike having them bring out a series under unsettled conditions between us.

Then there was the issue of Harriet's salary. Harriet decided she was going to finally push the issue and ask for a raise. Edna's surprising response was to ask for a full accounting of all the Syndicate's financials before she agreed to any salary change. That was the last straw for Harriet, who, despite enjoying the challenge of taking over her father's business over seventeen years earlier, had been taking on more and more responsibility to ensure the business remained profitable. This included creating two new series, seeking out radio and foreign printing rights, and investigating in the emerging television market. She was seeing the growth of children's stories that the publishers had predicted after the war had ended and felt on very firm footing in finally asking Edna for a raise.

(June 30, 1947)

Actually, the picture from 1942 to the present is a very good one, but I have yet to hear one word of commendation from you. And despite the ever increasing amount in your pocket due to new business, you keep silent, and let me be the only one in the office who has had no raise since 1942. I've had all the headaches, and have given increasingly of my time and efforts, but still the sum of 37.50 a week from you that I agreed upon as a starting salary has never changed. Frankly I cannot understand your attitude, and psychologically the effect does not make for good business.

There was one ray of hope for Harriet in early June of that year, but it came at a significant price, though not for her

Twenty-three ∾

Lillian knocked tentatively on Mildred and Asa's bedroom door. Mildred had been at Asa's bedside since he had taken a turn for the worse just the day before. They had called in the doctor, but he had said there was nothing he could do other than make Asa more comfortable. He had given Asa something to calm his labored breathing, but Asa still shuddered and shook with each breath. Lillian didn't know how her daughter could take sitting next to him listening to him struggle so.

There was a brown envelope in Lillian's hand with the East Orange, New Jersey address on top, a small light that she thought her daughter might grasp at during a time that was filled only with darkness. She had seen Mildred's writing career blossom from those first magazine stories from when she was a young girl to now writing stories under her own name, though that had dwindled of late to only two: Mildred's own Trailer Stories for Girls and her various mystery stories. Luckily she still had the three Syndicate series: Kay Tracey and Nancy Drew and now The Honey Bunch stories that she had just taken on that year. Lillian knew how much Mildred loved her stories. It was part of the reason she couldn't stop writing, despite all that she had to deal with.

Lillian stood just inside the open door but placed the large envelope behind her back. She was thinking better of the idea of showing it to her daughter. Mildred turned and looked at her mother's odd posture.

"What is it, Mother?"

Lillian hesitated, then stepped forward, handing Mildred the envelope. "From the Syndicate. I thought you might like a break from sitting with Asa," she said with a weak smile.

It was late. Peggy was already in bed, and Mildred had called into work, telling them that she wouldn't be making it in; she needed to stay with her husband. Everyone understood.

Mildred stood and stretched. She looked down at her wrinkled dress and pushed the hair out of her face. Her head itched and her hair felt thick, almost sticky as she ran her hands through it; she hadn't bathed in a couple days, afraid to leave Asa's side. But his breathing hadn't changed since the doctor had last been in early that morning, and even though it was a labored breath, his eyes were closed and his face held just a hint of tension.

"I could do with a bath," she said, standing and turning toward her mother. She took the envelope from her hand.

"It'll give me something to read in the tub," Mildred said with a half-smile.

Her mother gave her a soft kiss on the cheek. "Good idea, dear. Have a long, hot bath. I'll be here," she said, sitting down beside Asa and touching his hand. "We'll be just fine."

Mildred gently squeezed her mother's shoulder, then kissed the top of her head. "Thanks, Mom."

The steam rose out of the tub like billowing clouds of mist off a cold lake as Mildred undressed in the warm room. Mildred had never been to a Turkish bath, but she always envisioned it would be something like this. With her chenille robe around her, she adjusted the water to a more tepid range, poured in a cap full of bubble bath, then picked up the envelope off the toilet seat and opened it up, waiting for the tub to fill all the way. It was another book: *The Ghost of Blackwood Hall.* The outline was just two pages long, as had been agreed upon, but at the moment, Mildred wasn't sure that had been the best plan. It was how she preferred to work, of course, but with Asa getting sicker by the day, the thought of sitting at the typewriter had less and less appeal. Mildred dropped the outline down in her lap and sat back against the tank, exhausted. She had shed so many tears in the last few days, she didn't think she had any left. Her eyes closed, almost of their own volition, as she let the fragrant lilac scent of her bubble bath and the warm, moist air that engulfed the room, melt away her worries, layer by layer. She hadn't realized she had fallen asleep until she heard her mother repeatedly calling out for her to "Come quick!" By her tone Mildred knew the time had come, and she was instantly awake, running to Asa's side to find his chest still and his face an inert mask, all the pain fallen away. He was a young man again with not so much as a thought to hold him down.

Mildred dropped to her knees, draping herself over Asa's body as she wept fresh tears.

March 31, 1948

Dear Edna,

I have an idea I would like to put to you. I am thinking about this, in part, because of all the new opportunities that are coming our way, but also because of the continued pressure the publishing companies are putting on me to get outlines to them more quickly in addition to the issues I am having with them as I try to ensure the quality of the book artwork and content is up to our standards. Things appear to be moving faster and faster in this post-war period. The time of relaxed timelines and congenial conversation in a publishing meeting are long gone.

At any rate, my idea is to bring a partner into the Syndicate, someone to help me with the day to day tasks of working with the publishers and someone we could trust to do rewrites. The girls I have hired since your move have been very helpful, but they just don't seem to make the grade when it comes to the rewrites. To be fair to them, they were not hired with those skills in mind and have tried to help as best they can with their limited experience. I would also like help with looking into the different syndicating options. As I mentioned in my previous letter, I would like to get our movie rights back from Warner. Since they no long are making Nancy movies, I suppose because they didn't do as well in the box office as they had hoped, I would think they would be open to us buying back those rights.

I don't need to discuss this at length here, but it illustrates my point. We need someone in the office who can take on more responsibility, under my watchful eye, of course. Please let me know your thoughts soon.

Yours truly,

Harriet

Harriet was feeling the strain of running the day to day operations of the Syndicate, in addition to feeling a bit physically constricted. Other than the occasional long weekend to the mountains in upstate New York, or the two to three weeks at a small farm that she and Russell owned called Bird Haven Farm, Harriet had been stuck in the office. The family had not been free to travel as they had in the past. For Harriet, travel was essential, not only for her mental health, but she used her trips as research for the Syndicate's adventure stories, much as her father had done some thirty years earlier.

Perhaps it was Edna's earlier condemnation of her sister or the realization that Harriet did need help if the company was to grow – Harriet never knew why – but Edna did agree to hire a new partner in the firm, a thirty-seven-year-old sportswriter who had been working at the *Newark News,* Andrew Svenson. Harriet assured Edna that Mr. Svenson was a good man, besides being an experienced writer. "He's interested in the church, Sunday School, Scouts, Junior Chamber of Commerce..." Harriet explained, trying to illustrate the man's character through his various associations. This and the fact that he had four children and years of writing experience made him an easy choice. Harriet was particularly pleased with some of his ideas for the Syndicate in this new, and for Harriet – then fifty-six years old – sometimes confusing era.

Edna still held tight onto the purse strings, however, when a year later, she refused Harriet's request to give Andrew a raise, right at a point when Harriet was planning a nine week European vacation with her husband to sightsee and visit her daughter Patsy and her husband, who were living in England.

She only felt able to travel because of Mr. Svenson's wonderful grasp of the Syndicate workings. He fit right into the company from day one, being a respectful student of the daily tasks that Harriet had to undertake and gradually taking on an expanding list of duties. The Syndicate had pared down to only six series by 1948: Tom Swift, which had been running since 1910; the X Bar X Boys, coming in second in the race for the longest series having started in 1926; the Hardy Boys, which started in 1927 – Edward's last series, – Nancy Drew, in 1930; and the sisters' own literary inventions, the Dana Girls and Kay Tracey, both premiering in 1934. The sisters had also started the Mary and Jerry mystery series in 1935 but scrapped it after just a year due to sagging sales, along with Harriet's Mel Martin baseball series that Edna had finally agreed to. Mel made it through two volumes before the publishers politely declined to pick up the next book in the series. Perhaps boys' series were not Harriet's forte, as it had been her father's.

With Mr. Svenson securely on board, Harriet and Russell finally departed that June for a well-deserved vacation, while Mildred, still at the *Times*, moved on with her life.

(July, 1949)

"Come in, Mr. Benson," Lillian said, ushering the tall, handsome man in the suit and tie into the room and the shorter, more disheveled looking man with a box camera and large flash unit around his neck in behind him. "May I take your hats?"

"Of course. Thank you," George Benson said, as he handed his homburg to Mildred's mother. The man with the camera handed her his worn fedora. "You must be Mildred's mother," George said, extending her his hand. "It's a pleasure to finally meet you. Mildred has told me all the wonderful things you have done for her. She is so very lucky to have you."

Lillian smiled as a soft blush colored her cheeks. "Well...it's what any mother would have done under the circumstances."

"Relocating like that to take on a sick son-in-law and young grandchild? My mother would have done no such thing," he said with a chuckle.

"You shouldn't say things like that, George. My mother is apt to believe you," Mildred said, standing with her arms crossed, leaning in the doorway behind them.

Lillian, still red-faced, whirled around to face her daughter. "We didn't hear you come in. Mr. Benson just arrived," she said, still a bit flustered.

"I heard the door bell," Mildred teased.

"Oh, yes. I suppose." Lillian turned back to the men. "Can I get either of you anything to drink? I just made up some lemonade."

"I wouldn't want to put you out, Mrs. Augustine," George said.

"It's not a bother. I just have to put in a few ice cubes and it's all set."

"Then lemonade it is! Right, Denny?" George said, hitting the cameraman's chest to get his attention. He had been looking around the room and not paying attention to the polite conversation.

"Lemonade...Yeah. Just peachy."

"I'll be right back with a pitcher and some glasses," Lillian said, then headed into the kitchen.

"Don't you look lovely today, Mildred," George said with a broad smile.

"If you call melting in this heat lovely, then I think you need new glasses, George," Mildred said with a grin.

"It is unusually warm for July," George agreed, as he took off his suit jacket and hung it over his arm. "But as O. Henry once said, 'We may achieve the climate, but weather is thrust upon us.'"

Mildred nodded. The cameraman just looked confused.
"Here, I'll take that for you," Mildred said.

The tan jacket was made of a crisp linen and matched his slacks and light brown shoes, but even a light jacket was too much inside Mildred's apartment. There was a fan in the window that was moving some air into the room, but it was all warm air and did little to cool anyone. She took his jacket and with great care, hung it in their front closet, lingering to take in the earthy scent of the cologne George always wore. It was an aroma that filled his office and always introduced him before he even entered a room.

Just then Peggy, soft brown eyes and curly brown hair like her mother's, ran into the room and came to a screeching halt when she saw the two strange men. Mildred went over to her and helped her move closer to the men. "Peggy, this is Mr. Benson and Mr. Parker. They work in my office."

A soft pink blush filled Peggy's cheeks, and she nodded a polite hello, but didn't say a thing. George held out his hand to the thirteen-year-old.

"We're here to write a story about your mother, the famous author."

Mildred shook her head in amusement. Peggy stared at Denny and the camera that hung from his neck. "And take some pictures," she said.

"That's right. I think our readers would like to see what the real Carolyn Keene looks like, don't you?"

"I suppose," she said.

"Where should we do the interview?" George asked as he stood upright. "Do you have an office you write in?"

"My office is up in the attic room," Mildred said, leading them over to a door next to the closet. "It's not very big, but it suits me just fine." Mildred poked her head into the kitchen. "Mom, we're going up to my office. We'll be down in a few minutes for the lemonade."

"All right, dear," Lillian said. She put the last glass on an already full tray and put the pitcher of lemonade in the refrigerator to keep it cool.

"Peggy, you stay and help your grandmother, okay?"

"Okay," she said as she walked into the kitchen.

"This way, gentleman," Mildred said, leading them up the wooden steps.

They stepped into a sparse, low-ceilinged room half the size of the main floor that was separated from a storage space by a small door. The only things in Mildred's office were a moderate-sized wooden desk in the corner facing out with a typewriter perched on top and book shelves behind it and along one wall, bookshelves full of books. In addition to the typewriter, the desk had two neatly piled stacks of papers on top but not much else. George walked up to one of the bookshelves and pulled out a book.

"I know you said you wrote children's books, but I had no idea how many. Are all of these yours?"

"All one hundred and twenty six."

George pulled a notepad out of his breast pocket and wrote the figure down.

"You told me you wrote the Nancy Drew stories. What other books did you write for the Syndicate?"

"I actually started with Ruth Fielding."

"Can you pull out one of those for us?" George asked.

"Sure." Mildred went over to the bookshelf and pulled out a clean, unread copy. Other, more worn copies sat beside the cleaner ones.

"And...?"

"And the Dana Girls..."

"Keep pulling," George instructed.

As Mildred named off the different stories she had written, she pulled the same book off one of the shelves.

"The Honey Bunch, Kay Tracey, Penny Nichols, Dot and Dash, Penny Parker," she said, continuing to stack up the books on her desk, "but these last three weren't for the Syndicate."

"Keep going," George said as he wrote town the titles on his pad.

Mildred scanned the shelves and pulled *The Twin Ring Mystery* off the shelf. "This one was a set of mystery stories I did. I've got six different books of those so far. Then I did four trailer stories where three young women traveled around the country in their trailer solving mysteries."

"Any more?"

"Um..." Mildred stared at her books, then dove in when she found what she was looking for. "I did only three of these," she said, putting a Madge Sterling book on the growing pile.

"Do you have anything you're currently working on?" George said and walked over to her desk, peering at the stack of papers.

Mildred picked up a typed pile. "Cupples and Leon just picked up my Dan Carter Cub Scout Series. I guess they liked the Brownie Scout books they just published for me this last month." Mildred went over to a partially empty shelf behind her desk and took out *The Brownie Scouts at Snow Valley* and *The Brownie Scouts in The Circus* and set them on the her desk with the rest.

"You know, Denny, I think that would make a good picture," George said. "Mildred, you sit at your desk, behind your typewriter, and I'll stack the books on each side of you."

He began arranging the books in two tall towers, spines out, almost to the height of the petite Mrs. Wirt, then placed a small stack in front of one of the taller stacks and sat two books up so their covers were readable.

"There."

Denny stood in front of the desk and eyed up the shot. He flipped open the top of his camera and looked down through the lens. "She looks kind'a...kind'a stupid just sitting there," Denny said.

George looked at him disapprovingly, then stood beside him to stare at his setup. He picked up a book and gave it to Mildred. "Here, open this and pretend that you're reading."

Mildred complied. George stood back next to Denny. "That's better. Now smile," he said, smiling himself, as if he had to show her how it was done.

He didn't need to. Mildred loved the attention. She liked the fact that all her hard work would soon be displayed across the pages of the very newspaper she was working for, showing everyone in the newsroom and all the subscribers of the *Toledo Blade* the hard work it took her to get her where she was today. And getting such attention from the well-educated and handsome editor of the paper was something to smile about, as well. George could have had anyone write this story about her, but he had decided he was going to do it himself. George worked as a journalist before he was hired on as the paper's new editor, and editors rarely had time to write their own pieces for the paper. Mildred thought he might be writing the article about her because she was one of the staff, but she wasn't sure. Or perhaps he had an ulterior motive. A small part of her hoped it was the latter. It had been over a year since Asa had died and two long years before that without the intimacy Mildred now craved. But she had a daughter. What man would want to date a woman with a child? Mildred sighed and tried not to blink as Denny's flashbulb popped two, then three different times, blinding her for a second each time.

"That should do it," Denny said, popping the last spent bulb out into his hand, juggling it until it cooled, then stuffing it into his pants pocket with the others. Mildred put down her book and sat back, looking at her accomplishments stacked up in front of her.

"So when were you first published?" George asked.

"It was in *St. Nicholas Magazine* when I was just fourteen. The story was titled *The Courtesy*. I didn't get any money for it, of course, but I was definitely hooked on the idea of being a writer. Funny thing about *St. Nicholas Magazine*; they must have sold one of my stories to *People and Progress*, a company that makes children's readers. I found this out quite by accident when Peggy brought home one of her basic readers so she could show me one of my own stories. It was quite a surprise.

"I published my first book in college and started writing for the Syndicate in 1927 after Edward Stratemeyer put an ad in the *Editor* looking for writers. That was when I became the new ghostwriter for the Ruth Fielding stories."

Mildred stood and scanned the book shelves once more, eventually pulling out *Ruth Fielding and Her Great Scenario*. George wrote down the title. Mildred debated whether to go into the whole pseudonym thing and the fact that she wrote the stories from outlines, but she decided against it. She knew this was just a human interest piece, and she had learned from her years on the paper that the general public didn't care about those sorts of details.

"I didn't start writing Nancy until 1929."

George placed his hands on the edge of her desk and leaned in. Denny sat on the corner, camera still around his neck as if it were another body part.

"So how do you go about writing your stories? Are your characters created from people you know…" George cocked his eyebrow, "or after you?"

"No, they're not me," Mildred said with amusement. "And the people I know aren't interesting enough to write about. I find it easier to create my own characters."

"And your stories?"

"I create a fairly detailed outline from the information I'm provided, then I fill in the blanks."

"Well, that's interesting. I had no idea that's how book writers wrote."

"I can only speak for myself."

George closed his notepad and stood. "Well, I think I've got enough to go on. Shall we have some of that lemonade?" he said putting his hand on the small of Mildred's back and motioning them toward the stairs. Denny stood and followed Mildred and George down the stairs. He hadn't missed his boss's intimate gesture any more than Mildred had.

When they came downstairs, Lillian and Peggy were coming in through the front door. Peggy walked up to her mother with a fist full of letters.

"More letters for you."

"Thanks, sweetie," Mildred said, taking the small bundle.

"Fan mail?" George said, jokingly.

"Actually, it is. I get letters every week from my readers. It's sweet, really, and I answer each and every one. Probably a throwback to when I was a kid and I wrote to movie stars. I would hang around the village post office almost every day, hoping for a reply."

George pulled his notepad back out of his pocket and jotted down a few more notes before he put it away once more, then he pulled out his handkerchief and wiped his brow. He turned to Peggy. "I sure could use a glass of that lemonade about now."

"If you'll just have a seat," Peggy said, motioning to the living room furniture, "I'll bring it right out."

She gave George a polite nod and walked out of the room.

"Very impressive young lady," George said to Mildred.

"Thank you. I'm quite proud of her myself," Mildred replied, then motioned the two men to sit.

Twenty-four ᏅᏗ

(February 1950)

    Harriet took off her gloves and coat and stood waiting for the new managing officer at Grosset & Dunlap, Hugh Juergens, to take her coat from her, but he just went behind his desk and sat. Harriet sat down in front of his desk and put her coat over her lap. Harriet had wanted to meet this man in person. She had sent a letter to one of his editors, Mr. O'Connor, months ago, and she hadn't been pleased with his response. Since Mr. Juergens was new to Grosset & Dunlap it gave Harriet a good excuse to come and meet him for the first time and bring up the subject of her letter to someone who would be in a better position to do something about it.

    "How can I help you, Mrs. Adams?"

    "Well, I thought it would be appropriate for us to meet, since we do so much work with G & D."

"Right. Right. Of course. I was just reviewing our sales figures for your different series," he said picking up some papers that were sitting in front of him and examining them once more. "Nancy and the Hardy Boys certainly do you proud, and the Dana Girls, the Honey Bunch, and Kay Tracey are fairly steady as well, though not to the same level."

"Yes, I would agree. It's particularly those larger selling series I would like to discuss with you." Harriet stopped, wanting to choose her words wisely. She wasn't intimidated by this man, many years her junior, but she needed to be convincing, illustrating her position as best she could. "I don't know if Mr. O'Connor has shared the fact with you that G & D does not pay the Syndicate on the same increasing scale that is now typical in the industry."

Mr. Juergens shifted in his chair. "I *am* aware of that fact, but that is what you agreed to and at the present moment G & D is not in a position to change that agreement."

Harriet pursed her lips. "My father made that agreement in 1904. Times have changed, Mr. Juregens, and it's time for that agreement to change as well."

Mr. Juergens stood and came around his desk to sit on the edge directly in front of Harriet. "Mrs. Adams," he said in what Harriet took as a very condescending tone. "G & D has been a faithful business partner with the Syndicate for all those years, publishing hundreds of your father's books and now the books for you and your sister, as well. Why would the Syndicate want to kill the goose that lays the golden egg, so to speak?"

Harriet tightly squeezed the edge of her coat, her

knuckles going white. "Need I remind you that it's *the Syndicate* that is supplying you with those precious eggs, Mr. Juergens."

Mr. Juergens' eyebrows shot up. He hadn't expected this older woman to be quite so savvy. He had been warned about her, that she was old school and liked things handled just so with respect to the stories they published for her company. He knew that she perpetually gave his staff a hard time, though this had lessened of late since they were now able to deal more often with her new partner, Andrew Svenson. Mr. Juergens would have dropped the Syndicate when he came on board G & D if her book series weren't such steady sellers. And the deal he had with her company was a great one: a fixed royalty rate of only 4%, not the sliding scale he had to pay for other stories, the rate increasing as the sales increased. He realized he would have to handle this with a little more care.

"I'm sorry. Where are my manners? I never asked if you wanted some coffee. Or maybe tea," he said as he stood and walked partway to the door. "I can get Miss Miller to get us both a cup."

Harriet stared at him as if she were sizing him up before she spoke. "Yes…that would be nice."

Mr. Juergens let out his breath. He had broken the tension. Mr. Juergens was a master negotiator and by that simple question he had figured out how to manage Mrs. Adams. He felt confident now that he could convince Harriet into keeping the status quo, and he left her to put in their drink request with his secretary.

Even though Harriet's desire to change her contract with Grosset & Dunlap didn't work out the way she would have liked, she had another strategy she would implement in 1952. Her plan would increase the Syndicate's income and get rid of those pesky ghostwriters. Harriet was finding it increasingly difficult to keep them silent regarding their association with the Syndicate and the stories they wrote for the company, despite the frequent reminders of the contracts they all signed to that effect.

September 23, 1952

Dear Edna,

I am writing to discuss a new idea I have been mulling over with Andy. We both agree that the time is right for a change. My idea is this: I want to take over the writing of most of our stories. Not necessarily me personally, though I will probably do more than Andy since, initially, he will be busy with his new Hollister series.

I continue to have issues with writers not following our writing requirements, along with keeping their identities private in relation to the contracts that each of them has signed. Taking on the writing of these stories is the logical thing to do and will take care of both of these problems at one time.

Please think hard over this issue and let me

know your opinion soon. I am going to ask Mildred to do another story in the Nancy series, then I will be taking over that series. I have not been happy with the writers who have written Nancy Drew since Mildred left us in 1948.

Andy is currently writing the Hardy Boys, but I must admit, I have had to do more rewriting on these than I would like, so I am planning on trying William Halstead with the next volume since Leslie McFarlane is too busy making films, of all things, and is no longer able to help us.

I am glad you agreed to let Andy go ahead with "The Happy Hollisters." He thinks he can have three or four volumes done a year. I think that is a bit ambitious, but no reason not to let him try. He will be writing under the name of Jerry West, and he has already signed our standard contract. I'm not sure if I told you but Doubleday publishing liked the outlines of the breeders of the Hollisters, so he's already begun working on the first book. He has also thought of an ingenious way to bring back Tom Swift (the new project I mentioned in my last letter). He wants to create a book around Tom's children and call it Tom Swift Jr. That way they can have similar adventures but in a more modern setting. I think it's a splendid idea.

I don't know if you realize it or not, but we haven't had a new series since my Mel Martin Baseball stories in 1947, which if you remember, we restarted just last year. I expect three more of those to go out this year, as well.

Please let me know what you think of my proposal. I'll have Andy work on outlines for the new Tom Swift Jr. books, and I'll send them your way for approval.

Yours truly,
Harriet

(Spring 1953)

Mildred had just mailed in *The Clue of the Velvet Mask*, book number thirty in the Nancy series and book number twenty-three for Mildred, and she had agreed to do one more of the Dana Girls stories. She had married George Benson in 1950 and had switched over to covering the Toledo courthouse. These events were in addition to continuing her Brownie and Boy Scout series and keeping track of a very active sixteen year old. She was very happy with her current life and felt relieved that she would not be arguing with Harriet Adams much longer.

Edna didn't quibble with Harriet about the idea of eliminating the ghostwriters, unlike her reprimand a year earlier on the purchase of new typewriters and a new dictation system. Harriet supposed this was because Edna realized it was a cost saving measure for the company. So Harriet had her staff start to work up character sheets on the books they currently were running: the Hardy Boys, Nancy Drew, The Honey Bunch, The Happy Hollisters, and the Dana Girls, to be ready for the changeover when the time was right. Nancy, being one of the most popular stories, and one Harriet felt a special bond with, would be the one she would start with first, and she would be the one to write it. *The Ringmaster's Secret* was born that very same year.

But the harmony between the sisters didn't last long. Edna's husband had died in July of 1950, and the younger Camilla was away at college, so Edna's only source of income – the Syndicate – was even more on her mind than it had been. She scrutinized all that Harriet did, keeping a tight hold on the purse strings even to the point of refusing a second time to grant Harriet a raise in salary. This set Harriet on edge. But Christmas was just a month away, and soon Edna and her daughter would be coming to join Harriet's family at their Maplewood, New Jersey home for the holidays. Harriet felt a certain sense of obligation toward her younger sister, despite the years of mistrust Edna had shown toward her. After all, she was her only living relative and aunt to her children. Plus Harriet realized they weren't getting any younger, and Edna, now sixty-two, always had more health issues than Harriet ever did. Who knew what the future would bring. So Harriet sent a letter to Edna to lay it all out in the open in hopes of burying the hatchet once and for all.

Edna opened Harriet's letter and was taken aback at the content.

November 28, 1956

Dear Edna,

In your recent letter you mentioned Christmas and the thought came to me that the best Christmas gift which you could give me would be a change in attitude towards your sister.

Perhaps you are not aware how you have hurt me over a long period of years, sometimes directly, sometimes indirectly. Back in 1942, soon after I had suffered a tragic sorrow [Russell Jr.'s death], you told me that in my whole life I had never done anything for you. Since in my own mind I felt that both Russell and I had done a great deal for you, I told you a few truths. The matter was entirely a personal one and had nothing to do with business, yet I heard from two relatives that you said I had forced you out of the office because I wanted to get the business away from you. That was utterly ridiculous of course. Since that time you have harassed me by suspicious remarks in letters, but even worse by asking secretaries to spy on me...You have been away from the office for fourteen years. In that time I have built up the business from an annual income of 20,000 in 1942 to 115,000 so far this year, yet no recognizance of this has been taken by you.

Now Edna, I bear you no malice for the rift and the hurts, and I hope you will forgive me for any hurts

I have cause you. Let's make this a happy Christmas!
What say?

Your sister,
Harriet

Edna stared at Harriet's letter, read it over a second time. "'I bear you no malice'? And I'm supposed to believe that?" Edna folded the letter with slow, deliberate precision. "A happy Christmas…" She took the paper between her hands and ripped it in half, took it to the trash can, and dropped it inside.

It came as no surprise to Edna when Harriet tried to buy her out of the business a year later. Edna declined that, as well. So business continued on as usual until Harriet was asked to come to Grosset & Dunlap for an important meeting in early 1959.

"Thank you for coming on such short notice, Mrs. Adams," Mr. Juergens said, politely shaking her hand.

Harriet eyed the Grosset & Dunlap company president with some suspicion. She had not had an occasion to meet with him very often, and when they did meet, it was usually regarding some sort of dispute between the Syndicate and the Grosset & Dunlap office. She wasn't looking forward to this meeting.

"Won't you have a seat?" he said, pointing to one of the two wood and leather chairs in front of his expansive, wooden desk.

Mr. Juergens and Ann Hagan – the editor who worked on the Syndicate books – had both risen from their seats when Harriet was ushered into Mr. Juergens' spacious office. Being the head of the venerable and prosperous publishing company came with benefits. Harriet noted that Mr. Juergens' office was twice the size of the office her father once had in Manhattan, and the picture window behind his desk reflected the heights that the company had achieved both literally and figuratively.

Normally Harriet met with only Mr. Juergens or Miss Hagen alone, so Harriet suspected something serious was afoot when she stepped into the room and both were in attendance. And those weren't even all the people in the room; on almost every dark paneled wall there was a figure in a dark suit and tie or cravat, depending on the decade of the man, sitting or standing in matching gilded frames. Grosset & Dunlap's heritage went back even further than the Syndicate's, having put out its first typeset publications in 1898. These mostly serious-looking gentlemen all seemed to be staring directly at Harriet, and it put her even more on edge.

Mr. Juergens cleared his throat.

"I don't want to waste your time, Mrs. Adams, so I will get right to the point.

"You are well aware of the issues we have brought to your attention over the years from readers…well, actually parents of readers who have complained to us about the… let us say outdated references or language used in the older Syndicate stories."

Harriet felt as if the heat in the room had suddenly been

Counter argument

turned up, and she felt herself flush. She had gone over this with Miss Hagan many times over the years, explaining that the use of dialect by any number of nationalities or mimicking the speech of the colored help or villains in the stories did not show disrespect any more than the numerous white villains in those same series. Harriet didn't understand Miss Hagan's point when she tried to explain how these subservient and derogatory positions in the stories would be offensive to those same citizens who, after World War II, were protesting at universities and lunch counters across the South or who had family who had gone through the atrocities of imprisonment, torture, and even death in a war that was still fresh in the memory of many.

"I am well aware of these issues and have addressed them sufficiently at every turn. I really don't think we need to bring this up again."

Mr. Juergens looked at Miss Hagen then leaned on the polished desktop toward Harriet, who sat just opposite him. "Well, part of the issue for us, Mrs. Adams, is the plates that we use to print these older stories are showing significant signs of wear and really need to be redone. It's really quite amazing that they have lasted this long," he said, trying to add some lightness to the news he knew would not be taken well.

"At least for Nancy, it has been as long as I've been running the company," Harriet said with pride. "And it's been even longer for the Hardy Boys."

"Exactly!" Miss Hagan interjected, "and we want to take care of that legacy by bringing those early Nancy and Hardy Boys stories up to the times. I think the girls and boys of today would appreciate that for their favorite heroes and heroine," she said brightly.

Harriet looked at Miss Hagan a moment. The young woman was smartly dressed in what looked to be a navy-blue, cashmere sweater set to match her A-line, navy-blue skirt. It worked perfectly to bring out the color in her brilliant blue eyes. *Not too unlike Nancy*, Harriet thought. Then Harriet caught a glimpse of herself in the large plate glass behind Mr. Juergens' desk. She had worn a dark suit and tight-fitting jacket to mirror the times, but the face that looked back at her could not hide the changes that had occurred, changes that, since taking over the company, seemed to have accelerated her aging process. She was coloring her hair, as all the women her age were doing, but neither the fashionable suit nor the youthful mantle could hide her sixty some years from anyone's view.

Harriet relaxed her hands in her lap. "So what do you propose?"

Mr. Juergens and Miss Hagan looked at each other again. "What we would like you to do is start revisions on both the Nancy and Hardy series, starting with Nancy," Mr. Juergens said.

"Her original stories have the furthest to go as far as fashion and style to bring her up to the times," Ann explained. "That is less of an issue with a boy's story, as you can imagine."

"I've raised two of each, so I do know how different they can be," Harriet said with a strained smile.

Miss Hagan hesitated slightly before she continued. "And we'll work closely with you to ensure that all elements of the stories are up to date: the settings, the speech…really all aspects of the stories."

"And because of the issue with the plates, it's imperative that we get this done in a timely manner," Mr. Juergens said before Harriet could respond. "We need each of the first four volumes of Nancy redone in two weeks' time, Mrs. Adams. We think we can put off printing that long, but no longer. We get new orders for her books every day."

Harriet stared at Mr. Juregens as if she had been slapped.

"How can I possibly rewrite a book in two weeks' time?"

"Well, we've thought about that too," Ann interjected. "We would like the stories cut down from twenty-five chapters to today's more typical twenty. And Mr. Juergens has given me permission to help you with some of the editing, if you would like."

Mr. Juergens leaned back in his chair and smiled, obviously pleased with what he saw as a magnanimous gesture on his part. Harriet didn't smile back, she just stared across the desk in stunned silence.

"I can come to your office, if that would help," Miss Hagan said to try to soften the blow.

Harriet turned toward Miss Hagan. "Thank you, my dear, but I think I'm the only one who knows Nancy well enough."

Harriet looked into the eager faces of Miss Hagan and the Grosset & Dunlap president and sighed. She stood, her mouth set in a firm line. "Well, I guess I have some work to do, then."

Mr. Juergens and Ann stood as well. "Please let me

know what we can do to help," Mr. Juergens said, coming around his desk and extending his hand.

Harriet shook it politely and left without a reply. At sixty-seven Harriet knew this wasn't going to be an easy task, but Nancy was hers now, and she wasn't going to trust her revision to anyone else.

When Harriet got back to the office, she informed Miss Pearson that she didn't want to be disturbed for the rest of the afternoon. She gave her a brief explanation of what had transpired then shut herself in her office. She walked over to the shelf that was dedicated to the Nancy series and pulled off *The Secret of the Old Clock*. The dust jacket showed no signs of its twenty-six years since the office copies were for reference only and thus rarely used. Harriet stared at the blue-eyed blonde in the snug-fitting blue hat, matching blue knee-length dress, and three inch heels, who was walking briskly through the woods with a mantel clock under her arm, her neck scarf trailing behind her. Harriet ran her hand over the figure as if comforting a close friend.

"Well, Papa, I suppose it *is* time to give Nancy a new look." Harriet put the book to her chest and walked over to her desk. "But she's in good hands." She set the book down on her desk and pulled out a sheet of paper and a pen. "She's in good hands."

Twenty-five ∿

Harriet opened up the book to the title page.

"Illustrated by Russell Tandy," Harriet said out loud. "I think he did our illustrations for some time." She flipped through the book to find the first glossy page, a black and white illustration of Nancy in her roadster driving into the Horner sisters' barn, lightning threatening just behind her and Allie Horner standing just inside in an old coat and heels.

She turned back to the front of the book to look over the table of contents. It had been quite a while since Harriet had actually read any of the Nancy stories. She and Edna had both edited Mildred's early Nancy stories, but Harriet had taken over sole responsibility for Nancy well before Edna had left the company in 1942, and she had not left the final edits to anyone but herself since. So Harriet was familiar with the various characters in Nancy's stories, but the plots of the early stories were only a distant memory. Per their father's direction, characters in the various Syndicate series fared much better with their youthful reading audience if they never saw a gray hair in the mirror or wore a ring on their finger. Over time, Nancy had been aged from sixteen to the driving age of eighteen (the roadster now a sleek, blue convertible), but Joe and Frank were still fifteen and sixteen respectively.

But the boys would have to wait. Nancy would be the first to get pulled into the present decade.

Harriet sighed, looking at the Roman numerals that listed the chapter titles. Cutting the chapters from twenty-five to twenty was going to be a trick, but it had to be done.

She started reading the first chapter – *The Will* – taking notes as she went, listing the characters as they appeared or were mentioned in the story, adding obvious changes that had to be made for the revised edition:

> *Chapter 1: The Will (10 pages)*
> *Nancy - 16 years old (change to 18)*
> *Carson Drew - father, criminal lawyer, mystery-*
> *solver, former D.A. (change horn-rimmed*
> *spectacles)*
> *Richard Topham family - first in line for Josiah*
> *Crowley's fortune.*
> *Wife Cora - "vapid social climber" (tone this*
> *down)*
> *Daughter Isabel - "stuck-up"*
> *Daughter Ada - ill tempered*
> *Josiah Crowley (J.C.) - deceased, wife died*

following world war influenza epidemic
(change or eliminate war notation)
Two girls that were "pets" of the Crowleys
and other un-named relatives that should have been
named but weren't.
  Henry Rolsted - J.C.'s attorney who specializes in
wills

After Harriet read the chapter, she wrote down a brief synopsis.

Nancy doesn't like the Tophams getting
J.Crowley's money. It was rumored he was going to
change his will but the one found after his death gave
everything to the Tophams. Nancy's father mentions
he overheard J. Crowley and H. Rolsted talking about
a new will. Nancy convinces her father to talk with
Mr. Rolsted about a second will.

Harriet put down her pen and picked up the book again, leafing through the first chapter as she thought about what to do to change it. She read the beginning page.

"It would be a shame if all that money went to
the Tophams! They will fly higher than ever!"
  Nancy Drew, a pretty girl of sixteen, leaned over
the library table and addressed her father who sat
reading a newspaper by the study lamp.

"I beg your pardon, Nancy. What were you saying about the Tophams?"

Carson Drew, a noted criminal and mystery-case lawyer, known far and wide for his work as a former District Attorney, looked up from his evening paper and smiled indulgently upon his only daughter...

"It does seem to be a rather abrupt beginning, talking about the will right away," Harriet said. "I wonder if there is a way to ease into the story more but not make it any longer." Harriet wrote *soften beginning* on her notepad, then flipped to chapter 2.

Chapter 2: A Chance Meeting (12 pages)
Hannah Gruen - elderly maid,
    (make Hannah more motherly)
Helen Corning - Nancy's friend
    (change blue roadster and reference to
    Topham sisters as stupid)

Nancy's father invites her to a luncheon with Mr. Rolsted. She has to pick up a dress first and meets the disagreeable Topham sisters. Mr. Rolsted tells them that J. Crowley wanted to make a new will and cut the Tophams out. He was planning on making the will himself but Mr. Rolsted never saw it. Other relatives have filed a claim to Crowley's money, but without the second will, there is little chance they'll get it. Nancy decides to find the second will.

Harriet turned her attention to chapter three.

Chapter 3: Racing the Storm (9 pages)

There were only two new characters in this chapter: Judge Hartgrave, who Nancy was delivering a package to in Masonville for her father; and an un-named girl, who was standing in a barn on River Road. Nancy had decided to take a scenic drive home along the Muskoka River, that is, until a terrible rainstorm forced her off the road. This girl tells Nancy her sister is Grace, but doesn't mention Grace's last name or her own name. Harriet wrote this all down and read right into chapter 4 – *An Interesting Story* – so she could find out the mysterious girl's name. *How clever of Father to not tell the reader her name until the next chapter*, she thought.

She read on and added Grace and Allie Horner to her character list. She also made notes to change a few things related to the sisters and how they lived.

(change wood stove to oil)
Grace and Allie's farm is "a few acres" and they have a garden
Grace is a seamstress. Allie raises chickens.

"Two young women farming would be unlikely nowadays, but I would guess the chickens can stay."

Harriet read over chapter 3 where the caretaker helps Nancy out of the closet the robbers locked her into.

"Ah, here is some of the dialect they want me to change."

Frantically, Nancy rattled the door knob.

"Oh, you is a caged lion, dis time," a rather unsteady voice remarked. "You is one o'deses tough robber boys, is you? Well, you won't do no mo' pilferrin', cause I done got you surrounded."

"Let me out!" Nancy pleaded. "I'm not a robber!"

The sound of a feminine voice coming from the closet nonplussed the man.

"Say, robber boy, is you imitatin' a lady's voice to th'o me off de scent? If you is, it won't do no good 'cause I's a natural-born, two-legged blood hound."

Nancy thought of a way to convince him. She let go her longest and loudest feminine scream.

Harriet pursed her lips and put her chin in her hand, mulling over the page. "I don't want to cut him out completely, but if I made him white, I could more easily change the dialect to something less…less severe, then I would be killing two birds with one stone," Harriet said with a self-satisfied grin, and she wrote herself a note to that effect.

Harriet read into the next chapter to find that not only was Jeff Tucker colored but Mildred, (or her father, she couldn't be sure which) had made the man drunk.

"I guess I can see how someone might take exception to that, though a person certainly doesn't have to be colored to like the bottle. I suppose that's what father was thinking. Or perhaps he thought of it was an easy way for the caretaker to be bamboozled by the robbers. I think it works quite well, but

I'll have to check with Miss Hagan on that point, I suppose," Harriet said with a sigh.

Harriet finished reading the chapter and wrote down a synopsis.

> *Allie takes Nancy inside to meet her sister Grace. Nancy can tell they are poor by their surroundings but they still keep the place looking nice. Grace is making a cake and shares it with Nancy. They talk about their old neighbor, J.Crowley. They call him "Uncle." He told the sisters he was going to mention them in his will. Nancy suggests the girls tell her father what they know. The girls agree.*

Harriet read on, noting how the Horner sisters remembered that Josiah had said that he had made a new will and had hid it somewhere but didn't tell them where. Nancy overhears the Topham girls talking about another will, illustrating their anxiety about it and that they obviously hadn't found it and destroyed it. Abigail is very poor, as well, but remembered seeing it, plus a notebook that told where the will was kept. Nancy thinks it has something to do with Mr. Crowley's clock, so she goes about trying to find it. Nancy is able to get into the Topham home on the ruse of selling charity dance tickets. She finds out that Josiah's clock was moved to their cottage on Moon Lake, the same lake Nancy's friend Helen invited her to.

Nancy goes to Moon Lake, has a rousing good time with the girls at the camp, and manages to sneak into the Topham bungalow, which is being robbed. Nancy gets stuck in a closet by the robbers but gets herself out. She follows the robbers and is able to get the clock back from them – notebook and all – plus catch the robbers at the same time. What a girl!

Harriet added ten more characters to her growing list: Josiah's cousins, Matilda and Edna Turner of Masonville and nephews William and Fred Mathews, who live on a farm five miles from the Horner sisters on River Road; Abigail Rowen, a woman on West Lake Road who takes care of Mr. Crowley when he is sick; Jeff Tucker, who is the colored caretaker of the Topham bungalow on Moon Lake; and the police marshal of the town of Melborne, who helps Nancy catch the three un-named robbers of the Topham bungalow.

There was a soft knock on Harriet's office door.

"Come in," Harriet called out.

Miss Pearson stuck her head in the door. "I didn't want to disturb you, Ma'am, but I was wondering if you'd like some tea."

Harriet set down her pen and stretched her shoulders back. "Tea would be wonderful, Agnes. Thank you."

Miss Pearson pushed open the door fully, revealing a tray already filled. She set it down on a small cupboard close to Harriet's desk. She filled the delicate china cup, put in a half spoonful of sugar, stirred it in, and placed a small biscuit on the saucer next to it. She set the cup on the desk next to Harriet's papers.

"What would I do without you, Agnes?"

"I think you'd manage," she said with a smile. She stood

and watched as Harriet took her first sip. "Is there anything else I can get you, Mrs. Adams?"

"I don't think so." Harriet set her cup down and looked at her watch. "My. It's half past four already." She picked up her notepad and leafed through the pages she had so far. "With this old story fresh in my mind, I am going to work on an outline for revision right away. Would you mind calling my husband and telling him I won't be home for dinner?"

"Of course," Miss Pearson said, stepping toward the door.

"And before you go, send out for some of that wonderful Chinese food you ordered a couple weeks ago. I think it's my new favorite."

"Cashew chicken?" Miss Pearson asked before she left the room.

"Wonderful!"

The soft aroma of the chamomile filled Harriet's nostrils as she stared at her notes and slowly sipped her tea. She brought out a new notepad and wrote *The Secret of the Old Clock -Revision* across the top.

"I need a new beginning," Harriet said to herself. "Let's see…" She scanned the list of characters again and lit on Edna and Matilda Turner.

"I know! I'll bring the Turner sister into the first chapter. I think the name Edna is fine, but Matilda is a bit dated." She thought a brief moment then crossed out Matilda and wrote in *Mary* beside it.

"Now…the sisters have to be doing something worthy to get Josiah's attention, but what could it be?"

Harriet crinkled her eyes in thought. "How about if they were taking care of their niece or maybe great-niece – I'll have to figure out the ages later. Yes, that's it. The girl's parents died and the sisters are taking care of her with Josiah's help."

Harriet wrote her idea down in the new notepad and sat back in her chair, smiling with self-satisfaction.

"Now to get Nancy in on this."

Harriet took a moment or two more and hastily wrote down her next idea.

The girl (Jamie or Judy) is playing outside and runs in front of Nancy's car.

"No, no, not Nancy's car. I don't want Nancy to almost hit the girl." Harriet crossed out Nancy's name and wrote *a moving van*, then continued her train of thought.

The girl runs in front of the van and right off the edge of a steep drop. Nancy rescues her and brings her into the sisters, who tell Nancy their story including that Josiah was going to give them something in his will.

"There, that's an easy way to set up the story line. Now let's see…chapter 2 has to incorporate what went on in chapter 1 in the old book. I don't think there is any way in getting around that. Nancy's father has to be brought in on the whole thing and has to set up the luncheon with the lawyer, Mr. Rolsted. That all has to stay."

Harriet picked up the first notepad and circled the chapter 1 synopsis and wrote *Keep for chapter 2 of new story* in the margin. She then read the synopsis for chapter 2. "I don't think I can cut this either. I like how it introduces the Topham sisters and illustrates how ill-tempered they are."

Opening the book to chapter 2, Harriet paged through it until she came to the part where Nancy enters the department store, looking for a dress for an afternoon party.

"I don't think girls dress for afternoon parties nowadays. I'll have to change that in the new story."

Harriet wrote down *Nancy is buying a dress for an evening formal.* Then as an afterthought she wrote *perhaps a fundraiser for local children.*

Harriet read further. "Let's see...Ada throws down a gown she was looking at and steps on it as she and her sister, Isabel, leave.... How about if she ends up damaging it, or better yet, the good citizen that Nancy is, she picks up the gown and Ada tries to take it from her and rips it, then Ada blames it on Nancy. Yes, that works. It shows what a conscientious girl Nancy is and what a nasty girl Ada is.

Harriet wrote her ideas down. *Then Nancy offers to buy the dress, assuming it will be reduced in price.* "It shows how practical Nancy is," Harriet said, obviously pleased with what she had come up with so far.

"Add in the luncheon with Mr. Rolsted and chapter 3 is complete, so on to chapter 4."

In the original story, Nancy delivers the package to Mr. Hartgrave, then gets caught in a rainstorm, escaping at the last minute in the barn of the Horner sisters.

"I don't like the names Hartgrave or Horner." On the note pad with the new outline, Harriet wrote down under chapter 4: *Judge Hart* and *Allison and Grace Hoover.* "But I think the rest can stay."

Harriet wrote a note: *Use chapter 3 of old story.*

"I'm not cutting things down yet," Harriet said with some dismay. "I need to cut things out somewhere here." She hastily paged through the next chapter in the book. "But I can't very well do it here. She just arrives at the Horner, no Hoover sisters' house, so I have to keep that as well."

Harriet dropped back in her chair, obvious strain on her face, when there was a knock on the door. It opened slowly, seemingly pushed by the sweet, spicy smell of chicken and cashews, flash cooked and covered in a flavorful, syrupy sauce. It pulled Harriet out of her chair and over to the tray, but it was Patricia Doll carrying the tray, not Agnes. This dish was laid out on china with an accompanying pot of warm tea and a fortune cookie on a small saucer for dessert.

"Where did Agnes go?"

"She had to run home. Her mother is having some issues, so I said I'd bring in the tray. I was staying late to finish up on a few things anyway. Will you be eating at your desk? Miss Doll asked.

"Oh...Yes. Let me move my things."

Harriet hurried back to her desk and picked up the two notepads, the book, and miscellaneous papers and put them off to one side.

"This is a welcome reprieve. I don't know if Agnes told you but we've been asked to modernize the old Nancy Drew and Hardy Boys stories, and in addition cut them back from twenty-five chapters to twenty. I'm working on the first Nancy book, but so far, all I've managed to do is make it longer."

Miss Doll hesitated, "Could you use some help? Nancy is one of my favorite characters."

The cloth napkin was halfway to Harriet's lap when she was frozen in place. "Really? That would be wonderful. But I hate to impose on new staff. Though I should tell you, you seem to be catching on quite well to how we do things around here."

"Thank you," Patricia said with a smile.

Harriet placed her napkin on her lap and reached over to her papers. "Well, if you want to take a look," she said, shoving the pile toward the eager-looking woman. Patricia picked up the papers and sat in one of the wooden chairs in front of Harriet's desk. "There is one notepad with the old story laid out and the start of an outline for the new story on the other."

Patricia looked at the original story outline first then reviewed what Harriet had so far on the new one.

"I like how you started the new story out. I agree that the beginning of the old story could be improved upon."

Miss Doll stopped her critique when she realized she was disparaging her employer's father. She stared at Harriet, but her boss hadn't even looked up from her meal. Patricia let out a quiet sigh and looked back at the papers, studying them another few minutes before she spoke again.

"May I look at the book?"

Harriet dabbed at her mouth and finished chewing before she responded. "By all means," she said and shoved the book toward Miss Doll. She looked through the book and then at the notepad that outlined the chapters of the original story.

"I'm going to try something," Patricia said and got up and left the room, notepads in hand.

Soon Harriet heard the rat-a-tat of Miss Pearson's typewriter, and not five minutes later Patricia was back in the room. She handed Harriet a piece of paper.

"This is splendid!" Harriet said, as she set down her cup of tea and looked more closely at the paper.

Miss Doll had made two lists, side by side on the paper. On the left was a list of the original book chapters with a four- to five-word description. On the right were the four chapters of the updated book and blanks left for the rest.

The Secret of the Old Clock

Chapter	Original Version	New Version
1	Nancy and Carson D.	Judy, Mary, Edna, Turner
2	Topham sisters, Mr. Rolsted	Nancy and Carson D.
3	Mr. R., Judge H., rain	Topham sister, Mr. R.
4	Horner sister' story	Mr. R. Judge H., rain
5	H. sisters visit C.D.	
6	T. sisters break vase	
7	T. sisters talk about will	
8	Nancy visit Horner & Turner sisters, F. & W. Mathews	
9	Nancy visits Abigail Rowen	

"It will make it so much easier to see where I'm at and where I need to go!"

"As I was typing the list, I noticed that in chapter 6, Nancy has another run-in with the Topham sisters over a broken vase. I think that would be an easy chapter to cut, since she already has had an incident with them over the dress."

"Wonderful!" Harriet looked at the list again. "Then I can have the Horner sisters talk to Carson Drew in chapter 6 of the new version."

Harriet handed the paper back to Patricia. "Would you mind writing that in for me while I finish my meal?"

"Of course."

"So that leaves more room in chapter 6 for something else," Harriet said between bites. "I was trying to think of something else for the sisters to do besides farm. I think farming would be impractical for two young girls nowadays. Any ideas?"

"Right. If I'm remembering correctly, doesn't Grace Horner sew?"

"You're right," Harriet said, pointing her fork at Patricia. "Nancy can order a dress from Grace. That's a way for her to give them money without it being charity! Nancy wouldn't want to degrade the sisters' pride by offering them money," Harriet said as if Nancy were a real person she knew personally.

"Do the sisters have any other talents?" Patricia asked.

"Allison – which I'm changing to Allie, by the way, to modernize it a bit – she raises chickens."

"That seems reasonable for farm girls."

"I agree."

Both women sat still for a moment in thought.

"How about singing? I know music is very popular with the kids these days," Harriet said. "My daughters are always telling me about the latest singers: Frank Sinatra, Pat Boone…and who is that fellow from the South all the young girls swoon over?"

"Elvis Presley."

"Yes! That's him."

"That's a good idea."

"The sisters are baking a cake in that chapter. I'll have it be a birthday cake so they have to sing Happy Birthday, then Nancy will see how good Grace can sing and that can be something else she can do for them in chapter 6, set up a visit with a voice instructor."

Miss Doll wrote in the additions to the new chapter 5 and chapter 6 and handed the paper back to Harriet.

"Well, now we're back to dead even, because the new chapter 7 has to be the same as the old. That's where Nancy learns the Tophams don't have the old will," Harriet said, a bit disappointed.

"I agree. That's a critical piece of information,"

Harriet pushed her mostly empty plate away from her and studied the lists. "Nancy hasn't checked back in with the Turner sisters and little Judy yet. I would guess chapter 7 is where she ought to do that."

"Can the Turner sisters tell her about Fred and William Mathews and Abigail Rowen? That way, in the new chapter 8, she can visit both. "

Harriet sat upright. "Brilliant idea!"

Harriet wrote in the additions to the new chapter 7 and 8.

3	Mr. R., Judge H., rain	Topham sisters, Mr. R.
4	Horner sisters' story	Mr. R., Judge H., rain
5	H. sisters visit C.D.	*Hoover (Horner) sisters' story, dress order, sing*
6	T. sisters break vase	*Singing teacher, H. sisters visit C.D.*
7	T. sister talk about will	*Topham sister talk about will, visit Turners*
8	Nancy visits H. and Turner sisters, F. & W. Mathews	*N. visits F. & W. Mathews & Abigail Rowen*
9	Nancy visits Abigail Rowen	
10	Abigail remembers clock, Helen's ticket	

"And look!" Harriet said, handing Patricia the lists. "I'm finally ahead one chapter!"

"I would guess you'd have to leave chapter 10 intact."

"Yes, Abigail has to have trouble remembering about Josiah hiding something in the clock, and Nancy has to have an excuse to visit the Tophams so she can find that they sent the clock to their bungalow on Moon Lake."

"The same place Helen Corning just happened to invite Nancy to."

Harriet smiled at the obvious coincidence. "Indeed."

Miss Doll added the appropriate notations to the fast-growing list of new chapters and showed the new list to Harriet. "You don't think there is too much in chapter 10, do you?" Patricia asked.

"I've got to cut four more chapters, dear. I'll make it work!"

Miss Doll perused the list. "Don't you think we can cut Nancy's time at the camp down a bit?"

"I would agree. I thought the same thing myself," Harriet said, pointing to the notes she made about the original version. "We should be able to fit all of that into one or two chapters, plus having Nancy arrive at the Tophams' bungalow."

Patricia added the changes.

"You're three chapters ahead now!" Miss Doll said with glee.

Harriet paged through her notes. "So we only have two more chapters to cut," Harriet said, scanning the notes feverishly to find something she could eliminate. "Here! I made a note to have Nancy find the clock and the robbers all in one chapter."

"That sounds doable, and you're going to leave the two chapters at the bungalow as is?"

"Right."

"But don't you think she can get out of the closet in the same chapter as she is found?"

"I don't see why not."

Patricia amended the running list and handed it back to Harriet.

"And if she finds the clock and they arrest the robbers all in one chapter, we only have one more chapter to delete." Harriet said with some satisfaction. She handed the paper back to Miss Doll, who started to fill in the blanks. A broad grin brightened her face as she hastily finished her task.

"I hate to contradict you, Mrs. Adams," Patricia said, trying without much luck to portray a somber countenance. "But you're not down one chapter." She handed the paper to Harriet, no longer able to hold in her excitement. "You aren't down by any!"

7	T. sisters talk about will	*Topham sisters talk about will, visits Turners*
8	Nancy visits H. & Turner sisters, F. & W. Mathews	*N. visits F. & W. Mathews & Abigail Rowen*
9	Nancy visits Abigail Rowen	*Abigail remembers clock, Helen's tickets*
10	Abigail remembers clock, Helen's tickets	*N. visits Topham, visits the sisters, Moon Lake*
11	Nancy visits Topham	*Boat engine trouble, N. leaves, visits bungalow*
12	N. visits H. sisters, arrives at Moon Lake	*Nancy gets locked in*
13	More Moon Lake, boat engine trouble	*Nancy is found and gets out*
14	Leaves camp, visits bungalow	*Nancy and Jeff go to police*
15	Nancy gets locked in	*N. finds robbers and clock*
16	Nancy is found	*Nancy finds notebook, robbers arrested*
17	N. gets out and leaves with Jeff for police	*Nancy and D.C. read notebook*
18	Nancy and police, Nancy finds the robbers	*They find the will*
19	Nancy finds the clock	*Read will to all*
20	Nancy finds the notebook	*Nancy visits H. sisters, gets clock*
21	Robbers are caught	
22	N. and D. Carson read the notebook	
23	They find the will	
24	Reading of the will	
25	Nancy visits H. sisters, gets clock	

"How did you do it?" Harriet exclaimed.

"I just moved events a little closer together and it all worked!"

"How wonderful!" Harriet said and stood, extending her hand to her assistant. Miss Doll looked at the professional gesture a second before she took Harriet's hand. At the same moment her stomach growled.

"Oh, I'm sorry."

Harriet looked at her watch. "Well, look at the time. It's seven o'clock. No wonder you're hungry. You should get on home and make yourself some dinner."

"Yes. I think you're right."

Harriet walked with her secretary to her office door, then touched her arm. "Thank you again, Patricia."

"I'm just doing my job."

"Well, you went above and beyond this time," Harriet said. "And you'll be paid for the extra time you spent with me, to be sure."

"Thank you, Mrs. Adams."

Harriet hesitated, as if she was thinking something over. "Patricia…"

"You can call me Pat."

"All right. Pat, how would you like to do the revisions on the next two Nancy stories. I think you have a good feel for the work, and it would speed up the editing and rewrite process for me."

"I'd be happy to."

"Splended!" Harriet went over to her bookcase behind

her desk and pulled out *The Hidden Staircase* and *The Bungalow Mystery* and handed them to Harriet. "If you could start on *The Hidden Staircase* in the next week or so. That will give me time to work on the rewrites for the Old Clock story, then we can go from there."

Harriet started walking back to her desk but turned around again. "And don't forget to write up the release forms for us to sign."

"For you, too?"

"I'm no different than any of our writers."

"Oh, I don't think that's true," Pat said.

"Well, thank you, dear, but we have to make sure Nancy's readers never find out who the real Carolyn Keene is."

"Even though we know who she is," Pat said with a wry smile

"Yes, even though we know very well who she is."

It took Harriet two weeks each to finish the outlines, and manipulate the text for the *Old Clock* story and Nancy's next three adventures: *The Hidden Staircase*, the *Bungalow Mystery,* and *The Mystery at Lilac Inn,* to get them where Miss Hagan at Grosset & Dunlap wanted them.

In *The Secret of the Old Clock* in addition to cutting down on the dialect of the caretaker, Harriet was asked to make the man white. And Harriet was correct in her assumption that Miss Hagan didn't like the fact that the now white caretaker was drunk, even though Harriet argued for the legitimacy of the ploy within the story plot. Instead, Miss Hagan suggested that the man be tricked into going into the tool shed and getting locked in. Harriet still didn't see the need for the change. *As if there wasn't a drunk on every corner of every town in the United States*, Harriet thought. But she kept her opinion to herself. When Miss Hagan argued for the sensitivity of the children and the characters they should be reading about, Harriet could see her point. Harriet took great pains in keeping Nancy out of the more unseemly side of life. This and the fact that Miss Hagan's suggested change did work well enough for the story and allowed them to cut out some of the dialogue between Nancy and the caretaker.

In addition to the revisions, keeping up with what Andy Svenson was working on – The Happy Hollisters, The Bobbsey Twins, and the yet to be released Bret King – and continuing to expand the market that Nancy, the Hardy Boys, Tom Swift Jr., and The Bobbsey Twins were in, she had to come up with a new Nancy story for the spring of the next year, which Harriet titled *The Secret of the Golden Pavilion*. Nancy's adventure was to take place in Hawaii because Harriet had read in the paper that 1959 was the year that President Dwight D. Eisenhower was to accept the set of islands in the Polynesian archipelago as the fiftieth state in the Union. Harriet had been to Hawaii just the year before and knew at some point that it would be a location for one of the Syndicate stories. Unlike most people, Harriet knew that Hawaii wasn't already a state, but just a territory of the United States. In fact, Harriet had a cousin that was married to a territorial senator.

Much to her sister's dismay, Harriet hired on more staff. The Syndicate was up to eleven total now – most being ghostwriters. Harriet justified her hiring because of the aggressive revision schedule and her fairly routine absences during her research trips to Africa, Europe, or East Asia.

Twenty-six ∽

(1959)

Harriet wasn't the only busy working girl; Mildred had thrown herself even deeper into her work at the *Toledo Blade* after George died of a stroke that same year. She was the court reporter for the paper, but she also wrote such stories as, "New Treasure Found in Lost City of Mayas: Old Stone May Solve Mysteries," in June, 1960 after one of her archeology trips to Central America; and "Pat Worth Waiting for, Station Crowd Indicates" about Pat and Richard Nixon's visit to Toledo on Richard Nixon's campaign visit. Mildred also did a piece called "Cooking in a Radiation Shelter Found Easy Once You've Mastered Tricks" in 1961 when she went to her own kitchen and tried to make some dehydrated food. As with many of Mildred's culinary attempts, it didn't turn out so well, something she even admitted in the article, "My hope is that if war does come, a strenuous effort will be made to spare the hens."

Mildred had also fulfilled a dream she had been fostering for almost fifty years.

The gentleman in the leather jacket with the Federal Aviation Association patch on his shoulder held out his hand to Mildred as they stood next to the open door of the Cessna 150, a two-seat plane with wings that ran out directly from above the cockpit and spanned a little over thirty-three feet. Its single central propeller was run by a 100 horsepower engine and cruised at 120 miles per hour, all facts Mildred knew well after passing her written exam the week before. Now she was at the Wagon Wheel Airport just across the border in Indiana for her flight check. She and the FAA examiner had walked through the outside plane inspection and now she was ready to take flight.

"Aren't you a women's libber?" she asked, looking at the polite gesture.

The man dropped his hand. "My wife wishes I were, but my dad was a stickler for respect for women. It's a hard habit to break."

"I can't argue for respect for women, but I was what they now call a women's libber well before it became a thing to be. I was the first woman to graduate with a Master of Journalism from the University of Iowa in 1927, and I've worked as a journalist for the Toledo Times for twenty years."

"Well, I have to admit, I can count on one hand the number of women that I've taken up for their pilot's flight check, let alone someone of your..." The young man stopped himself when he realized what he was about to say.

"You were about to say, my age," Mildred said with a playful smile. "And I'll take that as a compliment."

Mildred stepped up to the door of the plane and boosted herself inside with little effort. The young man got in on the other side.

"So let's go over the checklist," the examiner suggested.

Mildred looked over the instrument panel in front of her. There were dials and gauges both in front of her and the examiner. Mildred ticked off the checklist out loud: "Ignition, on both; Master, on; Throttle, cracked; Mixture, rich; Fuel, both; Brakes, set."

"Good. Go ahead and start 'er up," the young man said.

Mildred primed the engine then turned the key. The engine slowly turned over, as did the propeller, then both quickly made it up to speed. The drone of the engine was loud enough that the examiner had to yell his next request. "Go ahead and start your taxi."

The plane cautiously moved forward and stopped just short of the runway. Mildred completed her preflight check, which included checking the magnetos and carburetor heat, and checking to make sure the controls, navigation instruments, fuel selector, and flaps were set for takeoff. Everything was working as expected, so Mildred turned onto the runway. They sat idling, facing down the long expanse of short cropped grass until Mildred pushed the throttle forward and the already loud engine roared like a caged lion. Moving down the runway, grass passing exponentially faster in her peripheral vision until it was all a green blur, a smile spread across Mildred's face. It happened every time and was the reason she was getting her license in the first place. She was nine again, an oversized leather flying cap on her head was flapping in the wind that whipped at her face and forced her into a squint. Mildred had first heard the roar of the plane's engine as she sat reading on her front porch on a warm summer's day. She instantly looked up to see the canary-yellow biplane circle her small hometown of Ladora and land not one hundred feet from their back porch. Mildred ran up to the pilot as he was getting out of the open, two-seated biplane.

"You got trouble?" Mildred asked.

The man put his goggles on his forehead and looked down at the young girl in rolled up jeans and a simple white blouse. "Nope, just takin' a break."

The man walked over to a grove of trees and disappeared behind a large oak, only to appear a minute later and head right back to his plane. Mildred offered him a drink from their well, which the pilot gratefully accepted.

"You ever take passengers?" Mildred asked as she watched him guzzle down the tin of water as if he had just crossed the Mojave Desert.

"Sometimes...for a price."

"What might that price be?" she pressed.

The pilot didn't hesitate. He wasn't sure he wanted to take up this young girl, so he thought if he put the cost high enough, he'd be off the hook and on his way.

"Fifteen dollars," he said then took another drink, watching Mildred out of the corner of his eye.

She hardly flinched. Mildred ran into the house and was back out in a matter of minutes. She stuffed the wad of one dollar bills and miscellaneous change into the pilot's hands. "Fifteen exactly," she said in triumph.

The pilot looked at Mildred in surprise, realizing he hadn't put the fee high enough. He was stuck now as he looked into her earnest, blue-green eyes. So he put Mildred in the front seat, buckled her in, and put his flying cap on her head.

It was all instantly back, the same broad smile, the lightness of heart, the freedom to soar like a bird with real wings as the plane raced down the runway. Mildred eased back on the yoke, aiming for the blue expanse that would loosen her tether to the earth and free her soul as it did each and every time she went up.

As with the other ghostwriters, Mildred was also starting to tell a few people about her work for the Syndicate. It wasn't something she did intentionally; people were seeking her out. Frank Paluka at her old alma mater, the University of Iowa, wrote her a letter in 1964. He was the head of the Special Collections department at the university and they were putting together a biography of some of the authors in the university's special Iowa Author's Collection and, of course, Mildred Augustine Wirt Benson came up on his list. Mildred had already been contacted in 1953 by the university. They were amassing a collection of books by Iowa writers and someone had given them Mildred's name. When they asked her what books she would be contributing, Mildred wasn't even sure how many books she had penned.

As for a list of my books, that will take some effort, as recently I've not bothered to keep track of them. At last count the number stood somewhere between 125 to 130...

Mildred also thought it was probably a good idea to have a list written down somewhere since, as of yet, there wasn't an accurate list anywhere, a fact for which Harriet Stratemeyer and Walter Karig were both partially responsible.

There never has been a complete listing of my books anywhere. The Library of Congress attempted to do it a number of years ago. However, the Stratemeyer Syndicate for which I did considerable work in such series as Nancy Drew, Kay Tracey etc., under pen names copyrighted by them, objected to any listing except in their name, and the library agreed to this. I wrote the books, and I think it might be well to have my complete list somewhere on record, as the Nancy Drew volumes in particular have been claimed by persons who had practically no connection with the series.

In 1937 Karig had asked the Library of Congress to credit the books he had written for the Syndicate to him. The Library contacted Harriet about his request, and she convinced them that neither Karig nor Wirt were the authors of any of the Syndicate stories (and per the contracts they signed, they could not claim to be). Unlike Karig, Mildred was well aware of this contractual obligation when she wrote to Mr. Paluka.

When I was young, they induced me to sign a release of all right[s] to the pen name, title, etc. As a result, there is today no published list of authors. I include this for informational purposes only, not to be used as a published statement.

Mildred wasn't looking to publicize this fact. Harriet had complained to her about what Walter Karig had done, so she knew better than to try and buck the contracts she had signed with the Syndicate. A contract was a contract; she couldn't argue that she hadn't signed the papers, ignorance of youth and inexperience notwithstanding. It still irritated Mildred that no one knew she had written all those books for the Syndicate. *At least it is going to be down in writing somewhere,* she thought, and she gave the university a detailed listing of *all* of the books she had penned under her name or someone else's.

what about the artrcle in the Times?

Twenty-seven ∿

(1964)

There was a tentative knock on Harriet's office door.

"Come in," Harriet said, putting down her blue pencil and the typed revised manuscript of the Nancy Drew book, *The Whispering Statue*. Harriet was pleased that she had fourteen of the Nancy stories revised so far, and ten of the Hardy Boys in the eight years since the Syndicate started the revision process. Harriet had the ghostwriters working on the revisions of the Hardy Boys and The Bobbsey Twins, but she didn't trust anyone with Nancy's revisions other than herself. Her conviction that she had done the right thing came in 1964 when *Mademoiselle* magazine ran a twelve page piece on Nancy, touting Nancy as "the girl girls have adored for the past 34 year…But no matter what her age, criminal lawyer Carson Drew's own intrepid, blue-eyed, blond-haired, indefatigable daughter, Nancy, of River Heights (state unidentified) has, from the moment of her first appearance, exhilarated all girl readers—and some of their brothers."

"Can I bother you?" Andy Svenson said, sticking his head in through the open door. Andy had tried to leave Harriet mostly to herself of late. It was not that long ago that she had come back to the office after the death of her husband and had thrown herself back into her work. He imagined work was a good tonic for her, but she was seventy-four and he wasn't sure how the news he had to share was going to affect her. Andy sat down in front of her desk and set the book he was carrying in front of her.

She picked it up and read the title. "*My Father Was Uncle Wiggly* by Roger Garis," Harriet said with some surprise. She opened the hardcover book and leafed through it. "I didn't know Roger was doing this. What a nice tribute to his father."

"Well...take a look at the page I bookmarked," Andy said with some unease. He had failed to note a section where Roger quoted an article that called the books Edward Stratemeyer produced "junk," saying they were written by "anonymous hacks." He knew better than that. He just had to make sure Harriet didn't read the rest of the book and find it. Of course, Roger disagreed with these terms, since he and his father were both one of those hacks, writing that junk, but Andrew knew that didn't matter. It would set Harriet off nonetheless.

Harriet found the scrap of white paper Andy had used to mark the page and started reading the section he had underlined. The passage told of how Howard wrote under a pseudonym and that he wrote from Edward Stratemeyer's "sketchy" outline that sometimes he followed and sometimes he didn't.

"This is disturbing, indeed," she said, shaking her head. "His father signed a contract not to disclose his relationship to the Syndicate, just like the other writers! Roger knows this as well as his parents did. Roger signed the contract too when *he* started working for Father," she said, her face visibly reddening. "His mother worked on The Bobbsey Twins and a few others, I think. Come to think of it, his sister Cleo wrote for Father, as well."

Harriet bunched up her lips in frustration. "Can we take him to court?"

"I have no idea. The only consolation is that the book probably will have a very small audience."

"Nonetheless, I'm going to contact our lawyers on the matter," Harriet said as she reached for the intercom. "Miss Pearson, get Max Krup on the phone for me."

"Yes, ma'am."

Andy had been thinking for some time about this anonymity issue related to the Syndicate writers, so he thought he might as well bring it up. He suspected Harriet couldn't stay in charge of the Syndicate much longer, and once she was gone, she would have less say in the matter. He thought his idea was a sound one and should be mentioned. In 1961 Andy had finally been made a partner in the Syndicate, something he had negotiated from the start. He was to gain a 5% stake in the company every five years of his employment, and at this point he had been working for the Syndicate for eighteen years, so currently he had a 15% share. This was less than the 37.5% that each sister owned, but he was a partner nonetheless, and he wanted to do what was best for the company, even if he had to push (or was it drag) the obvious head of the company beyond what she would consider her better judgment. Still, in eighteen years, Andy had learned a thing or two about negotiating with Harriet Adams.

"What do you think of finally telling the public about our ghostwriters?" he said in a very even tone – no purposeful dragging apparent in his voice or his manner.

Harriet looked at Mr. Svenson and dropped her shoulders.

Miss Pearson's voice interrupted her thoughts. "Mrs. Adams, Mr. Krup is out of the office today. Would you like to talk with his associate?"

Harriet pushed the intercom button. "No...no. Just find out when he'll be back and I'll try him then."

Harriet turned her attention back to Mr. Svenson and worked the fingers in her hands before she replied to his suggestion. She let out an audible sigh. "I *am* tired of this fight."

"If *you* come out with the information, then you'll have control of what the public hears. If you wait for someone to, say...interview Roger Garis, then Roger will have the first say, and first trumps correct every time."

"True." Harriet picked up a pen and softly tapped it on her desktop. "I actually had a woman from Life magazine contact me just the other day. She wants to do an article on The Bobbsey Twins."

Andy smiled. "Perfect! That would give you a chance to set the record straight about Howard Garis' involvement!"

"Or not. I could say that we had writers working on The Bobbsey Twins and not mention Howard. That way I could reveal that we did use ghostwriters but not give Howard direct credit. I wonder what his son would think about that?

Andy looked a bit surprised at Harriet's idea. "That's up to you, I suppose. It would still serve the purpose of getting the basic information out in the press."

Harriet nodded and smiled.

Harriet kept her promise and in the coming years was featured in numerous articles about her books and the Syndicate. In 1968, Judy Klemesrud of *The New York Times* came to her home for just such an interview.

The reporter looked up the flight and a half of wide cement steps to the white, two-story house that sat up off the street, as the rest of the homes on that block. It was a good sized home but not anything ostentatious. "I thought someone who sold all those Nancy and Hardy Boys books would live in something a bit more upscale," Judy said to the photographer standing next to her.

"I heard her husband was a broker," Roger replied.

Judy shrugged her shoulders and started up the steps. She opened the screen door and used the heavy metal knocker to let their presence be known. A middle-aged woman in a simple house dress and apron opened the door and led them into the small entryway just as the large grandfather clock struck one. A short, older woman, though Judy didn't consider her elderly looking, with a full head of curly, red-brown hair walked into the hall to greet them.

"You must be Mrs. Adams," Judy said, offering Harriet her hand.

"I am," she said, taking Judy's hand in a limp handshake. Then Harriet turned and walked into the next room.

Judy looked at the photographer and shrugged her shoulders, then followed Harriet into the next room. "Thank you so much for taking the time to visit with me, Mrs. Adams," she said, stepping up behind her. "And agreeing to have your picture taken. Our readership wants to know what the real Carolyn Keene looks like, you know."

"We can talk in the sunroom. It's brighter in there with more comfortable places to sit," Harriet said.

Roger and Judy followed Harriet past a couple antique chairs and two small tables with family group pictures resting on top, along with newer shots of younger faces that were obviously Harriet's grandchildren. The end of the long room was taken up completely by an ebony grand piano, a foot-and-a-half-tall Samurai warrior in full garb on a white steed stood on an embroidered cloth on top of its polished surface. Harriet turned left into a room that jutted off of the main home with large pieces of glass on the ceiling and walls. The glass was currently streaked and speckled with rain, but the room was bright despite the gray clouds outside. Harriet motioned for her two guests to sit on a long, L-shaped couch along the right side of the room. Harriet sat in an overstuffed chair opposite them.

The same woman who greeted them at the door, came into the sunroom and stood just to Harriet's left. "Can I get you anything to drink? Tea, coffee, water..." Harriet asked.

Miss Klemesrud looked at Roger and answered for them both. "We're fine, Mrs. Adams, but thank you."

"Thank you, Alice," Harriet said to the aproned-woman, and the woman turned without a sound and left the room.

"I'll try to not take up too much of your time," Judy said, opening her purse and pulling out a notepad and ballpoint pen.

Harriet leaned back in her chair and nodded with a subdued smile. She had agreed that getting information out about the Syndicate was good business sense, but she had been burned by the press so often over her thirty-eight years in running the Syndicate that she rarely enjoyed the experience.

"Normally I'd be at the farm on the weekend, but with such a cold and wet spring, I didn't feel like going."

"You own a farm?" Miss Klemesrud said in surprise.

"Forty acres in Califon. Not too far from here, really. We have over one thousand chickens and a substantial vegetable garden. I have a say in what goes into the garden each year, but the hired hands do all the work. It's getting too hard for me to manage."

Miss Klemesrud hesitated before she asked her next question. "May I ask how old you are, Mrs. Adams?"

Harriet let out a small chuckle. "Now if I told you that, it might keep the children from buying my books."

"I did a little research before our interview, and I wanted to confirm that you took over the company in 1930 after your father passed away. Is that correct?"

"Yes, he had left five unedited manuscripts, so I started there. But after those stories were printed, we had to start writing stories of our own. I think I'm up to one hundred books so far," Harriet said, crossing her legs and rocking back in her chair.

"That's quite an accomplishment. But you said 'we.' Who else has written for the Syndicate?"

"I currently have four writers. I give them a detailed outline for say, Tom Swift Jr. or The Bobbsey Twins, and they fill in the blanks, so to speak. No one works under their own name, including myself. Both my daughters wrote for me at one time, but they're too busy with their families to help me out any longer."

"I noticed from the pictures in the other room, you have grandchildren," Judy said with a smile.

"Eleven to be exact."

"That's nice. They must keep you busy, too," she said and turned the page in her notepad.

"I hardly have a moment to myself, but I wouldn't have it any other way."

"Do the ghostwriters work on Nancy and the Hardy Boys?"

"My partner, Andy Svenson, does the Hardy Boys and I'm the sole author of Nancy," she said with obvious pride. "We started revising Nancy and the Hardy Boys...oh, I think about ten years ago, and now we're doing the same for The

Bobbsey Twins. Those series started so long ago, we needed to change a few things. Now instead of getting in a carriage, the characters drive a car, or rather than taking a train, a character might take a plane. Nancy's car started out as a roadster, and we changed it so now in all her stories she drives her blue convertible."

"Of course, what would Nancy do without her convertible," Miss Klemesrud said with a grin.

Harriet squinted at Miss Klemesrud, unsure if that was a compliment or a slight.

"With those series having been around so long, are they still doing well? Sales wise, I mean," she continued.

Harriet straightened in her chair. "Nancy's sold 1.5 million copies last year, and she's been translated into seventeen languages," Harriet said with conviction. "And we've sold over one million copies of the Hardy Boys."

"That's quite impressive." Miss Klemesrud uncrossed her legs and wrote down the sales figures. "How do you account for their continued popularity? The characters are rather…rather straight-laced compared to today's standards."

"There isn't a hippie among them. None of the characters have love affairs or get pregnant or take dope. If they did, I'm sure that would be the end of the series."

"Can you tell me a little about your process? Your writing process, I mean."

"I try to get to the office by nine a.m. I've got quite a few people to keep track of so it takes me awhile to get down to my writing. I like to dictate at least three chapters or about 7,500 words every day. Sometimes that works, sometimes it doesn't. Then I have outlines to do for Andy and the other writers...There is quite a lot to keep track of, as you can imagine."

"I don't know how you do it, Mrs. Adams. I really don't," Miss Klemesrud said with sincerity. She looked down at her notepad, flipped through it until she was convinced she had all she wanted, then she shut it.

"Well, I think I have all I need. I'll write up the article, then it will go to my editor."

"Can I see it before it's published?"

"I...don't see why not," she said with some hesitation. "I'll let my editor know and he'll be in contact with you."

Miss Klemesrud rose to go. She turned and saw the photographer, half asleep in a stiff, upholstered chair.

"I almost forgot! We need to get a picture. How about one in front of your collection of Nancy stories?"

Harriet stood slowly. "Just a moment, I'll get some help to set them out."

Harriet walked out of the room and within minutes came back following a man close to her own age. He went to the bookshelf behind the piano and pulled out two stacks of books.

"Put them on the table, Roger," Harriet instructed, and without saying a word, the man lined the yellow-spined books along one edge of the shiny wood table.

"Thank you."

"How about if you sit right behind them," Miss Klemesrud directed. Harriet complied, her eyes blinking on occasion from the loud pop and flash as Roger took her picture from various angles.

"I think I've got it," the camera man said, looking down at his camera as if he could already see the developed exposures.

"Wonderful!" Miss Klemesrud came over to Harriet and shook her hand. "Thank you so much for letting us visit on your day off. My editor will get back to you soon."

The reporter headed for the front door but stopped when she noticed a glass cabinet filled with delicate dolls of every type and ethnicity. "My, what a lovely collection."

"This is just part of it. I have over two hundred dolls from every part of the world," Harriet explained as she walked up behind her. "I collect them when I go on my research trips."

"Do you mind if we take a picture of one of them? I know our female readers would be interested in knowing a little more personal information about you."

"Of course," Harriet said, and she took a Japanese figure in a colorfully embroidered, cream kimono out of the cabinet and set it on the table next to her books.

The photographer took two additional pictures of the doll and the books.

"I think one with Mrs. Adams would be good idea too, don't you think, Roger?"

"Up to you," he said, advancing the film in his camera.

"Mrs. Adams...do you mind?"

Harriet was getting tired, but she didn't want to be portrayed as being uncooperative. "Of course not," she said and sat back down behind her books, pasting on a pleasant smile.

And the articles continued. Mildred saw the one in the *Saturday Review* a year later, and after meeting with the freelance writer, Geoffrey Lapin – a gentleman who, after significant investigation into the identity of Carolyn Keene, had taken it upon himself to get the message out about Mildred's authorship of the Nancy stories – Mildred decided she was going to set the record straight, at least with the *Saturday Review's* editor. What the editor decided to do with the information was up to him.

June 7th, 1969

Dear Mr. Prager,

I read your article in the Saturday Review *titled, "The Secret of Nancy Drew," and I need to make a correction. I'm not sure where you got your information, but I am the author of the first twenty-five Nancy volumes plus an additional volume I completed in 1953. Like the other ghostwriters for the Syndicate, I had signed an agreement that would not allow me to publicize this fact or make any copyright claim to the works, but I wrote them nonetheless. Because of this fact, I can't ask you to write a retraction, but I wanted to at least let you know the facts. I have not had anything to do with the Syndicate since that time, so I have nothing to do with the revision of the original Nancy stories that have been published of late.*

And to set the record straight, along with writing the Nancy stories for the Syndicate, I wrote 10 of the Dana Girls Mysteries, 11 Kay Tracey stories, 2 Doris Force, 5 Honey Bunch, and 8 of the Ruth Fielding volumes until it was discontinued in 1934. In addition, I have published 72 of my own stories. I have worked as a reporter for the Toledo Times since 1943, so if you want to contact me, I'm available there Monday-Friday, come rain or come shine.

Yours Truly,
Mildred Wirt Benson

Feeling only slightly better about the whole Syndicate business, Mildred moved on to more interesting ventures, namely flying. The following year she convinced her editor to let her do a column on aviation, which she titled, "Happy Landings." It allowed Mildred to share stories of her exploits in the skies as well as those of the local Wagon Wheel Airport outside of Toledo. It was also a good excuse to travel to air shows in the neighboring state of Pennsylvania or as far away as Louisiana. Mildred made a special effort to take note of what other women were doing in the business. One such woman was Mary Gaffaney, an aerobatics champion out of Miami, Florida. Mildred had heard of Mary's win at the Women's World Aerobatics Championship in France in 1972, so when she was to appear at a Pennsylvania air show that fall, Mildred made sure she was there to do an interview.

And while Mildred was writing articles about women's rights and women in flight, Congress was passing the Equal Rights Amendment and Gloria Steinem was publishing *Ms* magazine. Harriet Adams decided to do a different type of publishing.

"She wants to do what?" Andrew Svenson said, a bit louder than he intended.

"She wants to publish a series of cookbooks based on Nancy Drew. She's going to meet with the publisher this very afternoon," Agnes said.

Andy dropped back into his chair and ran his hand through his hair. He had gone along with most of the franchise ideas Harriet had come up with so far, and the ever expanding list of foreign rights continued to help boost the company's bottom line, but a Nancy Drew cookbook published at a time in history when women were trying desperately to cut their ties to the kitchen, seemed like a ludicrous idea.

"I just found out about it this morning, when she wanted me to set up the taxi ride. She seemed so pleased with the idea...I don't think she really understands..."

"Yes, yes...I would have to agree." He let out a heavy sigh. "I'll have to say something to her, I suppose."

Andy stood reluctantly. "Thanks for letting me know," he said and headed for Harriet's office. The door was open but Andy stopped before he walked in. He wanted to think of a way to bring up the subject without breaking Miss Pearson's confidence. He tapped lightly on the wooden door panel and strode inside the lioness' den.

"Good morning, Harriet," he said with a pleasant air. "Do you have a minute? I wanted to update you on how The Bobbsey Twins revisions are going, if I could."

Harriet put down the newspaper she was reading. "Of course. Where are you at?"

Andy sat down on one of the upholstered chairs and relaxed back, trying to put on a mask of composure, glad she couldn't see the sweat accumulating in his palms. "We're up to 1930 with the revisions, so it's starting to get a little easier. I've got two people working on The Bobbseys, one writer helping me with the Hardy Boys revisions, and another working on the new Tom Swift." He crossed his ankle over his knee and adjusted the leg of his slacks. "Anything new with the Dana Girls or Nancy?"

"Yes, actually. I am quite excited about a new project I'm starting with Nancy. I was going to fill you in after I met with the publisher. I didn't want to bother you until I was sure it was a go," she said by way of an apology. Much like a good card player, Harriet usually kept her plans for the Syndicate close to her chest, so Andrew had gotten used to hearing of things at the last minute or from others in the office. "I was trying to think of other streams of income for some of our characters and, of course, our top-selling sleuth came to mind. Other than letting the Parker Brothers put out the Nancy Drew Mystery Game quite a few years ago and a few coloring books, we really haven't done much as far merchandizing

Nancy of late. I don't count that Madam Alexander doll they did of her. It looked more like a baby than a young girl," she said with obvious displeasure. "I'm actually going to meet with a publisher this afternoon about putting out a series of Nancy Drew cookbooks. I thought we'd start out with a general cookbook, and if that goes well, we can move on to a book on dessert or appetizers and party foods. We could name the recipes after some of the book titles." Harriet pulled her purse out of a drawer and took out a small notebook. "Let's see...I've written a few of my ideas here: Tapping Heels Tuna Casserole, Moss-Covered Mansion Meatloaf, or Velvet Mask Red Velvet Cake." Harriet looked up at Andy for a response when she didn't hear his immediate reply.

"Ah...sounds like it might work."

"I hope so. We need to do something to keep the company going."

Andrew uncrossed his legs and sat forward. "I agree with the marketing idea, Harriet, but a cookbook...at this time...might not be the best direction to go in for Nancy. The Hardy Boys cartoon seems to be doing relatively well; maybe we could sell the rights for a cartoon for Nancy, too," he said, trying desperately to come up with another alternative to a homemaking book for a very independent female character at a time when independent females were a commodity, not a liability.

Harriet's brow bunched. "I don't like how they have the boys in a music group. Who knows what they'd have Nancy doing."

"They're just trying to connect with the kids of today. You know, with the Beatles being such a hit…"

"I just can't take that chance with Nancy. I've worked so hard building her reputation, I have to be extra careful not to betray the trust parents have in her. I'm convinced that's why she continues to be our best seller."

"I suppose you're right," Andrew said, scratching his chin. "A cookbook is going to be different. You'll have to make sure they use a top-notch photographer."

"I plan on it. I don't do much cooking, myself, but I've done my research," Harriet said, and she pulled down five or six different cookbooks from a shelf directly behind her desk and set them in front of her. "I've got some examples of what I like and what I don't like here," she said, tapping her pile. "You can count on me to make sure this is done right."

Andrew smiled. "I have no doubt, Harriet."

(1976)
And the merchandizing didn't stop there for Nancy or the Hardy Boys. As Andy suspected, there was considerable negative press over Nancy's cookbook, so the Syndicate went in other directions with their two most popular characters. Nancy was found puzzling fans on a jigsaw puzzle and was immortalized in the form of another doll (this one more to Harriet's liking). In addition, she came out with a Private Eye Diary and another book on what Nancy did best – sleuthing. The Hardy Boys were even busier, tramping around on a board game, driving a toy truck, or solving mysteries in coloring and activity books. They could even be seen in 3D in

a Viewmaster set or heard rocking out on an RCA vinyl album. But it was Nancy, Frank, and Joe who would be appearing live on the millions of now mostly color television sets around the country. Frank and Joe were not big-screen stars like Nancy, but they had been featured in two live mysteries shows by none other than the Mickey Mouse Club in 1956 and 1957, then again in 1967 in an hour-long program titled, *The Mystery of the Chinese Junk.* Unfortunately, neither were popular enough to continue. But these new television programs for all three of the Syndicate's most popular characters promised to be a new venture, and Harriet was going to make sure it was done right.

"Thank you for meeting with me, Mr. Peterson."

"My pleasure, Mrs. Adams," Max Peterson said as he shook Harriet's hand, trying to keep the look of dread from showing on his face. He felt the woman's thin, delicate skin in his hand and was reminded that Harriet, at eighty-four, was older than his own grandmother yet still ran her own business. Max respected Harriet's fortitude in relation to their negotiations over a Nancy Drew and Hardy Boys Mystery television shows, but they had gone over this so many times now, he couldn't see how they were going to resolve their differences. The woman seemed to have an opinion on everything, from who would play the roles to what the actors would be wearing and the language they used.

"How can I help you?" he said, perching himself on the edge of his desk directly in front of Harriet.

"I've spent a lot of time and effort, not to mention a

considerable amount of money, getting back the television and film rights to the Hardy Boys and Nancy Drew, and my first ventures into television didn't work out so well. I just can't see squandering all that because we can't seem to come to the proper terms."

What Harriet was saying was true, she had spent a lot of money, time, and effort to get back the rights she had sold to Warner Brothers to make the Nancy movies, but it was mostly her three new junior partners who wanted Harriet to compromise with Universal Studios, which would produce the show, and ABC, which would air it.

Max nodded his head, a bit surprised at her declaration. "Go on."

"I'm prepared to make some concessions."

Max couldn't help but smile, though he wasn't all-out grinning. He had been meeting with this woman on and off for almost two years now, so he was going to reserve any downright jubilation until her concessions were spelled out. "Glad to hear it," he said, slapping his thigh. He sat down behind his desk, ready to take notes.

"I am prepared to concede that you know more about what actors would be best to play the roles of Nancy, Frank, and Joe, so I will leave that up to you. But I need to have your assurance…no, your word, that they will all appear, both in manner and in dress, as if they were taken out of the pages of my books," Harriet said with conviction.

"I think we have your answer, Mrs. Adams," Max said with a more convincing smile. "Since we last met, the networks have come up with a new concept. It's called the family hour. I don't know if you watch much television, Mrs. Adams, but it is an hour every Sunday evening from 6:30 to 7:30 that is used to air programs that are appropriate for every member of the family. I think Nancy and the Hardy Boys will fit perfectly in that slot," he said, leaning forward on his desk. "They've already been using the concept for a few months now, so the viewing public expects to see family-style programming during this time every Sunday."

Harriet was smiling now, too. "So where do we go from here?" she said with optimism.

"Well, we'll draw up a contract, pass it by you and your lawyers, then we can start casting and working on the script."

The thought of leaving these critical decisions in the hands of someone who had never even picked up a Nancy Drew book until two years ago, when Harriet had sent him a copy, was a bit unsettling for Harriet. She had suggested he read it to learn a little bit more about the young woman Harriet now commonly referred to as her daughter. Harriet was protective of Frank and Joe's images, but it was Nancy who had won Harriet's heart and whom she still quarreled over with Anne Hagan, the editor at Grosset & Dunlap.

I feel you have overstepped your position in trying to revamp Nancy's character. She is not all those dreadful things you accuse her of and in many instances you have actually wanted to make her negative.

Harriet and Anne had been working together for over

twenty years now, but Harriet had begun to feel that Miss Hagan was starting to overstep her bounds.

> *I must tell you quite frankly that you cause me a great deal of unnecessary work, which brings my creation of a new story to an abrupt halt... What bothers me even more is your supposition that you, not I, know what Nancy, Mr. Drew, et al. would say or do, like deleting Nancy's lovely gesture of putting an arm around an elderly woman who has just done the young detective a great favor. In the future will you please stick to the functions of an editor and not try steering my fictional family into a non-Carolyn Keene direction.*

It was understandable that letting go of any aspect of these characters was almost abhorrent to Harriet. But she knew she must acquiesce, if not for herself, then for the three young women that would succeed her. Even though her granddaughter, Cynthia – Edward Jr.'s daughter – and grandchildren, Karl and Cathie – Patsy's son and daughter, – had all helped at the Syndicate at one point in their lives, they had all started families of their own, and Harriet didn't see any family member who was willing or able to take on all that she had worked so hard to achieve.

A tear came to Harriet's eye, and she tried to blink it away before Mr. Peterson could see it. But he had seen the change that had come over Harriet.

"Are you all right, Mrs. Adams? Is there something else you would like to discuss?"

"No...no. I'm fine," she said. She pulled out a handkerchief and dabbed her eye since Mr. Peterson had obviously guessed at least some of what she was feeling.

He came around the desk and sat back on its corner, taking Harriet's hand in his. "I assure you, Mrs. Adams, we will take great care of Frank, Joe, and Nancy," he said, giving her hand a gentle squeeze. "I promise."

Harriet nodded and slid her hand out of his as she tried to compose herself. She eventually stood and extended her hand to Max once more. "Thank you, Mr. Peterson. It's been a pleasure."

Harriet started to leave the room and Max rushed past her to open the door for her and usher her out. Harriet was about to step out of his office but stopped and turned around. "Would you mind ever so much if I were allowed to read the script before it goes on the air? I promise, I won't try and change a thing," she said, putting up her hand as if she was a girl scout making a pledge. "I think it would just give me some piece of mind if I knew what was coming in that first episode."

Max's face softened. "I think we can arrange that."

"And I have your word about my characters," she said, her face easily changing from plaintive to commanding.

Max made an X across his chest. "Scout's honor!"

All the exposure of Nancy, Frank, and Joe was gradually paying off for the Syndicate when in 1977, Grosset & Dunlap sent Harriet a royalty check for $244,737.73. Unfortunately for Andy Svenson and his family, he wasn't able to revel in the year-end royalties. He had died two years before, leaving Harriet with large shoes to fill. Her sister's death in 1974, was also a blow to Harriet, even though, in their later years, they saw less and less of each other. Harriet had gone to the funeral in St. Petersberg, Florida, but since Edna had long ago given up the day to day workings of the business, Harriet was back behind her desk three days after the funeral, then in full ownership of the company. All that was left of her staff were three writing assistants whom Harriet had made junior partners in the firm: Nancy Axelrad, Lieselotte Wuenn, and her new secretary, Lorraine Rickle.

Even though they were working in the black, Harriet was not all smiles. In the back of her mind, she wondered if she was going to hear again from that old thorn in her side in the person of Mildred Wirt Benson. In 1975, when it was leaked to the press that she was negotiating with Universal Studios to produce a mystery series for both Nancy and the Hardy Boys, Harriet had heard, through her assistants, that the studio had gotten a letter from Mildred asserting her television rights as Nancy's initial author. The Studio and Harriet's lawyers assured Harriet that they had taken care of the situation. But Harriet felt that after forty-five years running the Syndicate, and most of those years outlining, editing, writing, and then revising the Nancy stories that everyone now knew, she was the real Carolyn Keene, not Mildred Wirt Benson.

346

When Mildred's continual supporter Geoffrey Lapin saw the new series on TV, he contacted Mildred to see if she had gotten any payment for the use of her Nancy character.

> *2704 Middlesex Dr.*
> *Toledo, O.*
> *April 24, 1978*

Dear Mr. Lapin:

Indeed I do remember you, and also I knew of your fine defense of my as the unknown author of "Nancy Drew,"...Intended to write you about it, but I've been on an exciting fly-your-own plane trip--the Louisiana Air Tour, and hadn't managed it....

I'm still on The Blade (ZIP Line now) but do very little creative writing these days as I'm so busy. I hadn't caught up with "Ghost of the Hardy Boys," and found it most interesting reading, especially the final chapters. I noted the author carries on the Stratemeyer Syndicate propoganda [sic] lie--that is, that Mrs. Adams started and wrote the Nancy Drews. Her publicity has been most effective. She's convincingly put it across that SHE originated and wrote them. When she couldn't explain [the] fact that the breeder volumes all were written before she even became associated with the Syndicate, she glossed over that one by saying her father wrote the first three volumes before his death. This, of course, was untrue, and at request of the publisher, I kept the volumes

347

going many years--until they were established world-wide. She then began re-writing and wrote the new volumes herself, so far as I know.

I'm most curious about one thing, so if you have the writer's address, would like to ask him a couple of questions. He mentions signing [a] release--the same as I did. But I signed two of them, and so far as I know they are ironclad. Would like to find out how he was able without lawsuit to claim authorship? In recent propoganda [sic] Mrs. Adams did acknowledge him, I think, as author. At least she didn't claim to be.

When the series hit TV I tried to assert TV rights. The Syndicate, network and producter [sic] all came down on me, threatening lawsuit. According to my contract, they insist I don't exist.

Nice to have one loyal fan and a million thanks.

Millie Benson

P.S. Until I read the autobiography which you so kindly sent, I didn't know who started the Dana Girls' books. I continued them, but never could make them tick as they weren't set up with a set of characters that one could put across. Very stilted, which apparently was the author's view also. Mrs. Adams, so far as I know, never made a success of any books that she started from scratch. Her fortune and success rest almost entirely upon Nancy Drew and the Hardy Boys.

MB.

And after the television programs got underway, they quickly dropped in the ratings. Pamela Sue Martin, the actress who played Nancy, was then asked to work on a new television program that included the Hardy Boys, teen heartthrobs Parker Stevenson and Shaun Cassidy. She refused the offer and went to the press with her story, including a racy, semi-nude cover of Playboy magazine, lambasting Nancy for her dullness and asexuality.

Harriet was livid, and she wasn't about to let this assault on Nancy go, despite attempts by her lawyers to convince her to do otherwise. She ran an ad in Playboy and five other publications denouncing what Miss Martin had done to the ennobled name of Nancy Drew. She wanted to sue the girl for defamation of character, but her lawyers had to remind Harriet that, as real as Nancy was to her and thousands of young girls all over the globe, Nancy was not an actual person.

Harriet and Mildred didn't cross paths again until that day in 1980, in the courtroom in New York City when Harriet realized that Mildred was still among the living.

Twenty-eight ∾

"Mrs. Adams. Mrs. Adams," a voice said again.

Harriet blinked twice and turned toward the sound. The clean-shaven face of the young prosecutor was leaning in close, concern in his eyes.

"Are you all right, Mrs. Adams?" came another male voice, this one from her right. Harriet turned in his direction. Judge Robert J. Ward observed the bewilderment on Harriet's face and smacked his gavel once hard on the sounding block on top of his bench. Harriet startled as if she had just woken up. "This court is adjourned for the day. We'll begin proceedings again tomorrow morning, 8 a.m. sharp."

The judge then stood and exited the courtroom, leaving Harriet staring out at all the people and the exponentially increasing then receding noise of the rapidly emptying room. A middle-aged court bailiff helped Harriet out of her chair and off the witness stand. Her lawyer was packing up his things and getting ready to leave. Behind him, Harriet spied Mildred, who still sat in place and was staring back at Harriet, a playful smile on her face.

"I thought you were dead," Harriet said as she stepped up in front of Mildred.

"I knew *you* weren't," Mildred said in reply.

"Why are you here?" Harriet asked, still unsure of what this trial all entailed.

"I've been called as a witness for the prosecution. I'm here to tell my side of the story."

"Your side of the story? I know your side of the story," Harriet said, incredulous.

Mildred tried to suppress a grin, then looked as if she was having trouble choosing the right words in reply. "You and I know the story, Harriet, but now the rest of the world is finally going to know the story, too."

Harriet straightened at Mildred's words, a look of sureness or defiance overtaking her; Mildred wasn't sure which.

"Yes, they will," Harriet said and left Mildred standing, watching her amble slowly out of the room.

❁

Epilogue

The trial lasted five days. The judge's verdict gave Grosset & Dunlap the rights to the hardcover stories of Nancy,

351

Frank and Joe Hardy, Tom Swift, Louise and Jean Dana, and the Bobbsey crew – before 1979 – and bidding rights for paperback versions of those same stories. Since G & D had a 1951 agreement for the paperback and hardcover rights to Tom Swift Jr., the judge ruled that this agreement was still valid. The ruling ended a sixty-nine year relationship that the Syndicate and its various owners had with Grosset & Dunlap.

This left Simon & Schuster the rights to publish any new Tom Swift, Nancy Drew, Hardy Boys, Dana Girls, and Bobbsey Twins series in both paperback and hardcover.

Two years after the trial, Harriet Stratemeyer Adams died of heart failure at the age of eighty-nine, apparently while watching *The Wizard of Oz* on TV at Bird Haven Farm.

The Syndicate was split 50-50 with Harriet's three children: Patricia (Patsy) Harr, Camillia McClave, Edward Stratemeyer Jr.; and her junior partners: Nancy Axelrad, Lorraine (Lorry) Rickle, and Lieselotte Wuenn. It was sold in its entirety to Simon & Schuster in 1984 for $4,710,000.

Twenty years, two months, and two days after Harriet's death, Mildred Augustine Wirt Benson died at a Toledo hospital at the age of ninety-six (2002 if you don't want to do the math). She was still working at the Toledo *Blade* (the *Toledo Times* folded in the 1970s and Mildred was hired at the *Blade*). She had allegedly handed in the copy for her column the day she passed away. At the time of her death, along with her private pilot's license, Mildred was also able to fly commercial aircraft and seaplanes.

Mildred stated quite accurately at the Grosset & Dunlap trial: "Mrs. Adams's style of writing Nancy is not the style I had, and I imagine that things I wrote in there did not hit her as Nancy. I mean, the Nancy that I created is a different Nancy from what Mrs. Adams has carried on...There's was a beginning conflict in what is Nancy. My Nancy would not be Mrs. Adams's Nancy. Mrs. Adams was an entirely different person: she was more cultured and she was more refined. I was probably a rough and tumble newspaper person who had to earn a living, and I was out in the world. That was my type of Nancy. Nancy was making her way in life and trying to compete and have fun. We just had different kinds of Nancys."

Now you, dear reader, can make up your own mind.

Acknowledgments

I have to first acknowledge Melanie Rehak and her book: *Girl Sleuth, Nancy Drew and the Women Who Created Her*. She and her book were invaluable to me for information about the people in Nancy's life. Second to Melanie is Cynthia Lum, who is the great-granddaughter of the original creator of Nancy, Edward Stratemeyer (her father also being named Edward). Cynthia was so kind to read my manuscript before publication and tell me where I had my facts wrong. A friend of Millie Wirt Benson, Geoffrey S. Lapin, was nice enough to give me a copy of a letter Mildred sent him, plus some previously unavailable (to me) information about one of the first three Nancy book outlines and about Patricia Doll. James Keeline, a Nancy aficionado, also read the book and gave me other corrections.

Then there are my other readers: Bonnie and Betty Davidson, Julie Luicks, Julie Johnson, ShaMecha Simm, and Jenna Nelson Patton, who did her dissertation on childrens' book production, including series books and research on the Syndicate. These women are all near and dear to my heart, and my book wouldn't be what it is without them.

I would also like to thank the helpful people at the New York Public Library's Manuscripts and Archives Division: Maurice Klapwald, Tal Nadan, and Kit Messick. I would have loved to visit the library myself and dig through their extensive Stratemeyer collection, but my situation would not allow it. They were a great substitute and the ones who put me onto Melanie's book.

Thanks to Christine Masters at Simon & Schuster for connecting me with Stephanie Voros and for S & S letting me use the copyrighted material from their Edward Stratemeyer collection at the NYPL, the excerpt from *The Secret of the Old Clock*, and for the gracious use of the name Nancy Drew.

Janet Weaver at the University of Iowa Women's collection was equally helpful in helping me find and allowing me to share information about Mildred Benson Wirt from their collection.

Also James Lewis and Tom Anker from the Newark Public Library; the unsigned assistance from the San Antonio Public Library; Mary at the Madison Public Library, who went above and beyond to help me find an article; the Local History and Genealogy Department of the Toledo-Lucas County Public Library; and Mike Linden, who allowed Mildred to take to the skys in a safe aircraft; thank you all.

Bibliography

The Courtesy, Mildred Augustine, St. Nicolas XLVL, no.8, June 1919, pg 762

Hardy Boys Named in Literary Suit, Lee A Daniels, June 10, 1980, The New York Times

100 Books—and Not a Hippie in Them, Judy Klemesrud, April 4, 1968, The New York Times

Court Rules on 'Custody" Of Hardys and Bobbseys, Lee A. Daniels, June 13, 1980, The New York Times

Funeral Tonight For E. Stratemeyer, May 12, 1930, The New York Times

Edward Stratemeyer, May 11, 1930, The New York Times

Will of Edward Stratemeyer, June 6, 1930, The New York Times

"The Rover Boys" Creator Is Dead, May 11, 1930, Syracuse Herald

Newarker Who Writs for Most Critical of All Readers Has

Far exceeded Standard of Success His Mother Set, June 4, 1927, Newark Evening News

The Newarker Whose Name is Best Known, December 9, 1917, Newark Sunday Call

Mr. Stratemeyer A Writer For Boys, March 9, 1902, Newark Sunday News, p.8
Richard Dare's Venture or Striking out for Himself - Edward Stratemeyer, 1894

Ghost of the Hardy Boys, An Autobiography, Leslie McFarlene, 1976

From Rags to Riches - Horatio Alger and the American Dream, John Tebbel, 1963

"Blowing Out the Boys' Brains," Franklin K. Mathiews, *Outlook*, November, 18, 1914 (http://www.unz.org/Pub/Outlook-1914nov18-00652)

Girl Sleuth, Nancy Drew and the Women Who Created Her, Melanie Rehak, 2005

Past and Promise, Lives of New Jersey Women, Joan N. Burstyn (HQ1438 N5 P37 State Historical Society call #)

Edward Stratemeyer and the Stratemeyer Syndicate, Deidre Johnson

Edward Stratemeyer, Brenda Lange

My Father Was Uncle Wiggly – The Story of the remarkable Garis family who created Uncle Wiggly and wrote countless adventures of the Motor Boys, the Motor Girls, Baseball Joe, the Bobbsey Twins, Tom Swift and the Outdoor Girls, Roger Garis

The Girl Sleuth, Bobbie Ann Mason

American Women in Flight, Deborah G. Douglas

The Mysterious Case of Nancy Drew and the Hardy Boys, Caorle Kismaric and Marvin Heiferman

The majority of the letters, though not all, and portions of other letters are taken verbatim from the Edward Stratemeyer collection held at the NYPL and are the sole property of Simon & Schuster. Since they are verbatim, I did not correct odd language or other errors in punctuation or grammer. Details of letter portions and locations within the collection can be given upon request of the author.

Excerpts of letters to and from Mildred Wirt Benson and University of Iowa: Mildred Wirt Benson papers, Iowa Women's Archives, The University of Iowa Libraries, Iowa City.

Letter from Mildred Benson to Geoffrey S. Lapin dated April 24, 1978, from Geoffrey S. Lapin

http://sdrc.lib.uiowa.edu/iwa/findingaids/html/BensonMil-dred.htm

www.Gutenburg.org - Repository for books that have lapsed copyrights

onlinebooks.library.upenn.edu – list of books by Edward Stratemeyer

www.series-books.com/mildredwirt/wirt.html

About the Author

Christine runs her own self-publishing company: CKBooks Publishing, that offers editing, designing, formatting and writing services. She enjoys sharing the information and skills she has accumulated in the many years she's been writing and publishing. Christine has written and published six novels to date – five historical fiction pieces and one memoir – and is working on her seventh – a middle-grade novel about a precocious twelve-year-old by the name of Agnes Kelly. Her first novel: *Rosebloom*, won an IPPY award for historical fiction.

In her free time she likes to read, watch movies and take walks in the great out there.

You can contact Christine from her website: ckbooksblog.wordpress.com. or if you're a writer yourself, her indie-publishing site is: ckbookspbulsihing.com. Come by and say hello. Christine would love to hear from you!

Christine's other books are:

Her Rose Series:
Rosebloom,
A Burnished Rose,
Rose From the Ashes
The Red Velvet Box
Living in the House of Drugs

If you enjoyed this book, please take the time to put a review on your favorite book website. Christine would greatly appreciate it, and she would like to hear what you think. Really!

—

Made in the USA
Columbia, SC
31 August 2017